THE HURTLE
OF HELL

AN ATHEIST COMEDY
FEATURING GOD
&
A CONFUSED YOUNG MAN
FROM HACKNEY

SIMON EDGE

Published by
Lightning Books Ltd
Imprint of EyeStorm Media
312 Uxbridge Road
Rickmansworth
Hertfordshire
WD3 8YL

www.lightning-books.com

First Edition 2018
Copyright © Simon Edge
Cover design by Anna Morrison, original artwork by David Shenton

British Library Cataloguing in Publication Data
A catalogue record for this book is available from the British Library

Printed by CPI Group (UK) Ltd, Croydon CR0 4YY

ISBN: 9781785630712

FOR MY LATE PARENTS,
MYLES AND KATHLEEN EDGE

The frown of his face
Before me, the hurtle of hell
Behind, where, where was a, where was a place?
I whirled out wings that spell
And fled with a fling of the heart to the heart of the Host.
My heart, but you were dovewinged, I can tell,
Carrier-witted, I am bold to boast,
To flash from the flame to the flame then, tower from the
grace to the grace

Gerard Manley Hopkins
The Wreck of the Deutschland

1

STEFANO MUST have blacked out. When he came round, he was looking down on an agitated crowd. They were clustered around something lying on the dark, wet sand, just clear of the waves. At the centre of the gathering crouched a squat, middle-aged man in improbably tiny Speedos, buttocks in the air. Bent over the body of a pale young man, he was trying to give him the kiss of life. The poor bastard, thought Stefano uncharitably. He would get a shock if he came round to find that guy sucking his face.

Craning to get a better look, it occurred to him that the stricken swimmer's candy-striped trunks looked familiar. Now he realised that so was the body, which really was shamefully pallid compared to all the bronzed onlookers. It was superficial to be so critical, but Stefano had every right, because that was his own body he was looking down at. That was him, lying there on the beach.

This was like the weirdest dream he had ever had, but he somehow knew, as surely as he had ever known anything, that this was not a dream. This was happening.

He watched the kiss-of-life guy come up for air, puffing it in with a great gulp, and then hunch over for another attempt. The scene was silent, and it took Stefano a moment to grasp that this was not because nobody was talking, but because he could not hear. There must still be water in his ears after being pulled under like that. If only his rescuer would stop the kissing thing for a moment and tilt his head from side to side, it might drain out.

He could see the onlookers' mouths moving as they jostled inwards. Now someone – Stefano recognised the soft-drinks seller who hawked Coca Cola from a cart in the middle of the beach – pushed them back. Give him some air, he would be saying, because that was what people always said in situations like this, only he would be saying it in Spanish, and Stefano had no idea what that was. And there, finally, was Adam, with only a hint of anxiety at first, turning abruptly to panic. Stefano did not need to lip-read to know that his own name was being shouted.

Then, abruptly, the scene was gone. He could no longer see himself, nor any of the people around him, and he was surrounded by specks of white light. As his eyes adjusted to the brightness, he saw that he was in some kind of tube. Not that he could see the sides – the lightness was everywhere and nowhere – but it felt like some kind of extraordinary tunnel because it was brighter up ahead, and now he was conscious of rising towards the far end of it. He felt light-headed, euphoric, as if the whiteness were shining inside him. It reminded him of the first rush of a pill, in the days when they still worked and you knew why it was called ecstasy, only there was nothing illicit about this. What was happening to him?

As he rose further and further up the long, white cylinder he was curious about what he would find at the end, but he felt no fear.

He blinked to focus better as the white walls rushed past him. There was definitely something up there now, different from the shining white, covering the entire end of the tunnel. His attention was drawn in particular to a pinpoint of pitch black at the centre, which gradually widened as he came closer. Now it became a deep, inky pit that he seemed to be moving steadily towards, a black hole at the end of the white corridor. All around the edges of this hole straggled translucent rivulets of white and grey, coursing over a glistening blue ground and pouring into the black abyss like water into a well. Beyond these shining trails of white, he saw, was something else: a border, like smooth rocks circling the pool of rivulets. Or maybe it was softer…porous, organic, alive.

It looked like an eyelid, he suddenly realised: the black hole was a giant pupil, the straggling rivulets over a shining blue ground were the iris, and that giant lid must belong to…

'He's breathing!' shouted someone, disturbing his concentration, and he heard a painful rasping sound accompanied by exclamations of relief. He blinked his eyes open, which was odd, because he could have sworn they were open already, and found he was looking at the kiss-of-life guy again, not from above this time, but from his own body, flat on the wet sand. He could hear again, that was for sure, and the rasping was coming from his own throat as he coughed up brackish sea water. The kiss-of-life guy smiled. With his wide, fat lips and gappy teeth, he reminded Stefano of a kindly toad. Then the face was replaced by an even more welcome one.

'I thought I'd lost you,' said Adam, and Stefano could see he was trying not to cry. 'How do you feel? Don't try to talk. We need to get you to a hospital. Can we get him to a hospital?'

Someone was shouting Spanish into a mobile phone. Adam kept turning away to talk to people, and it seemed an age before he was paying attention to Stefano again and there was a chance to tell him. To try to tell him, at any rate – it was hard to breathe, let alone talk, and his whole head stung with salt.

'Don't try to speak,' said Adam. 'Just stay there for the moment and then we'll get you to hospital. No, you mustn't try to move. Please, lie still.'

Stefano tried again to reach for Adam's hand, finding it this time and attempting to pull him closer. 'You don't understand,' he was saying in his head, only it would not come out like that. It would barely come out at all. But he kept trying, and Adam was eventually forced to stop shushing him and lean in close to make out what he wanted to say.

'I think…' said Stefano at length, concentrating hard to make the words separate themselves from one another.

'Yes? What?'

'I think I just saw the eye of God.'

2

THE HOLIDAY on this strange little volcanic island had been Adam's idea. They had started on the opposite coast, under a blanket of cloud. There were no beaches on that side, and the bad weather seemed so permanent that it was even cloudy in the postcards.

As the outermost part of the archipelago, the island had been celebrated in ancient times as the edge of the known world. This excited Adam. For someone who had always been interested in astronomy, the further discovery that this had once been the zero meridian, where the western and eastern hemispheres officially met, made the place all the more evocative.

Unfortunately, soaking up this conceptual geographical history was not Stefano's idea of a good holiday, especially when it rained ceaselessly on the day they trekked to the lighthouse that marked the western tip of the rock. There was not much to see, and Stefano was conspicuously unimpressed.

'There's not even a plaque,' he observed, after circling the lighthouse twice.

'What do you want it to say? This used to be the edge of the world and now it's not?'

'It feels like it still is.'

They heard the climate was better on the opposite coast, so the following day they were back in their hire car, threading across the mountainous interior. It took half the morning to wind around the ravines, up into the cooling mist of the ancient forest, and then to hairpin down into a terraced gorge, lush with date palms and banana trees, where it was a blazing eighty-eight degrees.

They found an apartment in the hippie-run resort at the bottom of the valley. It had a cushion-thin mattress on the bed and a door that took five minutes to unlock, but you could almost see the sea from the balcony and it was only two thousand pesetas a night. Stefano put his foot down about further attempts at sightseeing. For the sake of harmony, Adam decided not to mention the ancient villa which claimed to be the last place where Christopher Columbus had stayed before setting out for the New World; it would do for a rainy day, if it ever rained on this side of the island.

Instead, they went straight to the beach, where the sand was as dark as the volcanic rocks that framed it, and soft as pepper underfoot. The breakers were huge, especially in the shallows, and even Stefano, who tended to be fearless, was daunted by them on the first day. However, he discovered that the trick was to dive into the belly of the wave just before it broke on your head. This sounded terrifying to Adam, but Stefano assured him it was fine when you came out the other side.

'It's actually quite funny,' he said, 'because you can laugh at the wave knocking everyone else over as it goes higher up the beach, and you're fine. But you have to be careful there isn't another massive one coming straight after it.'

Adam was a much less confident swimmer than Stefano, and the sea was too rough for his liking, but he was happy lying in the sun, reading. He grew to recognise the other characters on the beach, who mainly seemed to be Scandinavians and Germans. On the third day he noticed that one of these Scandinavians was wearing his arm in a sling, which had not been there the previous day. It was only then that he noticed there was no lifeguard on this beach, which made him less inclined than ever to do battle with the monster waves. He could not quite understand why everyone else on the beach seemed so keen to go back for more.

He was snoozing at the time of the accident, and it must have been the commotion that woke him. He scanned the crowd of tanned figures clustering around the unfortunate on the sand, looking for Stefano among them. Adam was calm by nature, and not inclined to rush into an unnecessary panic just for the sake of the drama. As he got to his feet, however, there was still no sign of Stefano. He began to realise that, on this occasion, panic might well be justified.

He reached the crowd, pushing through to see who or what was at the centre of the huddle. The sight of a paunchy German crouching over the pale, slender body in stripy trunks confirmed his worst fears.

'Let me through! It's my…' Even here in the throes of terror he worried what word to use. 'Partner' sounded so uptight, but 'boyfriend' always seemed to invite ridicule when used outside the confines of their own world.

'*Er atmet!*' shouted someone, and then in English: 'He's breathing.'

'*Gracias a Dios!*' said someone else.

Amid the relief and jubilation, the German sat up to give Stefano room, and Adam flung himself onto the sand behind him.

'Stef! What happened? Are you all right?' he panted.

The green eyes looked up at him groggily through long lashes.

Adam gripped Stefano's hand, no longer minding what anyone thought, and called up to the little crowd: 'Has anyone called an ambulance?'

'I think so,' said a German accent. 'Yes, that guy is calling. It's coming.'

Adam turned back to Stefano.

'I thought I'd lost you,' he whispered.

Stefano was trying to say something, and Adam had to lean in close to catch it.

'I think I saw the eye…'

'Sorry, Stef, I can't really understand you. But don't try to talk now, you'll have plenty of time to tell me later. I'm so sorry, I didn't actually see what happened. I think you must have blacked out. But you're all right now. Lie back, don't try and talk.'

'But you don't understand, it was really weird…'

'I'm sure it was horrible, but don't talk now. You're safe now; try and relax.'

Looking up at the crowd again, he asked: 'What happened? I didn't see.'

'He was knocked down by a wave,' said the onlooker who had spoken earlier. 'They can be very dangerous.'

Others offered their own versions of what had happened. They had watched the English boy get knocked over, and they had all laughed, just as he had laughed when it happened to them, but then they could see he was in trouble because the waves were coming fast, one after the other, and whenever he tried to emerge, he was knocked down again.

'It was hard to help him because the force of the sea was so strong,' said one of them, apologetically.

From his prone position on the sand, Stefano was still trying to talk.

'Please, Stef, lie still. Help will come,' said Adam.

The guy who had administered the kiss of life was still there, a portly, near-naked shape outlined in the white afternoon sun.

'Thank you so much for helping him,' said Adam, squinting up at him. 'Is he going to be OK?'

'I'm not a doctor. I just know a little first aid. But I imagine yes. Don't worry.'

'Thank you,' said Adam again. It was strange for himself and Stefano to be the focus of concern from so many strangers. He had a sudden impulse to weep, and he fought it back.

After what seemed like an age, but could only have been five minutes, the burst of a siren – that funny, staccato dee-dee-dah chirp that was one of the hallmarks of abroad – announced the arrival of the ambulance.

The concerned but thinning gaggle that still surrounded

them parted and two men in black trousers and bright yellow t-shirts – one of them stocky, fortyish, the other younger, taller, ponytailed – pushed their way through.

'*Qué ha pasado?*' said the older of the pair, and one of the Spanish speakers answered. Adam could not complain at being sidelined: he still did not have a clear idea of what had happened, so could not have explained even if he had the language.

The ambulance man crouched next to Stefano and asked him his name.

He replied in a croaky whisper, but someone from the crowd had to step forward and act as interpreter for the rest of the conversation. How did he feel? Could he breathe properly now? How many fingers was the guy holding up? Did he know the name of the island they were on? What day was it?

Now a stethoscope was being applied to Stefano's naked chest and the ponytailed crewman raised his bare arm to apply the blood pressure cuff. Adam saw a telltale flicker of those green eyes, and was reassured that Stefano was out of trouble: if he was well enough to register a cute first-aider, he was no longer at death's door.

The older of the men was now standing up and asking Adam something.

'Sorry, I don't speak Spanish,' he said, appealing for support from the onlookers.

'You are together?' said a slim Spanish woman of about their own age.

'Yes,' Adam nodded, trying not to notice the brown nipples pointing up at him. '*Si.*'

The ambulance man said something else to her and she translated: 'He want to take your friend to the hospital, just to make sure he is OK, OK?'

'OK,' said Adam. 'Can I go too?'

Stefano was being lifted onto a stretcher now. The ambulance was parked on a track at the top of the beach, where the hot, black sand gave way to rough earth and rougher stones. Adam did his best to keep up, hopping in his bare feet.

'I'm coming too. Will you wait two minutes while I get our stuff?'

Their towels, cameras, watches, money were all still out there on the beach.

But the guy was shaking his head and saying something in Spanish, as his ponytailed colleague now closed the back doors of the ambulance.

'But we're together!' Adam bristled.

The bare-breasted Spanish woman laid a gentle hand on his arm.

'He say he cannot take you like this' – she gestured at his lack of clothing – 'so you follow behind in a taxi. It's not far.'

The ambulance was already pulling away, chirping away with short dee-dee-dah bursts to signal that it was on the move again.

The little hospital was at the top of the valley. The road sagged up the middle of the lush oasis in the side of the volcano which had made this side of the island habitable, and then wound back and forth in wide loops as the gradient began to show it meant business. Near the top, a turning pitched off at a tangent and led into what looked like a brand-new neighbourhood, with a gleaming white, flat-roofed hospital at the centre of it.

Adam paid his taxi-driver and hastened inside to track down Stefano.

'Cartwright,' he spelled out at reception, writing it down because the silent W was impossible to sound in foreigner-friendly English.

He need not have bothered. Not many tourists had been brought in on stretchers in the past hour, and they knew immediately who he meant.

Adam was directed to a ward on the first floor. He found Stefano in a bay at one end next to a tiny, brown, old man with wires attached to his chest, who was snoring loudly.

Stefano was propped up against a bank of pillows, wearing a pale blue hospital gown. There was an oxygen mask on the bed next to him but he was breathing perfectly well without it.

Adam gave him a discreet peck on the cheek.

'How are you feeling? What have they said? Have you seen a doctor?'

'I feel fine now. Did you bring my stuff from the beach? They need to see some kind of ID to keep me here. I don't see the point, but they say they want me to stay overnight. And I tried to tell them what I saw, but they wouldn't listen either.'

'What you saw?'

'I've been trying to tell you…' Stefano picked up his oxygen mask and took a few long drafts to fortify himself.

'Something really weird happened. One moment I was in the sea, getting knocked down by the biggest wave you ever saw, struggling to breathe, with water going up my nose, and I remember scraping my face on the sand, so I must have gone upside down. It was really frightening. And the next moment I was all calm. I was looking down on *myself* on the beach and I could see all those people standing around me, and then you arriving. And I couldn't hear anything at all, even though I could see people shouting. It was like everyone was on the other side of some…I don't know…huge glass screen or something.'

'It must have been horrible. I guess with the trauma, you were dreaming about what was happening. But like I say, don't dwell on…'

'It wasn't a dream, it was real. I was really watching it. And that wasn't the main thing. After I'd looked down on myself it all disappeared and I was going up this long white tunnel, and it was an amazing feeling, like the best rush you've ever had. And I thought I'd never get to the end, but then I did and I saw…'

'What?'

'It was an eye.'

'An eye?'

'Yes. I'm certain that's what it was.'

'A human eye?'

'Well, I don't really know. It could have been, but it's hard to tell when all you can see is an eyeball.'

'What colour was it?'

'Sort of bluey-grey. And it was veiny.'

'Veiny?'

'Yes, with kind of white vessels flowing across it.'

Adam had always found it tedious to listen to other people's dreams, which was what this sounded like.

'I'm sure it has all been really disorientating. But you're still alive; that's the main thing,' he said. 'You've had a lucky escape. Now you just need to get some rest.'

This was one time when he was not prepared to let Stefano get his own way.

In the morning, he was momentarily confused to find himself alone in their double bed. They had rarely spent a night apart in the past five years, and the extra space felt wrong, a luxury he had no wish to enjoy. It was frightening to think how close they had come to disaster the previous day, but he told himself there was no point in dwelling on that. It was all over now, and they just needed to put it behind them and make the most of the rest of their holiday.

He planned to have breakfast and then make his way back up to the hospital, but Stefano beat him to it by arriving in a cab before Adam had finished his coffee.

'They said I could go, but I need lots of rest.' He pulled out a packet of Marlboro Lights, which had been in the bag of belongings that Adam had left with him at the hospital. 'Have we got any Diet Coke left?'

'Go and sit on the balcony, and I'll bring it to you. Did they also say you could smoke like a beagle?'

'I've had a nasty shock. I can't not smoke.'

Physically he seemed fine, but he was much more subdued than usual.

Telling himself this mood would pass soon enough, Adam left Stefano listening to music on his headphones while he went to pick up ham, cheese and salad from the supermarket at the bottom of the next block. They had lunch on the balcony, napped, then Adam made them each a gin and tonic. He was not sure if alcohol was allowed, but it seemed important to get back into the holiday spirit.

'I've been thinking about the tunnel, and that eye,' said Stefano.

Adam's heart sank.

'Have you?'

'Don't say it like that. Something really big happened to me yesterday.'

'I know it did. I nearly lost you. You don't need to tell me. I'm still quite shaken myself, so it must be much worse for you.'

'I nearly died.'

'I know you did.'

'And I went somewhere.'

'Well…mentally, yes.'

Stefano crunched an ice-cube.

'I went somewhere,' he repeated, more forcefully. 'Nearly, anyway.'

'Where do you think you nearly went?' said Adam.

'You know where.'

Adam genuinely did not know what he was getting at. Then his eyes widened.

'You mean heaven?'

'You said it, not me,' said Stefano, putting another

21

Marlboro Light between his lips and reaching for his lighter.

'But Stef…'

'What?'

'You're an atheist.'

Stefano shrugged.

'Aren't you?' Adam persisted. 'You always told me you were. So, you know, you don't believe in all that stuff. God. The afterlife. Heaven.'

Stefano shrugged again.

'I've always been spiritual.'

'No you haven't! You've always burned joss-sticks and hung out with people who smoke too much weed. That's not the same thing.'

Adam was laughing, but Stefano did not join in.

'I know what I saw,' he said.

'You know what you think you saw.'

'It wasn't a dream. It was real.'

'How do you know?'

'Because I've had dreams, and I know what they're like, and this wasn't one.'

'Why? Because it was more vivid?'

'Yes.'

'But you were actually on the sand at the time, weren't you? And before that you were in the sea, being pulled out of it by all the people who rescued you.'

'That was my body. I left it behind, like you do when you die.'

'Except you don't. That's just a thing people like to believe, because they know they're going to die, but they

22

can't imagine not existing.'

'How do you know? You can be really patronising, you know.'

Adam was not quite certain why he felt so alarmed. They had different interests, which was fine, and he was much more cerebral than Stefano, which was not a problem either. But he had always liked the fact that they had both voted for Tony Blair and they both thought that religion was mumbo-jumbo, without one having to convince the other. Would it be a catastrophe if that altered, and one of them changed his mind? It ought not to be, but the prospect was unsettling nonetheless.

'OK, I'm sorry,' he said. There was no sense arguing about it now. They had both, he reminded himself for the umpteenth time, had a shock, and things were bound to settle down.

But he could not resist adding: 'I can promise you, though, that it's your brain playing tricks on you, just like it does when you're asleep.'

'How can you promise me that? How can you be so sure I didn't see God?'

Stefano's eyes were blazing, and Adam forced himself to change the subject.

'We've still got three days' holiday left,' he said. 'Shall we try and find a less dangerous beach tomorrow, and we can just lie in the sun and relax?'

On balance, he decided, it would be unwise to mention Christopher Columbus' villa.

3

ONE OF THE THINGS that distinguished God from some of the more developed creatures of his realm – such as the hominid master-race of the third rock from a middle-sized star in a spiral galaxy in a part of his universe that he technically classified as 'over there' – was that he did not have much stuff.

Having spun the whole thing into motion and then sat back and watched, for what those hominids would think of as thirteen billion years, he was not much of a maker. He had neither the tools nor the understanding of how to go about putting things together, never having been shown. Nor did he really have anywhere to put anything, what with objects tending to drift off into the ether whenever he let them go. The possessions he did have were either bits of cosmic jetsam to which he had taken a fancy over the aeons, or remnants of the mysterious, forgotten time before the present universe had got up and spinning, when objects had existed according to very different rules.

Of the latter, his most treasured item was his seeing-tube, a piece of para-dimensional magic that could be directed wherever he chose. Allowing him to zoom in as close as he wanted on whatever grabbed his interest, it was his entry into the scattered, teeming worlds that now spun according to their own magic. He could not imagine living without it, and he always kept it by his side, which was where it was at the moment Stefano Cartwright came so assertively to his attention.

The reason the creator treasured his seeing-tube so much was that he was not blessed with long-distance vision. He was excellent up close, which was not surprising, given how near everything in his universe had been back in the early days. As time had gone on, however, he had struggled to adapt to the ever-growing immensity of his realm. Big-picture views were fine, but if he wanted to see what was going on in any particular spot, he had to shift himself closer, which could be irritating if there was nothing much going on there after all. As the distances became ever greater, he could also never quite shake the fear that he might lose his way in some backwater galaxy and not be able to find his way back to the centre. His tube got around all those problems, allowing him to zoom in wherever he wanted without actually moving.

By contrast, his hearing was magnificent, as if he had been designed all along to exist in an infinitely expanding territory. He could pick up sounds from one end of his cosmos to the other, even if he sometimes had no idea what was making them. The problem with this hyper-sensitivity was that major and minor sounds threw themselves on his attention with equal weight. Stellar conflagrations made a primordial din, as loud as anything in the universe, but even if he was engrossed in watching a supernova – he never tired of the ever-changing colours – he could still be distracted by a much lesser commotion, something tiny and parochial that managed to penetrate through. It did not always happen: it was more of a random occurrence that the creator would have struggled to explain, if he had ever given it much thought. Since he had no real need to know how or why anything worked, he never had.

One of these random penetrations had now attracted his attention. The disturbance took the form of a crash and cry, unmistakably hominid, even to a deity with only sporadic experience of these creatures, but somehow primitive. It did not articulate anything beyond raw feeling: first pain, then anguish, and finally terror. It was also muted, as if it were being dampened by some great vastness, denser and more destructive than the enveloping nothing of space. Alongside it was a rushing sound, as of liquid, and a gurgling or bubbling, as if something gaseous were being forced through it. Then there was silence.

The creator turned away from his supernova – it would be there for a good while yet – and reached for his tube, which could be extended in whatever direction he chose to point it. Now he thrust it through the galaxies towards its target and peered through the nearest end. Light coursed down the dark cylinder as he did so, creating a massive torch arcing down to the surface of the rock. He was able to fix with remarkable accuracy – only two or three misses before he got it right – on the precise spot where the commotion had started. At first it was all a blur, and he had to twist the little wheel at top of the looking-end, which had been made slightly too small for divine comfort. When, after a little fumbling, he got it to work, he saw that he was not alone. Looking back at him were two large, green eyes, framed by long lashes, blinking in the glare.

As the light filled the length of the tube, the eyes seemed to accustom themselves to the brightness; they widened, first in astonishment and then fear, whereupon they vanished as quickly as they had come. Then the tube went dark and it was God's turn to blink.

The creator had been following the fortunes of this planet long before its hominid inhabitants had been around to call it Earth. He remembered the place when it was dominated by lizards, and he had watched those scaly machines shake the rock with their tread and beat the gassy surround with their wings. As they wrangled and sparred, he wondered which of them would win the battle for ascendancy.

In the event, none of them did. After a long observation tour taking in several million galaxies in a distant part of the universe, God had returned to find the planet barely recognisable. He had thought he had got the wrong place at first, and it was only after careful checking around the galactic neighbourhood that he could be certain this was the correct spot. Pushing his tube through a ring of dust and watching as the white light coursed down it, he saw that the lush, sprouting vegetation was smoking and charred. Nothing shook the ground or beat the grimy gas any longer. The creatures that had once done so now lay in an advanced state of decomposition, little more than stick frames to suggest their former shapes. As the planet turned on its axis, the creator traced his tube up and down its surface scouring for clues to what had caused this destruction. One third of the way round, he found what he took to be the culprit. Embedded in the planet's central belt was a piece of rock. It was a mere pebble by the standards of the cosmos, but it had clearly packed enough mineral punch to smash a smouldering crater into the surface of the Earth. Everything was much blacker here, at the centre of what had evidently been a fiery maelstrom. The stick frames that dotted what remained of this landscape were as black here as everything else, and the creatures must have been consumed by the inferno. Elsewhere on the rock they seemed simply to have expired.

The creator allowed the planet to spin for rotation after rotation as he surveyed the devastation. He wondered if he might have done something to prevent all this. He could perhaps have deflected the boulder, if only he had known it was coming. But he could not be expected to follow the trajectory of every flying pebble. Besides, how was he to know its impact would cause such destruction? Since the physical operation of his universe was a mystery to God, he had always judged it best not to meddle in what he understood so imperfectly. It was a shame about the destruction of the reptiles and pretty much everything else on this bushy little planet, but it was not really his responsibility, and he could not be blamed.

As it happened, the rock was not completely dead. He got into the habit of checking now and then, just to see if anything was sprouting. And sure enough, it was, and then some. New creatures rose from the ashes, dominated eventually by a race of apes. At first they seemed pretty basic creatures, tiny in comparison with their predecessors. Gradually, however, they rose onto their lower limbs, organising their shouts and moans into a form of communication that set them apart from the many other species that had also emerged from the devastation. This ability to talk, as they called it, did not make them unique in cosmic terms, but it was rare enough to raise Earth a good deal higher on God's list of rocks worth keeping tabs on. He might even go so far as to say he had an affection for the place.

He shook his suddenly darkened seeing-tube. It played up occasionally, which was not surprising considering how long he had had it, and he had been meaning to take a look at it when it was retracted. Now, however, it blinked back to life, which was a relief, allowing him to concentrate on the more pressing issue of finding what that disturbance had been.

The green eyes with the long lashes had definitely vanished. Instead, as he fiddled with the focusing rotor, the creator found himself looking at a strip of dark, grainy sediment where the dry part of the planet met the liquid part. On this strip were a number of scattered hominids who were instantly notable for having removed the garments with which these creatures normally covered themselves. God had noticed this ritual before: it involved prostrating themselves before their star. Sure enough, the strip of sediment was dotted with the bright woven mats traditionally used for this worship, although not all the hominids were prostrated. At the far end, a group of them – some completely ungarmented, others with a protective cloth at the top of their lower limbs – propelled a small, round object back and forth over a line suspended between two poles. At the near end, framed by the circle of his tube, was a different kind of gathering. Several of the creatures were gathered around a pale hominid shape stretched on the black sediment. One of this crowd, a furry male with a pendulous hide, was bending over it.

One of the onlookers shouted something in an Earth tongue and the furry hominid pulled back, giving the creator a clearer view of the prostrate figure. It made a rasping noise and opened its eyes, and he could see that they were the green ones he had seen down the tube.

The onlookers emitted a collective, high-pitched roar that made God wince. If only he could turn down his internal volume as easily as he could adjust the focus of his tube.

Now a self-propelling craft on rotors had drawn up at the edge of the strip, announcing itself with a searing wail that nearly made the creator drop his end of the tube. Two more hominids emerged from this craft, standing out from the rest of the creatures because they were fully garmented. The group around the prone creature parted to let them through. They lifted him onto a woven mat between two sticks and proceeded to bear it back to their craft. The craft gave another short wail – God was ready for it this time – and then it was back on the move. It performed a rapid manoeuvre to point itself in the opposite direction and then set off towards a collection of straight-edged hominid structures. Rather than stopping there, it turned towards the centre of what the creator could now see, as he panned backwards, was a free-standing rocklet. The craft joined a smooth, grey track that wound in broad, slow loops up the angled surface of the rocklet until it reached a larger collection of hominid boxes higher up. Here it wailed some more, making other craft shy from its path, and eventually stopped in front of the largest structure in the cluster. The two garmented hominids got down and opened the flaps to retrieve the stricken creature on his mat. Transferring him onto a raised pallet on rotors, they pushed him through a wide portal at the entrance of the structure and disappeared.

The creator continued to peer down the tube, irritated that he could not follow. Magical as his device was, it would not see through solid structures. This was frustrating, because his interest was well and truly roused. Homo sapiens had been shouting in anguish for tens of thousands of years, and if one of them managed to shout loud enough to attract the creator's attention over the general clamour of the rest of the universe, he was bound to be curious.

Something else bothered him too. As he looked straight into this hominid's eye, it had felt as if that eye was looking straight back at him. In all those aeons of existence, that had never happened. He had never been spotted before, and he was not at all sure he liked the idea of being spotted now.

4

IF ANYONE HAD asked Stefano before his mishap with the wave if he believed in God, he would have said without hesitation that he did not. He had described himself as an atheist for all his adult life and more, having decided at the age of fourteen that religion was make-believe, and had given it very little thought since then.

Until that point, his attitude had been very different.

His mother, while not a church-goer by inclination, had convinced herself when Stefano was small that regular attendance at their local Anglican church would help him gain entry to the better of the two available primary schools, which was run by the Church of England. So he had been taken there on at least a couple of Sundays each month from the age of four. He liked the place, because the vicar made everyone laugh with a stand-up routine that involved pretending to treat squalling babies as if they were hecklers, and sending the congregation home at the end of every service with strict instructions on what kind of roast they should eat for lunch. It made everyone hungry, as well as making them laugh, thereby giving the service not one but two positive associations in their minds for the rest of the week.

He was duly admitted to the C of E school, where the

vicar paid occasional visits, cracking more jokes to the class and making those children whom he knew by name, including Stefano, swell with pride. There were also daily prayers, where Stefano sang the hymns lustily and squeezed his eyes tight shut as he chanted *Our Father, who art in heaven, Hallo be thy name*, equally proud that he knew the words so well. It would never have occurred to him to peep.

He liked the stories they did in class, because the pictures took him to an exotic, far-away world full of nice animals like camels and donkeys, where everyone wore bright colours, including the men – unlike the grey jackets that men in the real world seemed to wear – and the weather was always hot and sunny. Aside from those obvious exceptions like the Flood and the Parting of the Red Sea, the stories were set in a world that always looked sun-kissed and sandy, like the slides of Spain that his Auntie Jill and Uncle Richard sometimes showed when they came to visit. It was refreshingly different from the rain-spattered, suburban sprawl visible through the window of their prefab classroom.

He also liked watching big biblical epics on television. His mother had a great fondness for Charlton Heston, who wore a short tunic and had thick, bronzed legs. Slightly disloyally, Stefano found that he preferred Yul Brynner: he was so handsome with his splendid pharaonic necklace nestling on his bare, hairless chest, and even though he played Moses' wicked royal brother, he prompted a wistful, breathless craving deep in Stefano's chest that he did not properly understand. He also knew that the poor Hebrew slaves, sweating and straining as they hauled great blocks of stone around, were being treated terribly, but he liked watching them, because they, like Yul Brynner, were stripped to the waist.

At his secondary school, which was for boys only, there were more daily prayers and school services at the end of every term. The singing of the hymns became more dismal, because no adolescent youth in his right mind could look as if he were enjoying them, and while Stefano took a certain pleasure in being different, he was not that perverse. Even for him, those assemblies were an ordeal: the headmaster droning on with his interminable thees and thous, as rows of fidgety boys shot peashooter pellets at one another. Unlike his classmates, however, Stefano did not loathe their twice weekly scripture lessons. These were taught by a lithe, hyperactive teacher of indeterminate age called Mr Thompson, who had never done any harm to anyone but had been nicknamed Tommy Tosspot by a previous, long-departed generation of boys, and had been known as such ever since. Stefano took a lively interest in Bible study and, because he had been paying more attention to this topic than to any other over a period of years, he got good marks, far better than in any other subject. He seemed so interested that, at one point, Tommy discreetly asked if he thought he might have a calling.

Life, however, was calling him in another direction. The stirrings occasioned by Yul Brynner and the Hebrew slaves had now made themselves more physically manifest as he grew into teenage maturity. The discovery that he was aroused by male beefcake, and not the big-busted nymphettes in the battered magazines that were passed around the class for nightly loan, did not alarm him. The pleasure he had already begun to take in being different had perhaps been an early intimation of this much more major departure from the norm, and it meant that he was happy to take the discovery in his stride, with a clear sense of the benefits of the situation. He and a boy in the year above him, Martin Morris, had been sucking each other off since Stefano was thirteen, taking them to a level that even the most confident members of his class could scarcely dream of in their courtship of girls from the school half a mile away.

His only concern was religious. He had never heard the act that he carried out with Martin Morris explicitly censured, not by the vicar, nor Tommy, nor anyone else. Stefano was not entirely naïve, and he knew that this was not because it would be smiled on, but rather that it was considered too shocking even to name. This puzzled him. He had always grasped the good sense of most Christian morality: if you accepted that you should do unto others as you would have them do unto you, it was obvious why it was wrong to kill, steal or lie. It was much less clear why it was sinful for Stefano to act on physical urges that he could no more control than he could change the length of his toes, and which were not doing anyone else the slightest harm. Yet he had an ominous feeling that there was meant to be a special place in hell for people who did this kind of thing.

His worry gave scripture lessons a more sombre twist,

but he continued to engage in debate with Tommy, raising his hand and taking a more willing part in discussion topics than the rest of the class put together. It was one of these discussions, in the December when he turned fourteen, that would prompt a wholesale reassessment of his religious worldview.

They were talking about the visit to the Holy Family of the Three Wise Men, with their gifts of gold, frankincense and myrrh.

Tommy wanted to talk about frankincense and myrrh. What were these things, and why were they valued? He brought out the lump of frankincense resin that he had acquired on one of his Holy Land pilgrimages, and passed around a little vial of myrrh oil.

'Smells like liquorice, sir,' said a boy called Morgan, who was good-looking and charismatic, with the effect that everything he said was confident and entertaining. If he was paying attention, the rest of the class did too. 'D'you think the baby Jesus liked liquorice?'

Drew, who always sprawled in the back row, reached forward and dabbed some drops of this essence behind the ears of Peters, whose glasses were held together with Elastoplast and was often bullied.

There was a muffled commotion as Peters tried to push him away and wipe the liquorice perfume off without drawing Tommy's attention.

'Why would anyone want it, though, sir?' persisted Morgan.

'It was highly prized,' said Tommy. 'It was used in medicine and in incense, so it was a very generous gift –

befitting the baby who they had been told was the king of the Jews. The same goes for frankincense.'

For Stefano, the interesting gift was the third one.

'Sir, sir,' he said, waving his hand. 'What happened to the gold, sir?'

Tommy brightened, as he always did when Stefano asked a question. This time, however, there was bemusement in his face too.

'What do you mean, what happened to it? I'm not with you.'

'I mean, it must have been worth a lot of money. Gold is gold, that's the whole point. And if an eastern king was giving gold to Jesus because he thought he was king of the Jews, he must have brought a decent amount, otherwise it would have been an insult. So what did Joseph and Mary do with it? Why didn't it make them rich?'

Tommy put his head on one side and rubbed the side of his nose with a long finger.

'Maybe they gave it to charity, sir,' suggested Morgan.

'No, I don't think that,' said Tommy. 'It's a good question, but you know, I don't think we have to take every element of these stories literally. Sometimes they're more…symbolic.'

Stefano frowned.

'Symbolic, sir?'

'The stories were told to make a point, and in this case the point was that the birth of Jesus had been foretold, and was treated as a major event by important people far and wide.'

'So they may not actually have brought gold,

frankincense and myrrh?'

The rest of the class was sniggering, assuming that this was all an elaborate game, designed to catch Tommy out. For Stefano, however, it was an utterly sincere question with no disruptive purpose.

'Not as such,' admitted Tommy. 'And they may not actually have been kings, of course. That's why they're known as the Three Wise Men, because the translation is ambiguous.'

Stefano fell silent and the conversation moved on, but he pondered it for days. If you did not have to take all of these stories literally, because some of them were only symbolic, how were you supposed to know which was which? He could not help feeling let down, because he had believed it all absolutely, in good faith. A week or two later, by complete coincidence, the *Nine O'Clock News* was reporting just the same issue: the bishop of somewhere had caused a controversy by saying he did not think the virgin birth should be taken literally, nor that Jesus had actually walked on water. These statements had met with widespread shock, so it was clear that this was not a mainstream view. However, Stefano began to wonder if some of the anger directed at the bishop was not so much for his modern heresy, but because he had let the cat out of the bag. He found himself going over all the stories he had believed all his life, and he was alarmed at how many of them seemed suddenly flimsy if you started to subject them to ordinary standards of plausibility. With some of them he realised there was an understandable chance of exaggeration, particularly if the tales had grown in the telling before they could be written down. With the Feeding of the Five Thousand, for example, it was easy to imagine that there were not really five thousand people, because it was hard to count crowds, and it would be very easy for the number to jump from five hundred in the telling, and that Jesus had more than five loaves and two fish; perhaps he had managed to make a big, watery stew, spinning it out as far as it would go, and nobody had got very much of it. However, if these teachers and bishops were saying that some stories were symbolic, that suggested they were not so much accidentally exaggerated but deliberately made up. To Stefano, that smacked of dishonesty, because it left him not knowing how much of any of it he could actually believe. Where, he wondered, did the symbolism end? Was he also meant to believe that God himself was symbolic?

And in a blinding flash, like a reverse version of the one that had struck St Paul on the road to Damascus, he had seen through it all: of course it was symbolic, whether the vicars and bishops knew it or not, because it was all invented, in order to make everyone feel better about dying. He ought to feel aggrieved, having been misled for so long, but he realised his reaction was quite the opposite. If God was not real, and nor was heaven, then neither was hell. That meant Stefano was not in any eternal trouble for sucking off Mark Morris. This was not just a tremendous weight off his mind; it was liberation.

He detached himself from his previous affiliation with remarkable ease. He stopped closing his eyes in assembly, he no longer joined in the mumbling of the Lord's Prayer, and he no longer gave any of it much thought, to the evident disappointment of poor Tommy Tosspot, who lost his most enthusiastic pupil without ever knowing why.

As an adult, it was all long forgotten. His only experience of Christianity was the crazies who stood outside the town hall to warn against the transformation of Hackney into Sodom-on-Thames, or the bishops on the *Today* programme, which Adam listened to in the mornings, who seemed to take much the same view, only in more sober language, as they explained their opposition to whatever new piece of homosexual liberalisation was edging its way through the House of Lords. It was true that he hung out with various vegan types who described themselves as spiritual. Nevertheless, it was clear to him before he and Adam set out for their island holiday in the Atlantic – as he assumed it was clear to all his friends and all the customers at work – that the Christian God was a made-up character whose primary function in modern life seemed to be to keep the gays down.

By the time they returned, some of his certainties were beginning to come unstuck. Since Adam seemed so reluctant to discuss anything that had happened during his blackout, his imagination had been left to its own devices, and it had begun to supply embellishments that made his memory of the incident more vivid. The eye, which at first he could not describe in any detail, was now the deepest blue he had ever seen, bluer than the sky above the beach or the satin curtains on the little cabaret stage at the Prince Edward – named, if the lawyers ever asked, after Queen Victoria's father – where Stefano was head barman. There had also been music, he now decided, of a celestial, harpish kind. And that white light of the tunnel was oddly wispy, like the cotton wool clouds you climbed through in an aeroplane.

He was keen to tell Rook about it all at the earliest opportunity.

'I'm so pleased to see you,' he said, when his oldest friend turned up at the flat the day after their return.

'And I thought that was a gun in your pocket.'

The August sun was beating down on the south-facing windows of the council flat, so the coolest place was the balcony, with the beats and sirens of a Hackney summer playing out beneath them.

'I'm serious. There was an accident on the beach and I nearly drowned. I had to go to hospital and everything.'

'Jeez, I never realised. Tell me everything, darl.'

Rook was an Aussie, about five years older than Stefano, and had been in London forever. His real name was Andrew Castle, but he used it so rarely that many of his friends would have been hard-pressed to state it. Crested with a scarlet mohican, he was permanently unshaven and had a thick ring through his nose. This punky look, together with a confidently gruff voice, made it all the more incongruous that he never knowingly used the masculine pronoun for another man, and addressed anyone he ever encountered, male or female, as 'darl'.

Rook started making a roll-up as Stefano gave his account of getting knocked off his feet in the sea.

'Wow,' he said, licking the paper down. 'So how did you

get out of the water?'

'I don't know. The next thing I knew, there was this big group of people standing around and a guy bending over me to give me the kiss of life.'

'Really! Was she cute? That should have been some consolation, at least.'

'Not at all. And stop interrupting, I'm getting to the most important bit.'

'What, blacking out in the ocean and nearly drowning isn't the most important bit?'

'No, that's the whole point! You're as bad as Adam.'

'You mean your boyfriend thought it was a big deal you nearly died? I wouldn't complain about that, darl. I'd be more worried if she didn't think it was a big deal.'

'The whole point is, I wasn't looking up at the guy giving me the kiss of life. I was looking down on him.'

'Like a sort of out-of-body experience?'

'No 'sort of' about it. That's exactly what it was.'

'Wow. So you could really see yourself just lying there?'

'I could even see Adam trying to push through the crowd.'

'Last on the scene, eh?'

'He's really sensitive about it. But then I couldn't see all that any more, and it was like I was going up this tunnel, with the sides all made of light. It's really hard to describe, but I was feeling amazing, like I was going up on the best pill I've ever had…'

'Now you're talking my kinda language.'

'And before I knew it I was lying on the ground, back on the beach.'

'Bummer.'

'Tell me about it. And I was looking right into this German's face, and now I come to think of it, he really wasn't cute. Then everyone was shouting and Adam was there and I was going in an ambulance. And I wanted to talk about what had just happened, but no one would listen. Thinking about it was making my head explode.'

'I'm not surprised, darl. And what would you have said if anyone had listened, like your Auntie Rook for instance? What do you think happened to you?'

'I reckon I actually died. That can happen, can't it? And when it does, you end up looking down at yourself. I saw something on TV about it once.'

'And you think this German gargoyle brought you back to life?'

'He must have done. And just before he did, I was about to go to…well…'

'Where?'

'You know… Heaven.'

'OK…'

'Why not?

'Well, maybe. If you believe in all that. But I thought you didn't.'

'No…I don't know…maybe I do.'

'I see.'

'Do you? That's why it's doing my head in. If you'd been up that tunnel and seen what I did…'

'Strictly speaking, darl, you didn't see all that much. If heaven was real and you'd actually been there, shouldn't you have seen angels and St Peter, and shit like that?'

'I did see an eye.'

'An eye?'

'Yes.'

'OK. And whose eye do you think it was?'

'Well…you know.'

'I know?'

'Yes, of course you know.'

'But you don't want to say it?'

Stefano glowered.

Rook helped him out.

'You think you saw God. Who, up till a week ago, you didn't actually believe in.'

'I don't think anything. I know what I saw.'

Rook relit his roll-up, which had gone out.

'This is pretty heavy stuff, darl.'

'Tell me about it.'

'You know I don't go for all that religion shit, so it's a bit of a stretch for me. But each to their own, eh? The main thing is, you survived. And now you're back with us, which I'm prepared even in my own godless way to accept as a minor miracle. So smile, darl. You're lucky to be with us and we're lucky to have ya.'

Stefano did not feel like smiling. It felt like nobody was taking him particularly seriously, which was irritating, but he also had a deeper, ominous sense that he might be in terrible trouble, of a kind that he had not contemplated for a very long time.

5

THE CREATOR HAD maintained a long, boring vigil, with his tube focused on the large structure where the hominid who had looked him in the eye had been taken. There was very little to do or see, and God had resorted to counting the number of building blocks on the front side of the structure to amuse himself – two hundred and forty-two across, sixty-odd upwards, and counting – when he heard a sound from elsewhere in his cosmos that mystified him.

The noises of the universe took many forms. There was the hum of life, the swoosh of weather and the fizz of blazing rocks, as well as the primordial roar of matter falling into itself or being created anew. There was also the whirr of constant orbit and the rush of space-wind as each cog of the machine turned. Finally, lurking beneath it all, there was the steady creak and groan of matter itself, as space pushed into non-space and the void grew ever larger.

This new sound was none of those. Barely discernible to start with, at first he thought he must have imagined it, because it faded out as gently as it had arrived. He turned away from his counting and listened as hard as he could, doing his utmost to tune out the myriad other sounds of the cosmos and focus on this one. For a long while there was nothing, and he was about to conclude that he had been mistaken. But no, there it was again – a faint but sonorous thrum. It was so soft it was easy to miss, but detectable nonetheless – and despite its softness, there was something peculiar about it. It sounded as distant as anything in the universe could be, but that was not the strange thing. The real oddity was that it seemed not to be coming from the same source all the time. As far as the creator could make out, it was alternating from one side of his cosmos to the other.

Again it faded, and again he focused as hard as he could, blotting out the roar, whirr and rush of everything else and attempting to mute the chaotic babble of life-forms all over the universe. There it came again, a humming vibration, now from one side, now from another. It was much too far away to make any sense of it. The fact that it seemed to be zigzagging about made the job all the harder.

He still had half an eye on the entrance to the hominid structure. As the vibration faded once more, he saw movement in the doorway and zoomed in to see the green-eyed hominid emerging. Walking now, rather than being carried by bearers, the creature got into the back of a small yellow craft with a beacon on top. For the moment, the oscillating murmur was forgotten.

God did not like the idea of any of the beings of his universe invading his privacy. He was particularly sensitive about this green-eyed hominid doing so, because these hominids had form in the matter.

Not so many Earth-years earlier, he had become aware that they were pitching objects off the surface of their own rock. These projectiles seemed to have the capacity to travel of their own accord. They also contained live cargo: other creatures at first and then, as their confidence in these missions grew, hominids themselves were dispatched. Initially they did not seem to want to go anywhere in particular: the earliest excursions were brief forays off the surface of the planet. Using his seeing-tube as best he could to follow their progress, God could see from the collective jubilation on their successful completion that the important thing seemed to be returning the hominid cargo unharmed.

He was not at all sure he approved of their trespass onto his domain. In a sense, of course, the whole universe was his domain, and they had trespassed onto that just by evolving into life. He certainly did not recall having any say in that matter. But as long as their life was confined to the rock that had spawned it, the creatures in question did not present any challenge to God, and they offered him something diverting to look at from time to time. Leaving the surface and venturing out into the universe itself was more unsettling. Where would it all end? That was his real fear. It was extraordinary how far they had come, and he took a degree of vicarious pride in that. But these hominids were a pugnacious lot, obsessed with expanding their own territory and trampling on everything beneath them. What if they were an evolutionary monster in the making, which might one day challenge his own position?

He remembered one occasion in particular, when his attention was caught by the roar of an explosion on the surface of Earth. Focusing his tube, he saw a slim, cylindrical canister, tapering to a point at one end, powering away from the surface of the planet. Behind it was a trail of fire, a tail-plume much longer and wider than the canister itself, which seemed to be propelling the craft up into God's realm. This was how they always did it: these hominids had learned to make their own comets now.

As the craft distanced itself from earth, the blazing tail-section fell away, leaving the stubby front end of the cylinder to continue on its route. It was heading in the direction of the dull, crater-spattered rock that spun around the Earth and had, as far as the creator could see, zero noteworthy qualities. What did they want from the place?

Through his seeing tube, God watched the craft drawing closer to the rock, and its three hominid occupants gathering at its windows, peering at the smaller rock, just as the creator was peering at them. He wondered if they would be able to make the craft stop once they got there. For all his reservations about this act of hominid hubris, it would be sad to see the canister smash into the smaller rock and crush the three travellers. For their part, they seemed unconcerned by this possibility, and were clearly captivated by the unremarkable lump that they had crossed the void to see. Only now did God notice, however, that the craft was off course. He had not seen it at first, but it became obvious the closer they came: they were set to bypass the rock altogether, which at least averted the risk of destruction. Perhaps they were set on a longer voyage after all. But no, now their craft was turning, hugging the curve of the smaller rock as if it meant to go round it. And now, finally, the hominid occupants began to show anxiety.

Although of course he could not understand what they were saying in their language, God worked out that they were somehow relaying communications back to Earth. From what he could gather from their bodily expression and the logic of the situation, they seemed to be worried that these communications would no longer work once they disappeared behind the cratered rock.

That gave him a mischievous idea. What if he were to pluck the vessel away when it was on the far side? It was tempting, and not just because it would bring their species down a peg. Reluctant as he was to admit it, God was sick and tired of being on his own. For aeon after aeon, he had been stuck in his solitary position in the cosmos, never having any living company, never a conversation, throughout the eternity of his existence, and sometimes it was all too much. He was meant to be the creator, the deity, the boss. Yet at times, he did not mind admitting to himself, he was lonely.

In that context, he rather liked the idea of three hominid familiars. He could snatch the craft, unseen by its controllers on the home planet, and spirit its occupants away to a new life at his side. It would be fun.

If he was going to act, though, he did not have long

to decide. Under pressure, he did his best to think it through. Would the hominids need care and attention to keep them alive? The creator was not the nurturing kind – he simply had no experience of such things. They needed sustenance, he knew that, which he had no idea how to provide. The craft was two-thirds of the way round now and this no longer seemed such a good idea. He wished he could be more impetuous, just act on a whim and never mind the consequences, but that was not how he was made. And now the opportunity was drifting away. Vacillation was an inevitable by-product of having to spin out an existence into eternity, he told himself, as the craft began to emerge from the lee of the rock.

A crackly voice from inside the canister told him they were back in communication with Earth. Through the windows, he saw the three travellers take turns to raise their upper limbs and slap each other's hands. He took this to be an expression of relief. The craft emerged fully into Earth-view and the creator waited for it to set a homeward course.

Oddly, however, its direction remained unaltered: it seemed to have fallen into the same kind of rotation that governed all the other floating objects on his cosmos. This seemed natural enough, but it might make it harder for these hominids to return to their own planet, if that was what they still sought to do. Wondering whether he ought, instead of abducting them, to give them a helping homewards nudge, he peered back into the interior. The travellers appeared calm, so they clearly meant to go round again. Was fate tempting him to reconsider?

There was again no chatter from the hominids as the craft rounded the far side of the rock, and the crackle of Earth-communication fell quiet. Maybe the creator could just cause a temporary diversion to give them a jolt. He could swing them out of their rotation and off in the opposite direction, perhaps show them a galaxy or two beyond their own. That would unsettle them, and confirm all their fears about disappearing from view of their own planet. But something, whether maturity or caution, continued to hold him back, and the craft began to nose into Earth-view once more. He was glad they were now going home. Aside from anything else, the whole episode had made him feel bumbling and indecisive.

Wait, though. Surely not? They were going round yet again! And again, it happened, and then again. Ten full rotations, God counted, before they finally changed their course and set off on the return journey to Earth.

This ten-times circumnavigation must have served some preparatory function. Not long afterwards, a new canister made another voyage in the direction of the cratered rock, adorned as it lifted off the surface of Earth by the same fiery tail-plume. This time, it headed straight there, landing comfortably on the rock itself. Two more hominids – or perhaps they were the same ones, since they all looked alike to God – emerged in a kind of garb they did not use on Earth and walked on the dusty surface. Now, perhaps, they would reveal their purpose in coming here. The creator watched carefully for any signs of what it might be. If there was one, however, it remained a mystery to him. They climbed back into their craft and embarked once more for Earth, after scarcely any time at all.

After that they came back a few times, but the novelty seemed to wear off. With familiarity, God became more relaxed about the whole business, and after a while he stopped watching. Soon enough there was nothing to watch anyway. The hominids seemed to have lost their enthusiasm for venturing into the creator's realm. Perhaps they had realised the truth that had been obvious to God all along: they would have to go a long way before they encountered a rock half as congenial to them as the one they already occupied.

Looking back at that period, he felt a certain sense of accomplishment, a satisfaction that he had conquered his anxieties. Coming back to the present, however, his encounter with a green human eye down his seeing-tube had shaken up him. Even at the height of his worries about hominid exploration of the cosmos, it had never occurred to him that any of them would actually be able to see him.

God was the watcher not the watched. That was how it had always been, and that was how he intended it to remain. As far as he was concerned, his realm was visible to him and he was invisible to it. He was not sure if this was literally true: if one of these space travellers had come into his presence, he had no idea whether they would have been able to see him or not. They seemed to live in fewer dimensions than he did, and it stood to reason that they could not conceive of vastness on the universal scale that he knew, or time on his eternal calendar. So it was perfectly possible that they did not have the physical capacity to perceive him. He could have put that proposition to the test if he had abducted the travellers but, now he came to think about it, that was one of the things that had stopped him going through with that impetuous plan. Exposing himself to needless scrutiny was something he had no wish to do. It was a question of privacy, of essential divine dignity.

That was why he was so unsettled at the thought of a hominid eye not only looking at him through his tube, but reacting as if it had noticed him. It had all happened so quickly, but he was pretty sure that was what had happened: the eye was unfocused at first, but then it had come to rest and visibly widened in...what? Awe? Horror? Fear? He had no argument with any of those reactions, but that was beside the point. The eye should never have been able to see him at all.

He looked on through his tube as the craft with the beacon on top descended the winding track, down the angled surface of the rocklet, conveying the green-eyed hominid back towards the little collection of shelters next to the strip where God had first witnessed the commotion. Another track, lined with structures on either side, ran around the edge of the rocklet. The craft now turned along it, heading away from the strip and stopping in front of one of the larger ones.

His quarry disappeared into an entrance and God groaned: observing hominids was next to impossible if they persisted in spending all their time within walls. He trailed his tube irritably up and down the structure and was about to pull it away when he noticed movement on an open section of the uppermost level. Here, a pair of bright sun-worshipping mats were draped over two white pallets, and the green-eyed hominid now emerged onto this open platform. The creator watched as the hominid shed all his garments, apart from a multi-coloured loin-protector, and sank onto one of the pallets. He then proceeded to set fire to a stick which he put in his mouth, sucking in the smoke and expelling it through his nose.

When the Earth turned away from its sun, he and his companion went inside the dwelling. The creator was able to maintain his watch for as long as it was illuminated, but then the pair of hominids extinguished their lights and he could not see a thing. He was vaguely aware that, during this dark-time, hominids lay motionless for hours on end – and he could see that this was going to be tedious even by his standards. Since the two creatures were not likely to go anywhere until their part of the planet came out of the shadows again, he decided he might as well see if anything else had been happening in his universe.

He was about to tug on his tube to retract it when, once again, he became aware of the same faint, sonorous vibration that had disturbed him earlier. As before, it hummed so softly that it was easy to miss. But once he had noticed it, the distant, alternating murmur was impossible to ignore, oscillating from one side of the cosmos to another. It was not a regular swing back and forth, but more random, with a long murmur coming from this side, followed by a short one from that, then a short one from the first side and a short one from that, and then a long one from each, with no discernible pattern. Abandoning his tube for the moment and turning to survey his glistening cosmos with his naked vision, the creator could see nothing out of the ordinary. That proved nothing, though. He needed to zoom in, to probe around the outer corners so he could trace the bouncing murmur. He retracted his tube from Earth, allowing it to clatter back across the cosmos and into his grasp, ready to be dispatched in whatever direction the noise dictated. By the time he had done so, however, the oscillating murmur had faded completely. He strained and strained to hear it, but there was now no trace of it, and he began to wonder if he had imagined the whole thing after all.

It was a puzzle, for sure. But at least it had stopped now, so there was no point in getting too worked up about it.

6

As a child, Stefano had often pictured himself at thirty-one. It was the age he would be when the twentieth century ended and the future dawned, a year so special that it was called 'the year two thousand', not 'twenty hundred', and it would usher in an age unimaginably different from anything that had gone before. Imagining himself in that year, Stefano pictured a handsome, strapping grown-up, driving an MG and working in gentlemen's outfitting, having left his parents' neat, bay-windowed semi in Woodville Close far, far behind.

He had spent his earliest years in one of the smaller houses in the Close, but his parents upgraded to a larger one on the opposite side when he was five, following the arrival of his sister, Katie. It had a separate porch, as well as an extra bedroom, and the move reflected his father's steady advancement at Hulme's – or Yume's, as it was pronounced locally – where he had started as a factory apprentice fourteen years earlier and now had his own office and one-third of a secretary. The Close was a neighbourly place, and Stefano's father shared a car to work with a couple of colleagues, each of them driving every third day, when the price of petrol soared. His mother was friendly with their wives. She mixed with most of the Close, but there were exceptions. Across the way was a lecturer at Liverpool Poly, called Dr Jeavons, who displayed the Close's only Labour poster whenever there was an election. Stefano's mother considered it a great irony that his was one of the four-beds, not a three. Mrs Jeavons was glamorous, and her hair sometimes changed colour in the evenings: it was normally brown and tumbled down over her shoulders, but if she and Dr Jeavons were going somewhere special, it would be yellow and piled up on top of her head. It would be back to normal the next day, which amazed Stefano. He wished his mother could be more like Mrs Jeavons.

His father told him he should be proud to come from the North West, but to Stefano, their part of it had always seemed a drab place. His favourite relatives were Auntie Jill and Uncle Richard, who lived Down South, and talked about having barths and walking on the grarss. At Christmas they sent him presents still in the Hamley's bag, and his favourite was a red London bus to add to his Dinky collection. There was a pole at the entrance and you could open the door into the driver's cab. On the front was the number 12 and a sign saying it was going from Peckham to Oxford Circus. He was of an age where he thought he might like to be a bus driver, which was no doubt why they had bought it, but now he dreamed of being a passenger, that he too might one day get on a number 12 bus and travel to Oxford Circus, or VISIT MADAME TUSSAUD'S, as the banner along one side advised.

His father made jokes about Uncle Richard, who

smoked cigars and called people 'squire'. 'Stee, run and get the red carpet from the garage, your Uncle Richard's coming,' he would say, and Stefano's mother would fuss and tut and fold the *Daily Express* in the rack. Whenever they arrived, Stefano would get the job of taking the coats up to the front bedroom. Auntie Jill's was light-brown wool with a fur collar, and it smelled of perfume. At the top of the stairs he buried his face in the fur, loving its scented softness. Uncle Richard's coat was a sober black, but the lining was as red as Stefano's London bus.

On one of these occasions he laid both garments carefully on his parents' bed, the pink candlewick clashing with the shiny scarlet. He folded his uncle's coat closed, and as he did so he read the label on the inside pocket: Austin Reed, Regent Street. He pictured the shop, with black-coated assistants bowing in the doorway and rows of immaculate coats; not anoraks like his father's. He vowed that one day he would go there.

Downstairs, Auntie Jill was asking for Cinzano, only she pronounced it 'Chinzano', and she wanted it with ice not lemonade. Uncle Richard had brought a bottle of Dubonnet, and he and Stefano's father were having that. Uncle Richard, who never called Stefano 'Stee', asked him about school and whether he still wanted to drive a London bus. Stefano said maybe not the bus, but he still wanted to live in London.

His mother shuddered.

'I couldn't live in London, not if you paid me. I know you like it, Jill, but I couldn't. Those crowds.'

'It's not really London, Marion. It's Amersham. There

58

aren't crowds in Amersham.'

But Stefano's mother shuddered again.

'I've never been and I won't go. The girls from the WI were organising a coach for *Jesus Christ Superstar*, and I said no, not if you paid me.'

'Well, young man, it looks like you won't be getting a visit from your mum when you've made your fortune,' said Uncle Richard. He winked. 'That means you can get up to whatever you like. Lucky devil.'

'Richard, don't put ideas in his head,' said his mother with a shriek that was meant to be a gay laugh. She had already sneaked one Cinzano before they arrived.

When everyone had clinked glasses – Stefano had a ginger ale and Katie was allowed squash in a real tumbler rather than her plastic beaker – they listened to Auntie Jill's description of their holiday in Spain. His mother would not go to Spain, not if you paid her. She had been nervous enough in Llandudno to hear Welsh spoken in shops, which she was certain they did deliberately, and they switched back to English as soon as you had gone. She listened to her sister's tales of sangria and bullfighting with a sympathetic smile. Stefano was transfixed, however. He treasured the flamenco doll his uncle and aunt had brought them, with her gypsy headdress and her tiny fan in one outstretched hand.

He had never been abroad. Their holidays were spent in the caravan in Whitby or the Lakes, where no black-eyed señoritas danced under the stars. His mother said she could not abide the smell of garlic, but it had to be better than the stink of damp face-flannel in his washbag, carried every morning to the muddy-floored facilities where men with hairy shoulders plunged their faces into bowls of water with the masculine fuss of public ablution. The showers were the worst: individual cubicles where you balanced your clothes on a slatted stool and had to have your wash quickly before your ten pence ran out, and then you had to dry yourself without trailing your towel on the wet floor. He also dreaded the toilets. At home he sat down once a day, but on the caravan site he only went when he really had to: leaving it till you had no choice made you think less about the horrors of the anonymous seat, at best stark and cold, at worst still warm from some grown-up's buttocks. His mother said it was much worse abroad, where you had to squat over a hole in the ground, but he did not see how she knew, if she had never been. He could not imagine Auntie Jill and Uncle Richard putting up with that.

Mostly, on these holidays, he kept himself to himself, teaching Katie to look in rock pools for crabs, but rarely making friends with children from other caravans. He preferred to sit and watch them, lying on his tummy on the grass if it was dry, peering under the tow-bar at games of catch or French cricket. He was not shy, and would have joined in if he wanted. But watching was more interesting, because you did not have to commit. You could lie there as long as it was entertaining, and when you were bored, you could go off and do something else. Only once was he properly intimidated, by an older boy with the whitest teeth and raven hair that tumbled shining down his shoulders. He was friendly-looking, with a ready smile that lit his face, but his obvious ease in his skin made Stefano feel awkward in his own. The boy was called Tim and came from a 'van five doors down. One day Stefano watched him sneeze into both hands, stoop to wipe the glistening snot on the grass, then stand up, run a hand through his silky hair and carry on his way. Stefano should have been disgusted – he hated putting his hand in his pocket if he had a dirty handkerchief in there – but instead he was awestruck. He felt a tightening in his stomach that he did not understand, just like with Yul Brynner and the Hebrew slaves.

When he was eleven he was taken to Liverpool to be fitted for his school uniform. They went on the ferry for a treat, but the real excitement was George Henry Lee's itself: five floors of soft carpet, a wooden lift with a cage inside, and women with glasses on chains asking if they could help you. Gentlemen's outfitting was on the top floor, next to the café where you got a separate pot of hot water with your tea. There were no windows, just racks of dark suits. The man who served them wore a waistcoat as well as a jacket, and he had a tape measure around his neck and called Stefano 'sir'. His grey hair was styled upwards in a bouncing wave that made Stefano think once more of the magical world of Austin Reed, Regent Street. His measurements were taken, and the man looked dignified even while he was kneeling down with his floppy yellow tape. Stefano's mother looked at the names above the racks.

'Pierre Cardin,' she read. 'Oh, I'd love to buy your father a Pierre Cardin suit.'

Back at his full height, the assistant showed the twitch of a smile that Stefano took to be recognition of his mother's good taste. 'Yes madam, Pierre Cardin is a very fine cut. And not unaffordable, you may find.' He pronounced it 'Car-dan', and Stefano was mortified at his mother's error. But she had not noticed and was looking at the tag on the sleeve of one of the jackets.

'Affordable, did you say? Not unless I win the pools!'

The assistant laughed, then winked at Stefano. It was like with Uncle Richard: he felt they were saying to him, 'It's all right, we can see you're cut from a better cloth.' In that moment, he decided he wanted to be a gentlemen's outfitter.

'Oh no you don't,' said his father, when it came out. 'No son of mine is going to measure inside legs for a living. That's a nancy boy's job. Is that what you want to be, hey, a nancy boy?'

It was still two years before his trysts with Martin Morris were to begin, and Stefano had given very little thought to the matter one way or another. As he bent over his plate and put a forkful of peas in his mouth, however, he made a defiant resolution. If becoming a nancy boy was what it took, then perhaps he would.

At school, he became more of a loner. He was neither particularly popular nor unpopular. Aside from scripture, he did not shine in class, which meant his profile was not high, and his peers did not pay much attention to his precise, strangely refined manner of talking, with the long a's that were beginning to creep in. He held himself apart from the rest of them, not so obviously as to appear aloof, but nevertheless with an instinctive, unconscious sense that he was different from them all and would not remain in this place forever.

His career plan remained unaltered. The school made a fuss about the need to knuckle down and get qualifications, and some boys took it seriously, but Stefano could not see the point. His ambition was to leave the Close and experience the glories of London. He would support himself by working in the kind of shop where refinement was valued and coarseness scorned, and he did not need exams for that. His father's disdainful attitude made him more determined.

It did not help their relationship that they had so little in common. They rarely, if ever, spent any time alone together. It was plain to Stefano that his father wanted someone to watch football with him on television on Saturday afternoons, or to help him change the oil in the car. He had no real way of expressing the horror with which he viewed both prospects, because he could not explain it to himself either, this visceral aversion. So his refusal to comply merely looked sullen and ungracious. His father was no better equipped to surmount the barrier between them. If he ever came into Stefano's room, the obviousness with which he averted his eyes from Boy George and Frankie Goes to Hollywood on the walls confirmed his son's every prejudice about his narrowness of mind. It was clear to both of them that Stefano's father much preferred Katie.

With each perceived slight, Stefano became more disconnected, such as the evening his father repeated a joke he had cracked in the office canteen about a new kind of tea that had appeared next to the water urn.

'I said, "I don't know who this Earl Grey was, but he must have been some kind of poofter!"' he related proudly, laughing so hard that the spit crackled at the corners of his mouth.

Stefano felt his lip curl, as he resolved to sneak a pack of the stuff into his mother's next grocery shopping.

He found himself coming back again and again to that phrase 'no son of mine measures inside legs for a living'. As far as Stefano was concerned, he was going to measure inside legs for a living. By the logic of his father's vow, that meant that Stefano was not his son. It was a contrived piece of reasoning, of course, fit only for Jesuitical debates in a world of immutable certainties where there was no room for give or take. But Stefano was a teenager, so that was just how the world appeared to him, and it was enough to plant the idea in his fertile adolescent mind that he did not owe his father the usual emotional dues. The man had as good as admitted that he was not really his father.

7

ADAM FIRST MET Stefano on Christmas Eve, when the most dismal Christmas that he had ever had to face suddenly turned into the best.

The previous year, he had been invited to spend the day with an older couple in their mid-thirties who had a large house in Streatham and were known for their generous hospitality. Adam had hoped the same invitation would come this year. When it failed to materialise, he worried that he had offended them in some way. That turned out not to be the case, and they had simply rented a cottage in Cornwall, so would not be at home. That was a consolation of sorts, but it still meant there was no invitation to join anyone.

Despite this, Adam decided to maintain the fiction, as far as his family was concerned, that he was spending the festive day with friends. Christmases back home in the Stour Valley, on the border between Suffolk and Essex, tended to be more tearful than jovial, despite the conspicuous jollity with which they were festooned. This was because the fun tipped, with wearisome predictability, into menace after Adam's father's third or fourth glass of Bordeaux. He was an angry patriot who regarded John Major as a pinko lickspittle to the Eurocrats, and not fit to carry Mrs Thatcher's handbag, so Adam was apt to get into fights with him about politics, and it was enjoyable for no one. His mother therefore made only the flimsiest show of resistance when he proposed staying in London that first year. He had a strong hunch that staying away a second year in succession would set this arrangement in stone, giving him permanent dispensation not to appear. Therefore, when the Streatham invitation did not arrive, he calmly assured himself that something else was bound to turn up, because it always did if you trusted to fate and did not give way to needless worry. By the beginning of Christmas week, however, fate was showing no sign of riding to his rescue. He told himself that he would survive, because the twenty-fifth of December was a day like any other, and it would be nice to have his flat to himself – he lived in a rental conversion above a bookmaker's on Balls Pond Road – now that his straight flatmate had left town for the holiday.

By the time he began to wobble, contemplating the gaping enormity of forty-eight hours of festive Christmas TV programming with nothing for company but his misery, it was too late to swallow his pride and head for East Anglia. He had not bought any presents, intending to pick them in the sales for a post-Christmas visit, and he had no confidence he would get on one of the last, packed trains from Liverpool Street. Venturing into the Prince Edward – which was technically his local, although he had never set foot inside it – seemed the best option out of a very limited range of possibilities.

'It's a terrible day to have your birthday,' he sighed to

the barman with green eyes and long lashes who served him a pint of frothy lager. Being born on Christmas Eve was a double misfortune for someone who came from a family that was congenitally terrible at celebrating Christmas. He usually tried to let it pass, but tonight he was in the mood for sympathy.

The barman looked surprised.

'How did you know?'

'How did I know what? I've always known.'

'You've always known that it's my birthday?'

'No, I've always known that it's my birthday. So wait… you're not serious?'

For Adam it was like meeting some long-lost relative, a fellow victim of the same stroke of ill luck.

'It's always been a rubbish day to have it,' said the barman. 'I used to think it was good, because I never had to go to school on my birthday like normal kids. But now I'd give anything to be born on some meaningless day in March or October. And everyone thinks you get double presents, when actually you get less than anyone else, because people either forget completely or they think it's OK to get one present and say it's for both.'

They smiled delightedly at each other, bonding at this sharing of a lifelong grievance.

'So go on then – what year?' said the barman.

Adam reddened.

'You first,' he said. At twenty-five, he had not yet begun to lie about his age to strangers, as his Streatham hosts did as a matter of course, but it was beginning to feel like a sensitive subject.

'Nineteen sixty-eight,' said the barman.

'You're kidding! Honestly?'

'Why, what year are you?'

'Same!'

Adam could not remember feeling so exhilarated. This was not so much like finding a long-lost relative as a long-lost twin.

'I'm Adam,' he said, offering his hand across the bar.

'Stef,' said the barman. 'Short for Stefano.'

'That sounds exotic,' said Adam. 'Is it Italian?'

'Yep, on my mum's side.'

'Oh yes? Where's she from?'

'Erm, she's actually a really strict Italian Catholic, from Rome. My dad met her when he was there on business. He used to import Vespa scooters, stuff like that.'

'Wow. *La dolce vita.*'

The barman seemed not to understand his reference.

'If you say so.'

'Do you speak Italian?'

'No... I was born there but I was brought up here. I don't see them any more. They don't approve of me. You know what it's like.'

Adam shook his head in commiseration.

They talked some more, but the pub was getting busier and Stefano had a throng of customers to serve.

'Don't go away though,' he said. 'What are you doing later?'

Adam blushed, an innocent reflex in contemplation of something less innocent.

He waited till closing time and then they went back

to Stefano's flat. Adam had never been in a tower block before, and he was amazed by the view of the City, with St Paul's beyond, lit up in a marble-white glow. He was further amazed by how much light there was in the morning, Christmas morning, which turned into all of Christmas Day, and it proved to be the most special, magical Christmas he could ever remember. It was romantic, which was not a quality he had ever associated with this day, nor indeed with anything he had ever expected to happen to himself. He felt a rare degree of confidence that Stefano was experiencing something similar, on the grounds that he, too, was highly unlikely ever to have spent Christmas Day with a quasi-soulmate born on the very same day.

They drank wine and attempted to make Christmas dinner, which was essentially a feast of all the junk food in Stefano's freezer, but Adam was in no position to criticise, because he had an uncanny ability to burn any kind of food he attempted to cook. Then they ended up back in bed, where they watched the Christmas *Two Ronnies* and Christmas *Top of the Pops*, *EastEnders*, *Birds of a Feather*, and even *Noel's Christmas Presents*. All this would have been an ordeal for Adam on his own, but with the two of them together, it was different. The combination of unseasonal carnality and seasonal naffness seen through knowing, merrier-than-usual eyes was entrancing.

In the evening they went out on the balcony. It was cold but the air was calm and, because there were no clouds, the sky was full of stars.

'The longer you look, the more you'll see,' said Adam. 'You need to let your pupils dilate to let more light in.' Sensing that waiting patiently might not be Stefano's strongest suit, he added: 'There is a short cut, though. Have you got some paper or a magazine?'

Stefano went back in the living room and emerged with a copy of *Boyz*.

'Yes, that's perfect.'

Adam took the freesheet and rolled it into a tube.

'See, if you look through that, it helps you filter out the light sources around you, and you can see more of the sky.'

'Oh yes!'

'The brightest one you can see is Jupiter, and that one over there is Mars. Can you see? It's less white than others, because it's got a red surface. Sometimes it looks completely orange.'

'I thought they were planets, not stars. How come they're shining the brightest?'

'They're reflecting the light of the sun. They're not really the brightest, but they seem to be because they're much, much closer than any of the stars you can see. And Jupiter is so bright because it's the biggest planet, ten times bigger than Earth. It's about forty times bigger than the moon, even though it looks much smaller, so that gives you an idea how far away it is.'

'And all the rest are stars?'

'Pretty much.'

'They really are twinkling.'

'They do that because they're so far away, and

you're looking at them through turbulence in our own atmosphere. They don't actually twinkle. They really are shining, though, because they're essentially massive nuclear reactors.'

Stefano scanned the sky with his tube.

'And where's the Milky Way? Aren't you meant to be able to see that?'

'It's all the Milky Way really. That's the name of our galaxy, and there's no way you could see any stars outside our galaxy with the naked eye.'

'Are there loads and loads of galaxies, then?'

'You could say that. Roughly a hundred billion.'

'You're kidding!'

'Seriously. And they all have more than a hundred billion stars in them.'

'Each one? So that means there's…a hundred billion times a hundred billion stars in the universe?'

Adam did the calculation.

'Twenty-two noughts. Ten thousand billion billion.'

'Can you actually do that in your head?'

Adam shrugged and smiled. It was not often you could impress a date with maths prowess.

'So is that an actual gazillion?' said Stefano.

Adam laughed.

'Gazillions aren't real. I think you'd probably call it a sextillion… Ten sextillion, to be precise.'

'Wow.' Stefano peered through his rolled-up *Boyz*. 'And I can see about eight of them.'

Adam had found himself another copy and was looking for himself.

'More than that. I can see about twenty, just over there. You have to look and look and let your eyes adjust. Just give it time.'

'How do you know all this stuff?'

'I was always interested. My dad got me into it. He used to be totally obsessed, and he bought me my first telescope when I was about seven. Apparently, the night I was born – the night we were born – it was all my mum could do to get him to drive her to hospital.'

'Why?'

'Well, you know, he was watching the Apollo mission on TV.'

'What Apollo mission?'

'You didn't know you were born on one of the most historic days in the history of the human race?'

'When they landed on the moon, you mean? Neil Armstrong?'

'No, that was the following summer. This was the first manned lunar orbit. Apollo Eight. It had to go round the dark side of the moon and they had no idea what they were going to find. You know the moon and Earth rotate in complete synchronisation, so nobody on Earth has ever seen the other side of the moon?'

Stefano nodded unconvincingly.

Smiling to himself, Adam continued: 'I've heard the tape of them talking about it. It was like sailors worrying about falling off the end of the world. But they went round the moon ten times and then came safely home.'

'And that was the day I was born?'

'We were born. Yes. They reached the moon on

Christmas Eve. You really didn't know?'

'Sorry, but I was otherwise engaged at the time.'

'They might have told you afterwards.'

'Nah.'

'Maybe they didn't show it on Italian TV?'

'Hey?'

'You were born in Italy, no?' said Adam.

'Oh…yeah.'

No doubt the thought of his family troubled him, and Adam made a mental note to be more sensitive.

'No, they just never mentioned it,' Stefano continued. 'Hey, I'm getting really cold. Let's go back inside.'

They were just in time for the start of *French & Saunders*.

8

STEFANO HAD always felt bad about telling Adam he was Italian. It was a simple, harmless invention which he had used so often since his arrival in London that he had almost begun to believe it. He had first said it years ago, on the spur of the moment, because it was an easier explanation – and a less embarrassing one – than the true story of how he had acquired his incongruous name. Once he had used it another couple of times after that, it became his reflex response to the question, repeated by rote, so that while the thinking part of his brain knew perfectly well that his mother was not really Italian, the unthinking part trotted out his habitual line without conscious effort to deceive.

It had never posed him any problems before, largely because nobody had been interested enough to follow it up in any way that was likely to catch him out. Only when it became clear that he might see a lot more of Adam did he realise that he had boxed himself in. Extricating himself from the initial falsehood risked exposing his fantasy in a damaging light, and the longer he allowed it to continue, the harder it became to back away from it. At least he had fought against his initial instinct, he consoled himself, which was simply to flee by not returning Adam's calls.

He had been sorely tempted at first, but he had a sense that this was worth pursuing, whatever the risk of later embarrassment. He was glad he had followed that wiser course.

The painful reality was that the most Italian thing about Woodville Close was his father's collection of Mantovani albums. His mother regarded Heinz Alphabetti Spaghetti as dangerously foreign and she referred to pizza as 'pitt-ser'. Their suspicion of anything alien was part of the problem.

In the year he turned sixteen, Stefano had applied himself with more dedication than he had ever shown, certainly exhausting himself by his own standards, to revise for the mixture of O-levels and CSEs which it had been decreed he would take. The three, relentless June weeks of exam after exam were a horror for him, and surviving to the end was so liberating in itself that he was past caring about his results. His mother wanted him to stay on into the sixth form, convinced that he might be polytechnic material, even if he was not cut out for university. His father, keen to nip Stefano's more airy-fairy notions in the bud as quickly as possible, thought it would be better for him to go straight into an apprenticeship at Hulme's, as he himself had done. It had been agreed – or at least, his parents had agreed – that they would wait to see how he had performed in his exams before making a final decision.

Stefano had his own ideas. He had no wish to stay on at school, but if he was going to become an apprentice, he did not see why he could not train for a job he actually wanted to do, rather than one he knew he would detest, even if it were not in his father's shadow. He had attempted to tell them this, but they would not listen, which had merely amplified his growing sense that he had been born into the wrong family in the wrong place. He was nearly an adult and, if his parents persisted in denying him a say in his own future, he would pursue that future without them.

He had already been courting danger at home. One afternoon when he was meant to be revising, his mother had come home unexpectedly and nearly caught him with Martin Morris. Martin just managed to get his trousers up before she came in. She looked from one to the other and then at the open window.

'Have you two been smoking?'

'No,' lied Stefano.

They had shared one of her low-tar Silk Cuts.

'Well, close the window. You're letting all the heat out.'

Later, when Martin had gone and she was peeling potatoes at the sink with her back to him, she said: 'I won't tell your father, but if I ever catch you...'

'We weren't smoking,' he protested, almost beginning to believe it.

'I'm not talking about the smoking.'

He was impressed. He had not realised she had the imagination. And even though he knew the answer, he asked: 'Then what are you talking about?'

This was dangerous territory, but he wanted to make her say it.

She wheeled around, and he was shocked at the disgust

in her eyes as she jabbed her peeler at him.

'Just be grateful your father doesn't know.'

She turned back to the sink, and dropped a handful of clean white chips into a plastic bowl.

Stefano wanted to retreat, but it would be a sign that she had won. After a pause in which the silence seethed with the fury of her accusation, he tried a different tack.

'Am I adopted?'

It caught her off guard, as he had known it would. Her back stiffened, but her voice was calm and cold when she spoke.

'I'm sorry to disappoint you, my lad, but you're not. You may not like it but we're the only parents you've got, and as long as you're under this roof you'll do what we tell you.'

She was virtually inviting him to go, he told himself. As it turned out, though, the real clincher was Rock Hudson.

Stefano did not as a rule pay much attention to the news, but he knew instinctively that there was something malign and cruel about the way the gaunt, emaciated actor was being hounded by the media. The jostling press pack was desperate to get close enough to see the fear in the sick man's eyes, without ever relenting on their core message that getting too close would be fatal.

'It's a terrible shame,' said Stefano's mother, leaving her knitting unattended on her lap as they all watched the stricken star blinking in the light of the flash bulbs on the evening bulletin. 'I loved him in *Pillow Talk*. He was so masculine, you'd never have known he was "like that".'

Stefano kept his eyes on the screen, willing her to stop

talking.

'And to see him now,' she continued. 'He's so thin, look.'

Stefano's father snorted.

'They've brought it on themselves, men of his sort. It's not natural what they do, so this is Nature's way of fighting back. If you want to feel sorry for anyone, what about Linda Evans, hey? He kissed her on screen, when he must have known he already had it. If anyone's the victim, it's her.' He tutted to himself, but his voice suddenly brightened. 'Hey, have you heard this one? You know what 'gay' stands for? 'Got Aids Yet?'! I love that.'

He burst into a guffaw, but nobody joined him.

'Dad, that's horrible!' said Katie. 'Tell him, Mum.'

Now, for the first time, Stefano took his eyes off the screen and looked at his mother, waiting for her to rebuke her husband. He could see she was frowning, that she had no time for a crack which, as well as being nasty, was painfully unoriginal – it had been going round Stefano's school for at least a year.

The item had ended now, and she picked up her needles again.

'Alan!' she chided.

Her tone was gentle, but saying anything at all was a start.

'You shouldn't say things like that in front of Katie,' she said.

Stefano glared at her. She did not look up to meet his eyes, but the damage was done. She had implied it would have been all right to talk like that in front of Stefano, which he was certain was intended to make a point, after their showdown over Martin Morris. That, if anything, made her attitude worse – because she knew that Stefano had reason to take the jibe personally. He did not expect any better from his father, but from his mother, this was a betrayal.

He had two years' birthday and Christmas money saved, as well as the proceeds from his Saturday job at the newsagent's by the station. He would go to London, where he could be himself and live his own life. He had no idea how much cash he would need to get started, but he reckoned he could easily forego the suburban comforts his parents took for granted, and he was confident he could rough it if necessary. He felt bad about abandoning Katie to their parents, but he would try to make her understand when she was older.

He slipped out early one Monday morning in late July, a couple of hours before his father got up for work. He walked the mile and a half to the M53 and waited in the dawn on the slip-road with a cardboard sign for London.

He got his first lift from an old man in an Austin Allegro with a mat of orthopaedic beads down the driver's seat. He was only going a few miles, but it was a start, and it would get him away from a place where he might be spotted by neighbours or, worse, by his father on his way to work. Then a young couple in a Dormobile reeking of joss-sticks took him as far as the M6. He told them he was a first-year student returning early to his digs in London before his next term began.

'London,' shuddered the woman, who wore her hair

in braids and had badges on her dungarees. 'Rather you than me. I don't know how you stick it.'

'It's all right really,' said Stefano. 'When you get used to it.'

Another couple of rides took him as far as Newport Pagnell services. The next one, a van from a wholefood shop in Brixton, took him all the way to London. This time he could not say he was a student there: as a Londoner himself, the driver would soon realise that Stefano had never set foot in the capital. Instead he said he was on his way to visit his uncle and aunt.

'Oh yeah? Where do they live?'

The guy had a way of nodding encouragement before Stefano said anything.

'Near, erm, Euston,' he said, because that was where you ended up if you got the train to London. At least he knew it was a proper place.

'Yeah?' The guy looked surprised. 'It's mainly offices round there.'

Stefano noticed that the distance to Central London on the road signs had dwindled into single figures, so they could not be far away.

'Maybe they're in one of the streets down the side,' the guy was saying. 'Or up towards Camden. You got the address? I can drop you, if you want.'

'No, honestly, Euston Station's fine. They said to ring them from a phone box when I get there, and I should really just follow those instructions.'

Stefano did have Auntie Jill and Uncle Richard's address, but it was in Amersham, which was probably nowhere near Central London, and in any case he had no intention of contacting them.

It took an hour to get from the outer reaches of the city to the centre. The driver dropped Stefano on the Euston Road, giving him a goodbye toot as he rejoined the traffic. It was nearly seven o'clock, long after his father normally finished work, but the pavement was full of men in business suits streaming toward the station entrance. Everything was so much taller, wider, deeper than Liverpool, which had always been the big city for him until now. Despite the bewildering scale of it, everyone seemed to know where they were going, and Stefano was in their way.

He found a burger place and broke into one of the fivers he had stuffed into his underpants, not wanting to take any chances with pickpockets in London. He asked the girl who served him if she knew of any cheap hotels, but she either did not know or did not understand the question.

'Up to the lights and turn right, love,' said a woman behind him in the queue. 'There's loads of hotels along there. Just try and avoid the ones with red lights in the window.'

She had a smoker's wheezy laugh, and it set her coughing.

She was right, there were plenty of hotels in that street. He chose one, and went in to ask the price. He was horrified to learn it was fifteen pounds. He tried another, and then a third, but they were even more, and he ended up returning to the first one.

'The traveller returns,' said the landlady, and he knew she was mocking him. But she gave him the room without asking how old he was or what he was doing in London on his own. All he had to do was sign the register.

He wrote 'S. CART…' but then hesitated. It was stupid to put his real name. Instead of '…ER' he wrote '…WRIGHT'. He liked the sound of that anyway. He added a false address, made up from his own birthday, Martin Morris' road and the town of Cockermouth, because it had always made them laugh. He had no idea what county it was in, but the woman did not seem bothered. She did not ask for the postcode.

The bed was lumpy and had nylon sheets, and the noise outside – of traffic, sirens and people laughing, shouting or breaking bottles – seemed to go on all night. Instead of excited, he suddenly felt very small in this enormous, grimy city, which seemed more tawdry than glamorous.

In the morning, he packed up his things, paid for his room, and splashed out on another burger for breakfast. He could not really afford it, but he reasoned that this was his big day and he should not start it on an empty stomach.

He had memorised the address he wanted, and he queued up at the Underground ticket office, amid a throng of tourists, to ask which was the right stop. The man behind the counter, who was very dark and spoke like Ben Kingsley in *Gandhi*, told him he wanted Piccadilly Circus, which was easy to find because it was on the Piccadilly Line, with no need to change. The flow of commuters and visitors cramming onto the escalator was daunting, and he had to stand his ground to check the map at the bottom, to make sure he was not carried along in the wrong direction. It was exciting, though, when the Tube train squealed into the station and he squeezed onto the hot, smelly carriage, because he was confident that he knew where he was going and he felt so grown-up for being able to find his own way. He worried he might not be able to fight his way out of the carriage when he arrived at his stop, but plenty of other people were getting off too, and he allowed this great human tide to carry him up to the surface. He took a moment to savour the bustle of Piccadilly Circus, where the first thing he saw was a number 12 bus. That was surely a good omen.

It was difficult trying to work out which one of these roads with their cliff walls of high buildings was Regent Street, and when he did work it out, he had to cross at three different sets of traffic lights just to get there. Austin Reed turned out not to open until ten, so he walked up and down Regent Street. He looked at the Londoners striding past, every one of them with a sense of purpose, and marvelled to think that he too might shortly have his place in this world. But at eight minutes past ten he was back on the pavement with his rucksack, humiliated by a thin-necked assistant who did not bother to hide his contempt when Stefano asked for the manager. They did not hire people off the street, he sniffed; Stefano should write to head office instead.

He gave him the address, but Stefano wanted to blurt out: 'How? Tell me how I'm meant to write! I haven't even got paper, let alone a return address, and I need a job now, because my money's running out and I haven't even got enough to go back to that stinking hotel tonight.'

But he did not say that, and he even managed not to cry until he had reached Green Park, where he flung himself under a tree with his face in the grass.

He spent the rest of the day wandering. He ate a packet of bread rolls from a mini-supermarket, with a couple of tomatoes to make them less dry. He checked phone boxes for reject ten pences, trying not to think about the night ahead. Suddenly roughing it did not seem so romantic. He saw a boy of around his own age in a doorway, sitting up in a sleeping bag and asking for change in an empty voice. He quickened his step, and reminded himself that he still had Uncle Richard and Auntie Jill's phone number if things got really bad.

He noticed that he was in Jermyn Street. It seemed a lifetime ago that he had longed to see these places: Pall Mall, Charing Cross Road, Shaftesbury Avenue. It should have been exciting, a dream come true; but now it scared him.

A few streets further on he found himself in what he realised must be Soho, mere mention of which would set his whole class sniggering at school. He saw shops with blacked-out windows and signs promising XXX-RATED MAG'S 'N' VIDEO'S. One of them had a window display of magazines which were familiar from the top shelves of the newsagents back home, but among the inflated blonde cover girls and coquettish Asians was a tanned, bare-chested man with sleek hair. Stefano's eyes widened.

So this was London. The magazine was openly displayed, and nobody was throwing bricks, laughing or calling the police. For a moment, he forgot the problem of where to sleep.

A boy walked past, not much older than Stefano, with his hair in a New Romantic flick, and chalky white thighs peeping out of the rips in the back of his skin-tight jeans. He had clearly noticed which magazine Stefano had been looking at, and he smirked, but it seemed like a smile of complicity, not derision. He moved with a rolling confidence, a proper swagger, even though he was no more than five foot seven, had spots on the back of his neck and a complexion that was nearer blue than white.

Stefano watched him flick a cigarette expertly into a drain and disappear around a corner, and he was drawn to follow. He rounded the same corner, aware that he could get very lost in this bewildering, not-quite-grid of similar-looking streets, just in time to see the boy slipping into a pub. Another teenager, even scrawnier, with a tweed cap pulled over his face, entered from the other direction, followed by a bald man in a suit and then a second, younger man in a leather jacket. Stefano felt excitement begin to conquer despair. This was surely the shadowy, nether world that people like his mother shuddered even to imagine; yet here Stefano was, on its threshold. As he watched, the door swung open again and an older boy emerged, briefly registering Stefano's presence on the opposite pavement, followed by a pudgy older man in an anorak. The man walked a couple of steps behind the boy, but by the time they turned the corner they had fallen into step.

Stefano had little experience even of normal pubs. Despite early maturity below the waist, he was late shaving, and the shame of being turned away on one humiliating occasion had put him off trying again. However, here were other boys of his own age, and he did not want an alcoholic drink, just a Coke. He sensed that this was where he might belong in this busy, hostile city, and the fact that it was a million miles from the values of Woodville Close, from anything that anyone there could imagine in their worst nightmares, made it all the more enticing. If he did not go in now, he might never find it again in the maze of streets.

Taking a deep breath, he pushed open the door, forcing himself forward as half a dozen faces turned to look.

Slightly to his disappointment, it was what he supposed an ordinary pub interior to look like, with green leather seats, flock wallpaper, horse-brasses and plumes of smoke rising from along the polished bar. Jimmy Somerville's falsetto blaring from the juke-box, loud enough that those customers who were trying to talk had to lean into each other's ears, offered some confirmation of the kind of place he was in. Many of the customers stood alone, he noticed, as if they were waiting for someone or something. All were male.

The two boys he had seen going in were stationed on opposite sides of the bar room, each in conversation with an older man. A third, wearing a sleeveless singlet that revealed a bush of hair under his arms, stood with his back to the bar, blowing moody smoke rings.

Stefano approached the bar.

'Haven't seen you in here before, darl. What'll it be?' said the barman. His hair was shaved at the sides and rose into a bleached brush on top, and dark stubble came up his cheeks. He wore a tee-shirt with the slogan 'They call it sodomy, we call it fun'. His accent sounded Australian, although Stefano was not certain: he had never met an actual Australian.

'How much is a Coke?' he said.

'How much you got? No, don't answer that. Put it away, it's on the house. Just don't tell her over there.' He gestured with his thumb, and Stefano looked in vain for a woman.

'Her with the white hair and the gut the size of Leicester Square,' the barman clarified, and Stefano realised he meant the stocky man in a plaid shirt in the doorway at the back of the bar – evidently the landlord.

The barman leaned forward.

'Hey, would you like a shot of vodka in that? You look like you kinda need it.'

Stefano shook his head.

'No, really. No alcohol. I don't like the taste.'

'Vodka doesn't taste, darl, it just kicks. But you know best. Maybe it's better to keep your wits about you in this place, with all these old monsters.'

He winked and swung to the other side of the bar, where one of the monsters was waiting to be served.

Stefano tasted his drink and congratulated himself on coming in. The free Coke was the first kindness he had received since arriving in London.

Of course, it did not solve the problem of where he was going to sleep. He hoisted himself onto a high stool and reconsidered his options, but they had not increased. He had heard of free hostels you could go to if you had nowhere else. He wondered how you found them.

Across the room, one of the men in suits was staring at him. Now, as he caught Stefano's eye, he smiled.

Stefano smiled back, because that was what he had been taught to do. But he realised his suburban good manners might not be the most appropriate behaviour here. Encouraged, the man was coming over.

'Haven't seen you here before, have I?' he said, putting his near-empty pint glass on the bar beside Stefano.

It was what the barman had said, but this time it had an edge to it.

Stefano shook his head.

'Thought not,' said the man. 'I'd have remembered.'

He had cracked veins in his cheeks and a growth on his forehead that looked like there was a marble trapped under the skin.

'What's your name?'

Stefano told him.

'I'm Terry. Let me buy you another drink.'

Stefano still had half his Coke. What he really wanted was food.

'Have they got any crisps?'

'Hungry, are you? Me too, as it happens. If you like, we could go and get something to eat. Do you like Chinese? Indian maybe? Don't worry, it's on me. And then afterwards…'

As he left the sentence dangling and Stefano understood what was going on – the strange mix of clientele, the boys talking to the men in suits and not to each other – he found that the idea did not horrify him. His immediate reaction was relief, as he realised he might not have to ask a policeman for a hostel, trek to Amersham or, worst of all, phone his father. He would do what he had to do, and he was proud to discover that he was not squeamish. In fact, he was curious to know what it might entail. If money was to be involved, he wondered how much it would be. He imagined Terry would know about that.

'What do you say?' Terry pressed. 'Have a drink first, then make your mind up, eh?'

The barman approached, and before Stefano could say he wanted Coke, Terry asked for two pints of lager and a bag of salt and vinegar.

'Is one of the lagers for him?' The Australian's friendly manner had evaporated. 'Because he's underage. I'm not serving him alcohol, and you should know better.'

'But…' started Stefano.

This was unfair. He had not even asked for beer, so he did not really care, but this very same barman had offered him vodka only ten minutes earlier.

'Zip it, darl, I'll deal with you in a minute.'

He turned back to the older man, but Terry had already drained his pint and picked up his briefcase, and was on his way to the door without a word to Stefano.

'Good riddance to bad rubbish. Now listen, darl. What's the story?'

The barman's tone was friendly again, and Stefano was

thoroughly confused.

'Hey?'

'Come on, darl, don't play the innocent with me. Run away from home, is that it?'

He nodded at the rucksack.

'All your worldly goods?'

Stefano flushed.

'So tell me where you're staying tonight,' the barman demanded.

Stefano looked at his hands.

'I thought so, darl. And you reckoned you'd go with that creep so you could get a roof over your head?'

Stefano was suddenly furious. He looked the barman in the eye, no longer embarrassed.

'What business is it of yours? And now he's gone, where am I going to stay?'

'Hey, keep your wig on, darl. You'll stay with me tonight. And don't worry, there's no funny business on the agenda: chicken isn't my thing. You sit tight there for the evening, OK, try not to pull any more punters, and we'll go to my place when we close up. Then you can tell me your story. Deal?'

Stefano forced a smile. This was a better offer than Terry's. Even if the barman was lying and was planning on 'funny business', he was far less horrible.

'I'm Rook, by the way,' the barman said, extending his hand over the bar. 'What's your name?'

'I'm Steven. Though generally people call me Stee.'

'I think I'll call you Stephanie.'

Stefano took his hand away in horror.

'Why?'

'Don't worry about it, darl. I give everybody girls' names, you'll see. I don't mean anything by it.'

'I don't want a girl's name.'

He looked back around the bar. Maybe Terry had come back.

'OK, darl,' said the barman. 'I'll make an exception just for you. I'll call you Stefano. How does that sound?'

Not only had Rook given him his name, he had also quite likely saved his life. It was nineteen eighty-five when he arrived in the capital, and its gay bars and clubs were not immune from the horror that had engulfed Rock Hudson. Here it was mostly still invisible: the customers who fell by the wayside simply stopped turning up, and there was always someone else to fill their place at the bar. So it was perfectly possible for a naive young runaway from the North West to plunge into the illicit pleasure-bath that London offered, with little sense of the jeopardy he was in.

But Stefano Cartwright, as Steven Carter now became, had the benefit of Rook's older, wiser tutelage. Having saved him from the clutches of his first would-be punter, Rook gave Stefano a home in his spare room for four years until he managed to get his own place around the corner, and he also gave him a no-nonsense education, setting out in graphic detail what he could and could not do in bed, or the bushes of Hampstead Heath, if he wanted to stay alive in the age of plague. He sometimes wondered what would have happened to him if this bleach-plumed saviour had not taken him under his wing that night. He did not imagine he would be alive to see in the new millennium.

Instead, another four years later, he had met Adam, with his pleasant, wholesome-looking face, his neat haircut and his ears that stuck out just enough to glow a luminous pink when the light came through the top of them. Their chance encounter on both their birthdays had surely been a sign that something was meant to be.

Adam had also helped Stefano raise his horizons, reminding him of the ambitions he had once had for his life in the big city, back when he dreamed of Austin Reed and all that went with it. Those ideas had fallen gradually away as he slipped into a life where the brightest lights he saw were over the bus stops on Dalston Lane. But Adam was much better educated than he was, and more at home in the kind of places that Stefano would have been nervous to venture into on his own.

They went, for example, to the National Gallery. Stefano had assumed that dusty collections of Old Masters demanded a reverential attitude, especially the religious ones, but Adam helped him shed that vestige of his childhood piety by showing him how much fun there was to be had sniggering over the various martyrdoms of Saint Sebastian. He showed him a pale, smooth, improbably pretty youth, naked apart from the diaphanous wrap slung low over his hips and knotted casually as if it were a cashmere jumper. This boy looked out at Stefano with head aslant and an eyebrow raised, and it was easy to overlook the fact that he was being executed. Not that there was any avoiding the circumstances of his dispatch: surrounded by villainous, hairy bowmen in canvas after canvas, the boy was pierced by darts in the tenderest of places, and there was even one in the soft vee between the tendons of his neck, drawing attention to the sweetness of his skin. What was lacking was a proper agony. The martyr's refusal to suffer made it look as if the cords that lashed him in place were part of a game that had nothing to do with death; the look of boredom seemed just another element of that game, taunting the archers, as perhaps the model had taunted the painter.

'Maybe the artists are just a bit rubbish,' speculated Stefano, his critical confidence growing. 'I mean, not up to getting the facial expressions right.'

'I think it's all part of the story,' said Adam.

'What, that they put him to death and he wasn't bothered?'

He did not remember Tommy Tosspot telling them about this saint, so he was genuinely interested.

'Well, it's partly because he's just discovered Christianity, which gives him a superiority over the pagan Romans trying to kill him. That's the idea, anyway. It's also to make the point that he doesn't actually die. In the legend, he was a Roman captain caught preaching the new religion, who was then sentenced to death by the emperor. He survived the arrows and was later rescued by a Christian woman who nursed him back to health, so what we're looking at is meant to be a kind of miracle. Actually it didn't end there, because he had a bit of a death-wish. He carried on preaching, was caught again and was sentenced to die. By clubbing, this time. But as far as these pictured are concerned, he survives.'

'My friend Rook nearly clubbed himself to death,' said Stefano. 'He went out every weekend for a year and ended up on a drip.'

He liked making Adam laugh, but was also in awe of his knowledge, even on a subject where he himself had once been something of an expert.

'How can you remember so much stuff?' he said.

'It's an idiot skill,' Adam shrugged.

They had wandered through the galleries that day and ended up in Spanish Masters, a room that was dominated by a giant Christmas-card image of Mary and Joseph kneeling on either side of a saccharine-sweet five-year-old with Silvikrin curls, eyes gazing into the middle distance and head magically aglow. Directly above the child's head was a fluttering dove, which in Stefano's scurrilous imagination was about to land a direct hit on Jesus' tresses. Like the Christ-child, the bird also emitted a radioactive glow. Way above all that, floating on a cloud of well-fed cherubs, was a bearded old man in a flowing pink robe, gripping onto a rock in the sky.

'Funny how God hasn't got any lines on his face, isn't it?' said Stefano. 'He's got white hair, but he clearly moisturises.'

'He looks like Charlton Heston in *The Ten Commandments*. You know, where he plays Moses? He comes down Mount Sinai and he's gone grey overnight. It's meant to be a huge shock for the Israelites but you can still see it's only him in bad make-up, and he's got perfect skin underneath it all.'

'I used to love that film! I had the real hots for Yul Brynner. Funny, I'd forgotten all about that until now.'

'We'll have to get it on video some time,' promised Adam. 'I'm glad you're an atheist too, by the way. I'd feel awkward laughing about this stuff if you weren't.'

'Don't worry, I stopped believing in all of that a long time ago,' said Stefano.

They never got round to watching The Ten Commandments. If they had done, it might have been strange for Stefano to re-enact a childhood activity that he had once carried out with his mother. But they never did, so the memories of his family faded.

Aside from sending a card to Katie every birthday, which he did for the first few years, he found it was easier to act as if they did not exist at all. That became his antidote to the occasional pang of guilt he felt for turning his back on them so completely. In time, the guilt faded and, in some ways, his made-up Italian mother was as real as his actual one.

9

IT WAS TWO WEEKS since his accident, and they had been back home for ten days. For Stefano, life stubbornly refused to return to normal. He had been shaken to the core by his experience, and his fears were so profound that he would have found them hard to share with anyone, even if they were prepared to listen properly and take him seriously.

At work at the Prince Edward, he knew he was irritable and aloof, but snapping out of it was easier said than done. Although he had always been good with the customers, now he found himself reluctant to be drawn into the usual burble with the regulars on their high stools at the bar. There was Tony the Tory, Three-Necks Neil and Pool-Cue Patty, a tattooed lesbian who acted as the pub's unofficial muscle in the event of trouble, and they were used to a level of spiky repartee which Stefano had learned from Rook in the early days and which normally came as second nature nowadays. He knew he ought to make the effort, but it would involve flipping a switch in his head to turn his worries off and his barman's persona on, and something was actively stopping him doing that.

One of them must have grumbled to Kevin, his boss, because he asked Stefano to stay behind for a word when he had closed up.

'Everything all right, Stef?' he sniffed.

Kevin sniffed after every sentence, in the manner of someone who did too much cocaine. He was an East Ender who had run to fat: he could afford all the rent boys he wanted, so had no need to take care of his appearance. He was a benevolent employer, offering generous bonuses at Christmas and other bank holidays. But his normal bonhomie quickly fell away if anything threatened his takings.

'I'm just a bit distracted. I'll be OK.'

'I hope so, sweetheart, because that scowl of yours is curdling the lager. Whatever's going on up here…' he tapped the top of his own skull, '…remember to smile at the punters, and everyone's happy. Capeesh?'

Smile. That was what Rook had told him too. It sounded like nothing: a tweak of the facial muscles on this side, and then a matching tweak on that side and, hey presto, you were no longer depressing to look at, and with luck you had magicked away your misery at the same time. If only it were so simple.

He had given up confiding in Adam. It was hard to speak openly about his worries to someone who would not listen patiently to his account of what had happened. In any case, Adam's mind was closed on the issue that was of most concern to Stefano. It was easier to trust Rook, who at least understood how shaken he was, and had shown his concern by paying him plenty of attention.

Rook worked as a part-time social worker these days. The afternoon after Stefano's dressing-down from Kevin, he brought a colleague to see him at the flat. This Ronnie – short for Veronica – was a trust-fund girl with a Roedean drawl and platinum hair cut into short spikes.

'I hear you had a near-death experience?' she said, when Stefano had made them mugs of camomile tea. 'That's really interesting. My sister Pandora had one of them. She was kicked in the head when she was sabbing.'

Stefano winced in sympathy.

'By a horse?'

Ronnie laughed throatily.

'No, by this guy Noz that she was going out with. She was trying to lie down in front of the horses and he didn't see her. The police wouldn't take her to hospital and they had to go in Noz's Morris Minor, which would never go above second gear. When they got there, she was in a really bad way and there was a point when it was touch and go, but afterwards we found out Pandy was loving it. She was having this massive out-of-body thing, looking down and thinking that Noz would have to get rid of his dreads if he went any balder on top. Then she went down this long, white tunnel into a really bright light and she says she saw all her previous lives at once. Because she believes in reincarnation, yeah?'

'I went down the tunnel too,' said Stefano excitedly. 'And yes, it was long and white, with a really, really bright light at the end of it. I didn't see my previous lives, though. Do you think that's significant?'

'I think it depends on what you believe in, darl,' said Rook. 'Like Ronnie said, her sister believes in reincarnation, and you don't. Do you?'

Stefano shook his head. It was a relief to know that there was something that, no, he definitely did not believe in. But he wanted to know more about Ronnie's sister's experience.

'Did she see God?' he asked.

'No, but she doesn't really believe in one God, you know, like an old guy with a beard.'

'I saw him, and nor do I. At least, I didn't at the time.'

'Wow,' said Ronnie. 'What did he look like?'

'Well, all I saw really was his eye.'

'An eye, darl. You don't know whose it was.'

'Whose else would it have been?'

'I dunno, darl. It's hard for me to say, when I don't really believe in any of that stuff.'

'But nor did I!' cried Stefano.

'And now?'

'And now I…just don't know.'

He leaned forward, cradling his head in his hands and rocking from side to side.

'But Stef,' said Ronnie, putting her own hand on his arm. 'Would it be so bad if you changed your mind? So you saw God and now you believe in him. Why the big tragedy? That could be a lovely thing, if you let it.'

Stefano lifted his head and looked from one to the other. They were both staring at him with pity on their faces, like he was a sick puppy.

'Because I…' he started, but the words were too hard to say and he felt himself choking on them.

'Take your time, darl. It's OK.'

Stefano put his head in his hands and started rocking

again.

'You don't understand,' he whispered.

'No, we don't, darl, because you need to tell us,' said Rook, attempting to fold him into a hug.

Stefano pushed him away. He knew that Rook was right, he could not expect them to understand if he would not explain. The truth was, he was so frightened of the words themselves, he could not get them out of his mouth.

They eventually excused themselves because Rook had somewhere he needed to be. Stefano remained where he was for a long while, still rocking back and forth. At length he realised he was thirsty. Looking in the fridge, he discovered that they had run out of Diet Coke. He would force himself to leave the flat and buy some. It was a beautiful summer's day out there. Perhaps the sun on his face would make him feel better.

It was hot outside. He had come down without his sunglasses and he squinted in the glare as he waited to cross the main road at the lights. When they changed, he had to step back to avoid being mown down by a speeding cycle courier who raced through on red.

'Don't mind us,' said a woman at the crossing beside him, rolling her eyes at Stefano.

He nodded in acknowledgement. He liked that about where he lived: you could talk to strangers all the time if you wanted. It was not true that Londoners were unfriendly, and often the human contact could lift the spirits. The only unwritten rule was not to keep it going too long, which constituted clinginess. This woman clearly knew that. She looked sixtyish and sounded posh, one of the downwardly mobile Hackney middle classes, with greying hair cropped into a wiry bob and a lop-sided way of holding her mouth that made her look readily amused.

Now the road was clear and they were making their separate ways across, each minding their own business once more.

The pavement was busy for a weekday afternoon, and up ahead he could hear a commotion from the direction of the town hall. It was one of the usual crazies, he saw as he came closer: a bearded black man in a pork pie hat, with a heavy Caribbean accent, shouting angrily into a whistling loud-hailer.

'We accept you as a human being,' he cried as Stefano drew near, addressing everyone and no one, as the rest of Hackney trudged past with supermarket carrier bags, manoeuvred buggies or pushed through to get on buses.

'God wants the best for you…'

He seemed to look at Stefano, mainly because Stefano was the only person paying him any attention.

'But we refuse to accept you remaining the same. The Church does not define family. The Bible does. And God defines family as a male and a female, a male and a female with children, by the Bible's standards. The Church is here to represent what God says to society, and God says no, it is not acceptable for a man to lie with another man!'

Now he was looking at Stefano full on, eyes flashing.

Once he would have shrugged this kind of sermonising off with a laugh. Today, however, he stood transfixed.

This was what he could not express to Rook and Ronnie, the words he did not dare try to get his tongue around. It was the essence of his problem. What if the guy was right, after all?

His mouth was dry and he began to tremble. He scarcely noticed the tap on his arm, and he jumped with a start when a voice said in his ear: 'Don't take any notice of him.'

It was the woman from the crossing, giving him her lop-sided smile.

'God didn't say anything of the kind, you know. Or if he did, it was in the Old Testament, which is full of all kinds of other nonsense that people like this man choose very conveniently not to take literally. What ought to matter for all people who call themselves Christians, as I do, is that Jesus did not say a word about homosexuality one way or the other. Not one word. Just you remember that.'

She clapped him reassuringly on the shoulder, smiled again, and went on her way, waving her hand dismissively at the preacher as she passed him.

He barely heard her, however. All he could see was the abyss of his own fate.

10

GOD HAD BEEN ON an expedition. It was rare, these days, that he moved about within his realm, but on this occasion he had gone one better. He had ventured outside it.

Over the aeons, he had lost the habit of travelling around his cosmos. Early on, he had been quite happy to waft about within his realm, but as it expanded and the distances became ever greater, he lost the inclination and, after a while, he tended to forget it was even an option. Now, however, he had heard that strange, oscillating murmur again. It was beginning to give him the creeps, with its stop-start humming in the background of all the other sounds of his universe, and it had roused him from his usual torpor into venturing away from the bridge of the universe to find out what was going on.

From the centre of it all, the stars of his world were a continuous, regular spatter of blazing lights in all directions. But now, as he left his seeing-tube behind and passed through them, the patterns changed. On and on he roamed, alert for the humming, which always seemed to be further ahead or a long way behind. Gradually the rocks and burning stars thinned out, in a sign that he was drawing near the periphery of it all. He thought back to the time when his universe was scarcely bigger than he was, and the period immediately after that, when it dawned on him that the place was somehow programmed to get bigger and bigger all the time. He wondered, as he had wondered more than once before, whether it would ever stop doing so. Perhaps there would come a point when it would hit some kind of limit. It might even start shrinking again. He was not sure what he would make of that. The whole thing would become more manageable, or at least more watchable, but it would be odd and not a little threatening to see his realm diminishing. What if it shrank back to a tiny point, like it was where it all began? Would there still be room for him? That was purely hypothetical, he reminded himself, and there was no sense fretting over mere conjecture. He really must stop inventing catastrophes to worry about.

Looking about him, he realised that he had arrived at the outer edge of his world. The oscillating murmur had ceased once more. While the place was not silent, exactly, because his universe was never that, it was more tranquil here. He might at least take the opportunity to enjoy it.

One of the strange things about this outer extreme of the cosmos was that there was no abrupt end. This was a moving boundary, seeping ever onwards, and there was a fuzziness about it that seemed to get inside him, making the creator feel he too might blur into foggy oblivion if he stayed there too long.

There was, though, something tantalising about this fog. What was on the other side? The riches of his own universe were immense, but they were known to him. Out there was completely unknown. Slowly, almost without knowing he was doing it, he found himself edging into that blurry boundary, just to see what would happen. Would he reach a point where it pushed him back? It seemed not to do so, and so he continued a little further. If he passed through it, would he be able to return? He edged forward, and then reversed the same distance. There did not seem to be anything stopping him going back. He ventured a little further, and then experimented by reversing again. Once more, it was quite possible to return. Pushing through a little further still, he began to see through to the other side of the mist, to what seemed to be a vast, colourless, multi-dimensional void. Surely it would not do any harm to go just a short way further, he told himself, and now he was able to reach out so that part of him was outside his own world. Not quite abandoning all caution, he reversed one more time, to make absolutely sure that it was possible to get back, and when he found that yes, it really was, he pressed on again, excited and emboldened. Now, at last, the cloud around him lifted completely, and he found himself outside his own universe, adjusting to the enhanced sensation of lightness that came with hovering outside space.

He scanned the dizzying expanse of nothing, so different from his own busy, noisy realm. In every direction it was empty. As his vision began to adjust, however, he thought he made out the distant glow of what he could only assume was some foreign cosmos. He wished that he had thought to bring his seeing-tube. There was another one, a little to the right, and, yes, a third, off in the other direction. Perhaps one day he would venture towards them to investigate but, for the moment, he had come far enough. He turned back to survey the wall of mist that was his own world. It seemed somehow smaller from this angle, and deceptively tranquil, revealing nothing of the violent conflagrations within.

He gazed back out into the multiverse. It was strange to think there could be other creators like himself out there. Would they be friendly or hostile? Would they look like him? Perhaps they were as isolated and solitary as he was, never removing themselves from their own domains. Or maybe the other universes had no creators. That was a weird concept, and he was not sure he liked the idea. Fret as he sometimes did about the deity-strangers who might be out there, he really would not want to be on his own in the entire multiverse.

He scanned the vastness looking for signs of divine presence, whatever that might look like. There were still just the three distant glows. There was something strange about the third of them, though. He was sure it had been the faintest when he first saw it, but now it was just as bright as the other two, if not brighter. And it seemed larger than it had been before. In fact, the more he looked at it, the bigger and brighter it seemed to become. Even as he watched, it began to take on the recognisable form of a great swirl, spinning on its own axis, just as his own universe did. A chill ran through him. This foreign swirl was on the move, and it was coming his way.

He told himself not to be so alarmist, that it could not do him any harm. But there was no getting away from the fact that the spinning swirl was getting larger and larger, and heading in the direction of his own cosmos. What would happen if one universe crashed into another? That was a question he had never had any need to consider. It was just about possible that the two would fuse neatly, boosting his realm and making everything suddenly more interesting. What if the new cosmos came with its own creator, though? He would learn soon enough what it was like to have company after all this time. The newcomer might be a hostile invader and God could end up being a junior partner – or worse, a prisoner – in the expanded realm. In any case, harmless fusion seemed an unlikely outcome. He knew from watching objects collide in his own universe that such events caused immense damage. If the oncoming cosmos was larger than his own – it was impossible to judge at this distance – it might blast his poor domain to bits. It was time, he realised, to set aside the laissez-faire approach he had favoured in his own universe. It was all very well to let cosmic events take their course internally, but a threat to the survival of his realm needed serious and urgent attention. The question was, what, if anything, he could do about it.

Bolder now, with such danger encroaching, he pushed himself further out into the void, with the aim of somehow attempting to position himself between his own cosmos and the advancing foreign one. On and on it came, bigger and bigger all the time, approaching very rapidly now. He would have to brace himself, and he wondered what kind of impact to expect. These worlds were blurred and fuzzy at the ends, which was what allowed him to pass in and out of it. So what if the foreign universe sucked him into it in the same way, and he was transported away into the far depths of the multiverse inside some alien world? On the other hand, it might operate according to completely different physical principles to his own. It was, after all, a mobile universe, tumbling through the void without a thought to its proper place in the order of things, so who knew what other properties it had? If it had hard edges, it might be heavy and powerful enough not just to obliterate a few million of his own galaxies, but to knock him flat along the way. And maybe that was the point. He had assumed that this runaway cosmos was on a random trajectory, heading for his own purely by coincidence. But what if its motion were the work of a warring rival, a deity who had learned to pilot his or her own universe and splatter innocent creators, whose only crime was to mind their own business? If only he had taken more heed of this Greater Multiverse all along, and made the effort to encounter some of his fellow deities, he might have some better idea of what to expect – or who to call on for help.

It was coming ever closer now. On the upside, it really did appear very much like his own world: blurred at the edges, as if it too were expanding from its own central point. On the downside, it was beginning to look seriously big. God could not say with the remotest degree of confidence that he would be able to deflect it.

Suddenly, however, he saw that he would not have to. Whether it was following some winding meander of its own design, or it had been diverted by a vigilant divine helmsman, the mobile universe was skirting off to one side. As he watched, it tumbled past and away off into the emptiness. After a while it faded completely from view as it sped on its course, corrected or random, with barely a wake in the void to say it had ever been there.

God remained where he was. His creation was safe but it felt like this had been a close call, and the experience had unnerved him. He had never been aware of any such dangers before, never even contemplated the possibility, but now he had witnessed it, he could not shake the thought of what might happen if he were not permanently there to act as a divine shield. Maybe such near-misses happened more often than he had ever realised, and they were not as hazardous as he thought. Perhaps the two universes really would just have bounced off each other, and if he had been in his normal place at the centre of his own cosmos he would never have known about it. Or maybe this was a freak event, in which case it was unlikely to happen again any time soon and there was no point staying out here, tubeless, wearing out his tired old vision. His panicky side began to concede that it was out-argued, and God gradually returned to a state of something approaching calm. At length, with no further dangers visible, he was ready to go back inside. He made his way back, without difficulty, through the cloudy blur. It was actually a relief to get properly back inside his own world, surrounded by what now seemed an ineffably enormous expanse, and this illusion of internal vastness boosted his confidence. It gave him a sense of security that defied the logic of the multiverse outside.

Retracing his route back towards the centre, he

eventually reached his normal place at the bridge of the universe and picked up his tube. By force of habit, he sought out the place where he knew he would find the green-eyed hominid. His adventure outside the confines of his own universe had been a major distraction, but he was still shaken by the idea of such a creature being able to look directly at him. Whether it was a freak accident or something more unsettling, continued surveillance of the creature in question seemed a sensible plan.

Something had changed, however. The location was the same, he was sure of it, but other hominids now occupied the sun-worshipping pallets where he had last seen his own special hominid. His own green-eyed one was nowhere to be seen, for as long as he looked.

Again and again he scrutinised the cluster of hominid structures beside the shoreline on the craggy rocklet. There were hominids there, all right, but he was absolutely certain that they were different ones. One spin of the Earth passed, and then another, with God observing most of the time. After a few more spins, he concluded that this rocklet was some kind of facility for temporary occupancy, where hominids came for seven spins of the planet, lay on sun-worshipping pallets, and departed again, to be replaced by another batch of creatures doing exactly the same thing. Panning inland from the shoreline, he watched as swarms of travellers were delivered via flying conveyances several times a day, and an equivalent number were removed. There seemed very little point in waiting for his own particular creature to come back.

That meant the creator must search out the green-eyed hominid for himself, which presented an obvious challenge. God had no idea how many of these creatures there were on Earth, but it seemed to be a lot: fewer, it was true, than there were stars in the average galaxy, but that was still a heck of a lot. He directed his seeing-tube at various points on the surface of the Earth in a desultory fashion. All he saw were endless random hominids in different environments – he had not realised they came in so many shades – but never the one he actually wanted.

He was close to giving up the whole business when he made a chance discovery. He was peering irritably through his tube at some crowded hominid settlement where the faces of the population were the same deep brown as their eyes, and concluding that he was in totally the wrong place yet again. He closed his own eyes for a moment, visualising the features he wanted to see instead: the green eyes and long lashes of his special hominid. As he did so, he felt the tube begin to move of its own accord, and when he opened his eyes to look back through his device, he found himself looking at the very individual he had visualised. The creature was not on the craggy rocklet this time, but on the upper level of a red, people-moving conveyance in a large, grey settlement on a part of the Earth that had turned away from its star and was now lit by the hominids' own substitute yellow lighting.

God laughed out loud. He had used this tube for the best part of fifteen billion years in the hominid measure, and he had never known it could search out any target he told it to find. This was the problem of having nobody to explain things to him: he was somehow meant to pick it all up for himself as he went along. Sometimes he was embarrassingly slow on the uptake.

As he watched, the Special Hominid descended to the lower level of the red conveyance, which stopped to let him and another couple of passengers off. Hunching over to put a white stick in his mouth, to which he then applied a flame, he walked along the flat, grey pathway beside the main conveyance track and stopped at the base of a tall pillar that towered over its surroundings. He pushed opened a barrier to gain entrance and disappeared from view. Ordinarily, at this point, God would have been stumped, not knowing how to follow his quarry any further. Having newly wised up to this seeing-tube's capabilities, however, he refused to accept this as a setback. Visualising the Special Hominid as precisely as he could, he was rewarded right away, as the distant end of the tube nosed up the outside of the tower, where rows of windows clearly correlated to levels within the pillar. The lens found its own way up these levels until it reached the tenth one. A notable feature on this level, unlike on the others, was that all the windows were wide open.

Bold and unbidden, the tube now snaked its way into one of these openings where, as God watched, it focused on the Special Hominid, who was now entering the dwelling and exchanging greetings with his companion. The latter had been lying prone on a long, padded seat, large enough for him to extend himself to the full. He now retracted his legs and folded into a seated position.

Had God been able to understand their form of communication, he would have been able to follow perfectly, because he could hear it all very clearly. As it was, he detected hostility in the air, as the green-eyed hominid went around the dwelling, snapping shut each of the transparent panes that normally sealed the windows, with what seemed like irritation. The last one he came to was the opening through which the creator's tube now intruded. The creator was nervous for a moment that his presence might be detected, but his seeing-tube was evidently invisible to hominid eyes, because the Special Hominid paid no attention to it. Instead, he was making an effort to get behind a large, rectangular item of furnishing equipment that had been placed in front of the window, and which made it awkward to close this particular pane. The Special Hominid's grunts increased as he exerted himself until, finally, he secured the pane shut.

Rapt by all this hominid domestic activity, which he was unused to witnessing at such close quarters, it did not occur to God until it was far too late that it might be sensible to pull his tube out of the way. Now, as the Special Hominid returned to the main body of the room and continued to engage in spoken exchanges with his companion, the creator tried tentatively to pull his tube back. He still had a perfect view through it, but it did not want to retract. That did not bode well. He pulled again, a little harder. This time it grew tauter across the vastness of the cosmos, straining right across its length, but it did not budge at the far end.

The creator was trying not to panic, but it was hard to avoid the most obvious conclusion: his precious seeing-tube was stuck fast.

11

'By any yardstick, the rush of showy construction projects up and down the country, first and foremost in the capital, has brought heady times for British concrete as the twentieth century draws to its close...'

Today, being the second Tuesday of the month, was Adam's press day. Hanging from a strap on the Victoria Line, having failed to get a seat, not just at Highbury and Islington, but also at Euston, where enough people usually changed to the Northern Line to free up some space, he was rehearsing the intro for the feature he had to write by the end of the day.

For the past five years, he had been on the staff of an unglamorous but profitable fortnightly magazine which reported on the cement industry. His paper had been the butt of satire among his friends ever since it had been the guest publication on the headline round of *Have I Got News For You?*. But his link to the construction industry had made life in London infinitely more interesting this past year, as the city rebuilt for the new millennium. New tunnels were being bored and new stations constructed for the Jubilee Line extension; a vast, plastic Dome was being raised on an abandoned peninsula on a remote eastern loop of the river; a giant, temporary Ferris wheel was about to be hoisted onto the South Bank; the Tate Gallery was expanding into an old power station somewhere in Southwark – and Adam had enjoyed hard-hat previews of all these twenty-first-century wonders. He was not one of the national journalists who, having bitched and griped about the spiralling costs and timetable overruns which the British public expected to read about over breakfast, would be invited to drink champagne at the opening parties; but he knew how much cement held up each stanchion, how many concrete panels held back the river mud on each section of the new Tube tunnel, and how much load the foundations of the London Eye would have to bear. As far as he was concerned, there was honour in that.

A small part of him still missed the undulating Suffolk of his childhood. His father had once run a thriving business in an improbably elongated chocolate-box village that was famous for its mile or more of antiques shops. Fortunately, Adam's father had seen the rise of the cut-price Scandinavian design aesthetic, with its devastating consequences for purveyors of brown furniture, long before most of his competitors, and he had managed to sell up and offload the bulk of his stock without incurring too much damage. He had put the proceeds into the stock market, and he seemed to have the knack for it, transitioning into a comfortable retirement of gardening, Mediterranean cruises and claret. He watched from his double-fronted, expensively repointed Georgian house on the village green as his former rivals made way for less ambitious businesses selling corn dollies and gingham-clad teddies to the tourist trade.

Not that Adam's father was always ahead of the curve. At the time of the New Labour landslide, he had supported the crazed billionaire Goldsmith in his failed bid to whip up fervour for a referendum on Europe. It had made no difference in Suffolk, which would always return Conservatives to Westminster; but Adam's father had actually joined the Referendum Party as a card-carrying member, thereby helping defeat a clutch of Tory incumbents in more marginal seats, and making Tony Blair's triumph all the greater. Adam enjoyed pointing this out whenever his father raged about the appalling drift to socialist tyranny – although these days he was preoccupied with stockpiling food and water in the cellar against the threat of the Millennium Bug. It seemed that most computer equipment was likely to fall over at midnight on the thirty-first of December, because it had only been programmed to recognise dates beginning with '19'. The national supply chain would grind to a sudden halt, Adam's father insisted, and only those with the foresight to stock up would get through the crisis. It was easier to let him get on with it than to argue.

As well as raising three children – Adam was the youngest – their mother had spent her life making sure the interior of the house lived up to the perfect pointing of the brickwork. She was good at matching rugs and cushions to wallpapers and paints, and when she discovered that having her husband at home all day was a mixed blessing, particularly as his lunches and the subsequent afternoons became steadily more liquid, she opened up a boutique in one of the defunct antiques shops, selling luscious silks and tasselled accessories.

His parents personified a county mentality and culture that Adam did not miss. However, there were some aspects of the metropolis to which he could never fully reconcile himself. The fact that it never really got dark at night, for one; and the grime – because the black stuff that came out when you blew your nose was altogether different from the more obviously organic, country dirt he had grown up with. Above all, it was the needless mess. He understood that air pollution was a by-product of mechanised life, and it needed some big technological fix that was beyond the reach of any single consumer to implement; but litter – the discarded McDonald's cartons, tin cans in gutters, gum on pavements – was the result of woeful individual failing, multiplied many times.

It was not so bad here in the West End, he noted, as he walked past the Palladium and into Great Marlborough Street, having forced his way out of the crammed Tube carriage at Oxford Circus into a morning that was surprisingly cool for September. Here there were daily collections, litter wardens and fines, so the place was generally tidy. It was the return journey that often filled him with gloom, as he picked his way through the paper, cardboard and plastic detritus of Hackney, wondering how many pieces of litter a benevolent resident would have to pick up to set an example or make a difference. So far his stance had only extended to Stefano, whom he had finally trained to dispose of cigarette butts as litter, rather than just treading them out on the pavement. But at some stage, if he was serious about the obligations of citizenship, which he found himself rehearsing in his head whenever he walked to and from the bus stop, he might have to start doing a little more.

The office was on the third floor of a small, unremarkable Sixties tower on the outer fringes of Soho. His employer, a family firm which had grown and eventually gone public, owned the whole building. There it housed its eclectic portfolio of trade titles: *Carrot Weekly*, *Rubber & Plastics Monthly*, *Freight Forwarding Quarterly*. These publications were not meant to be exciting, Adam wearily explained, whenever he was cornered into admitting where he worked, but they were valued by their readers, who could not do their jobs without them, which meant the pay was not too bad. The art of working for his publication was to make himself care enough to get through the day with a measure of enthusiasm, without ever letting himself get carried so far away that he became the kind of person who genuinely cared about cement contracts. However much Stefano might snigger, Adam liked the fact that he could follow the bidding process of a public works project from the point where the scheme was still a gleam in the client's eye, through the tender process, to bidding and then to award, knowing that the care with which he cultivated his contacts within this uncomplicated industry would make all the difference if he was to scoop his bitter rivals on *Cement & Concrete Intelligence*. Sometimes, as today, he had the chance to pull all his knowledge together and assemble it into a more discursive piece about the fortunes of the industry as a whole. This was the kind of writing he could imagine landing as a cutting on the desk of the construction editor of the *Guardian*, who would be so impressed that he or she would write a memo to the editor-in-chief advising that, next time they were hiring, there was a bright young chap at the very acme of cement reporting who might be just the ticket.

His concern about Stefano remained at the back of his mind throughout the morning. He had been quiet and withdrawn ever since their return from holiday, and Adam wished he could help, but he did not know what he could do about it. It was natural to be shaken by an accident that had brought him so close to death, and Adam had been shaken by it too. That surely ought to wear off, though. Instead, Stefano's malaise was getting worse. He had mentioned some kind of friction with Kevin, the landlord of the Prince Edward, and he seemed increasingly reluctant to leave the flat. They had been out of crisps and chocolate for days now, which never usually happened. Whatever had happened in Stefano's mind while he teetered between life and death was now preying on it, and Adam could see that his own scepticism had made matters worse as far as Stefano was concerned. The incident had virtually become a taboo subject, which was an unwise way to leave it when it was clearly bothering Stefano so much.

The one thing Adam could perhaps do was to read up on similar incidents himself. At lunchtime, after picking up a baguette from an Italian sandwich shop in Broadwick

Street, he went up to the fifth floor, where the group library served all the titles in the Murphy Magazines empire. Run with quiet but ferocious authority by a tall, angular woman called Chrissie, it was lavishly endowed with reference books and periodicals, as well as all the serious national newspapers going back for a year, before they were packed off into storage off-site. The papers were hole-punched all the way through and laced with string onto a hardboard mount, which deterred the light-fingered or lazy from removing individual editions and not returning them. It also made single articles notoriously hard to photocopy, particularly if the desired paper was at the bottom of a stack. The officially sanctioned way to do it was to secure Chrissie's permission and then unlace every paper from its mooring, returning each one to its proper place under its custodian's watchful glare once the photocopy had been made. But the more usual option was to try and twist the stack back onto itself to cram the page in question into the photocopier, without damaging the archive in the process. Either way, it was a laborious undertaking.

The library also contained a large collection of magazines: not just every gleaming jewel in the Murphy Mags crown, but proper titles, the kind that normal consumers paid money for: the *Spectator*, the *Economist*, *New Scientist*. These, too, came in their own binders, with an index at annual intervals.

After assuring Chrissie that he had no intention of eating his sandwich until he returned to his own floor, Adam asked to see the *New Scientist* binders. He found the most recent index and ran his finger down to N, looking for 'near-death experiences'. There was nothing. Nor was there anything under O, for 'out-of-body'. But that was just one year, and the binders contained at least ten. There was no need to be discouraged yet.

When he had gone through the whole decade, however, he was losing heart. He went back to Chrissie's counter to ask for any health magazines on file, and she passed him the binders for two different journals.

'What is it you're looking for?' she asked, when his sighs of frustration had grown progressively louder with each binder thumped back shut.

He hesitated: it was not strictly work. But she was not to know what he was working on downstairs and, even if she did know it was extra-curricular, it was unlikely she would care.

'I need anything that looks at the science of near-death experiences,' he said.

She beamed.

'Why didn't you say so before? I saw just the thing only the other week. Let's see... I didn't bind it yet, I don't think...' She flipped through a stack of magazines, as yet unmutilated by hole-punch or binder, on the counter in front of her. 'No, I did. So it'll be over here. Yes, here you go.'

She handed him a royal blue binder with the name *Paranormal Today* stencilled on the front.

Adam's face must have registered his disappointment, because she said: 'Don't worry, it's proper science. I skimmed through it myself when it came in, because I was surprised to see it there. That's it, look, the issue on the top.'

Extraordinarily, she was right. It was an article by a neuroscientist with an interest in explaining apparently paranormal phenomena in rational terms, having been through a near-death experience herself. Notebook and pen at his side in order to jot down the key points, Adam settled down to read.

The first thing to recognise, this woman said, was that the experience which all these people reported was real. They weren't making anything up. They really did feel they were looking down at their own bodies and then travelling up a bright, white tunnel amid feelings of euphoria. She knew, because she had done it herself. She noticed that everyone who reported the phenomenon seemed to describe much the same thing, across a wide variety of cultures, belief systems and educational backgrounds. So she had set out to find a scientific explanation. She also claimed to be able to explain the sensation of people looking down on their own bodies.

Her hypothesis was that, under stress, any sensible biological system would try and work out what was happening even when its senses had packed up. Citing further research that people tended to picture themselves from above, she concluded that the memory was providing the brain with a bird's eye view of what was most likely going on. She then made a computer model to show what an increase in activity in the relevant part of the brain might look like in the run-up to death. The result, which she showed in various illustrations, was a blizzard of white dots getting more and more concentrated towards the middle. It looked like a speckly tunnel with a white light at the end. As people seemed to move up the tunnel, their brains then showed them the sort of things they expected to see when they died. That was why, she explained, people from Christian cultures reported angels, while people in India said they had seen the Hindu god of the dead.

The crucial point, she added, was that this probably happened to everyone when they died, but it was only those people who were revived at the last minute who came back to talk about it.

Adam devoured the article with growing excitement. He was sure this was helpful. It certainly helped him understand what had happened to Stefano, without having to dismiss the experience as fantasy or a figment of his imagination. Maybe it was a figment – but of an entirely legitimate, scientifically explicable kind. The question, however, was how he could convey all this to Stefano, who was likely to glaze over at all the technical detail.

It was nearly two o'clock. He had spent too long in the library already and he was about to close the magazine and return the binder to Chrissie when he noticed a box in the text, separate from the main article. It was illustrated by an early Renaissance painting – by Hieronymus Bosch, he saw from the caption. The image was tall and thin, and was set in a sludgy night sky. In the bottom two-thirds were suggestions of clouds, while four versions of the same cluster of figures ascended the canvas like a strip cartoon. A naked figure of indeterminate gender was being carried by an escort of fluttering angels and, in each version of the tableau, the group gazed up at a large tube suspended in the sky. Its most striking feature was the white light emanating from its far end and reflecting off the sides. A tiny silhouette stood against the brightest point, waiting for the arrivals and waving. It looked remarkably like ET standing in the doorway of his spaceship, and in ordinary circumstances Adam would have laughed at it. For now, however, the content of the image was what mattered.

It showed exactly what Stefano and all the other people reporting near-death experiences said had happened to them. That suggested that these experiences had been around for ever, long before modern medicine had started resuscitating people in greater numbers. With his own professional hat on, Adam noted that the tunnel looked as if it was made of reinforced concrete, a detail he found troublingly exciting. What mattered far more, however, was that this image offered him a route to gaining Stefano's confidence.

He shut the binder, thanked Chrissie for her help and returned to his own floor, where he spent the afternoon finishing his feature. He managed to raise two of his friendliest contacts to give him quotes about the millennium building boom. One of them obligingly agreed that these big projects would 'provide a strong foundation' (ho ho!) for the industry in the twenty-first century, and he left the office at five-thirty with the satisfaction of a job well done.

It was barely any warmer now than it had been in the morning, and he walked briskly, vowing to make sure he wore a jacket tomorrow. Instead of going to Oxford Circus, he headed for Piccadilly by way of Wardour Street where, among the tattoo parlours and sleazy DVD outlets, there was a bargain bookshop which he knew had a decent art section. Just as he had hoped he might, he found a glossy, inexpensive picture book featuring the collected works of Bosch. A quick check revealed that the near-death picture – its proper name was *The Ascent of the Blessed* – was included. This was turning out to be a good day.

In the early days of their relationship, he had found it difficult that he and Stefano worked such incompatible hours. They could never go out together in the evenings, watch television companionably, or even eat together. But they had evolved a routine which Adam now quite liked. He could go to the cinema to see whatever he liked, and on nights when he was going straight home, he would cook for himself, leaving enough for Stefano to eat when he eventually got in. He could watch whatever he wanted on TV, without having to wage a fight over Stefano's trash diet of *Brookside* and *Who Wants To Be A Millionaire?* that he was generally doomed to lose. Instead he could curl up in front of *Cold Feet* or *Ally McBeal* without being disturbed by a fusillade of ostentatious sighs of boredom.

Tonight he made dinner as he watched TV. He was so distracted by Alan Titchmarsh hiding behind a wall to surprise Nelson Mandela with a garden makeover that he forgot to put water in the pan when he put the potatoes on to boil for bangers and mash. The smell did not alert him at first, because he thought it must be the sausages in the oven. It was only when the stink mutated from gentle browning to full-on burned that he came running back from the sofa. Seeing what he had done, he threw the blackened pan into the sink and blasted it with the cold tap, creating a hissing cloud of charred-potato steam. The smell was truly noxious now. He tore around the flat opening every window that would open, even the one in the living room that was never opened because you had to clamber around the TV to get to it. It was cold, but the smell was making him feel sick. Since the potatoes were ruined, he put some pasta on instead.

After eating, he often tended to nap on the sofa before Stefano returned. It was a middle-aged habit that he was happy to adopt if it meant they could spend some time together of an evening without him becoming chronically sleep-deprived. Tonight was no exception. With the windows still open to get rid of the smell, he crawled under a rug and settled down for a snooze.

The bang of the front door jolted him awake.

'It's freezing in here. Why have you got all the windows open?' said Stefano crossly, going around closing them.

It was true, it really was cold now. Adam had been dreaming he was lost in a snowy waste land, looking for a concrete piping manufacturer by the name of Hieronymus Bosch.

'Sorry. I burned something, and I was trying to get rid of the smell. What time is it?'

'Half eleven. Same time as it always is when you ask that. What did you burn?'

'What?'

'You just said you burned something.'

'Oh yes. The…potatoes.'

Adam was good in the mornings but always woke at a complete loss if he slept in the evenings. This usually amused Stefano, but he was in short supply of good humour these days.

'Looks like you burned the pan as well,' he said.

'I know. I'll clean it.'

Stefano was leaning over the TV to close the last window.

'I can't believe you even opened this one. You know how hard it is to close.'

'Sorry. The place smelled pretty bad.'

Stefano grunted as he finally pulled the offending window shut, snapping the catch into place.

'Please don't open that one again, OK?'

'Sorry. There's pasta instead,' Adam remembered. 'With sausages and peas. It's quite nice. Oh, and I got you this.' He held out the Bosch book. 'Look, this guy painted pretty much what you described, more than five hundred years ago, in fourteen something. I want you to see it, to show you I don't think you're making anything up.'

Stefano took the book, examining the page Adam was holding open for him.

'It was just like that,' he confirmed, after studying it intently. 'I didn't notice any angels carrying me, and there was an eye at the end, not a whole figure. But it's the same tunnel.' He looked up, his eyes softer now. 'Thanks. I'm glad you believe me.'

Adam pulled himself up off the sofa.

'Everything will be OK, you know,' he said, pulling Stefano into an embrace. He yawned as he did so. 'Sorry, I'm going to go to bed. I'm zonked.'

He did his teeth, rubbed moisturising cream into his face and changed into pyjama bottoms and a Tom of Finland t-shirt that he had never dared wear outdoors.

'Night,' he called, leaving Stefano poring over the Bosch book.

He was pleased that the book had been a good idea, and it was also encouraging that they seemed to have got over the taboo and could talk about Stefano's tunnel. After feeling so powerless for the past few weeks, it was reassuring to feel that he had found a way to help.

12

STEFANO WAS pleased that Adam seemed to be listening at last. The book of paintings was a thoughtful touch, because it was immediately obvious that this guy Hieronymus Bosch was on his wavelength. The painting that Adam had shown him was a five-hundred-year-old representation of his own experience in the tunnel of light. It felt like vindication.

He stared at the picture for a long time. The one thing that was missing was the eye. He wondered how many other people who had been through this experience actually saw God looking back at them.

He shivered. It was still so cold in the flat. Normally, he would put the food Adam had left for him in the microwave, but now he put the gas ring on, to warm the place up as well as to reheat his dinner.

Having heaped the pasta, sausages and peas onto a plate, he sat down again and put his art book on the arm of the sofa so he could turn the pages as he ate. He glanced at the introduction, skimming through the basic facts about the painter's life, and then started looking at the big colour illustrations, one by one. At a stroke, his appetite vanished.

Instead of painting transcendental images that might

speak to Stefano's soul, the artist was clearly obsessed with the torments of hell. There was page upon page of the stuff, some of it enlarged in detailed plates in case any reader failed to get the point. One painting was full of naked sinners hanging upside down, being tortured by demonic monkeys against a nightmare backdrop of gibbets and a burning sky. In another, a naked man in a hood climbed a ladder, with an arrow jammed between his buttocks; it did not require much imagination to guess what sin he had committed. Naked bodies were piled high in every direction: living ones writhing in torment, corpses strewn in hellish tangles. Victims were shown being carved up with swords and knives or fed to a pack of wolves. In the centre of one panel, a bird-headed giant sat on an enormous toilet, devouring human corpses and shitting them whole into an equally giant potty. What kind of sick imagination thought all this stuff up? Stefano wanted to look away, but each picture drew him in: there was so much detail, so many tiny tableaux of ever-more inventive cruelties and indignities being inflicted on human beings, all of them naked. Despite the lavish nudity, there was nothing erotic about any of these pictures, not because the bodies were obese or grotesque, but simply that in the context of all these indescribable agonies, seeing anything sexual in them was unthinkable. It was like those photographs of the naked corpses after the liberation of the Nazi death camps. The difference was that these pictures were designed to be shown in churches, not as a monument to man's barely imaginable brutality to man, but as a warning of the torments yet to come if man did not behave.

He went to bed, eventually, because it was late and he ought to try and sleep. But he was dazed and tormented. Was God watching him now? If so, he would see that he was in bed with another man. That was bound to count against him, even though the pair of them had barely touched each other since the incident on the beach. And tomorrow night, as usual, he would have to go back to the Edward, which was tame by the standards of some of London's other fleshpots, but was hardly going to help his cause. He turned onto his side, as far away from Adam's side of the bed as he could get, and tried to get images of eternal damnation out of his head. When he finally slept, he dreamed he was being stalked by a giant cockatoo that lived in the public toilets at Tottenham Court Road station and was seeking to add Stefano to the rotting pile of naked corpses it had stashed in the end stall.

He did not wake till mid-morning, long after Adam had left for work. The Bosch book was still on the sofa where he had left it, and the mere sight of it made him feel queasy. To make matters worse, he had run out of Marlboro Lights. He pulled on a jacket and travelled down in the lift to the street.

'All right, Stef?' said Mo, who was about his own age and had served behind the counter of the local Costcutter for as long as Stefano had lived there.

'All right. You?'

He did not feel all right, but people did not want to hear that.

As he was paying for his cigarettes, he noticed a set of

amber prayer beads next to the till.

'Mo, can I ask you something?' he said.

'What's that, boss?'

'You believe in God, right? You pray, and that?'

'Yes, boss.'

'But you sell all this beer and wine and spirits, that your God doesn't like. You don't worry that he'll punish you for it?'

'Nah, cos I don't drink myself, innit? As long as you live according to your scriptures, you'll be all right, know what I'm sayin'?'

Stefano thought about this as he walked back to the estate. He had once known his scriptures very well, but his loss of interest once he had decided that he no longer believed in God was so absolute, he could no longer remember half of it. That, at least, was something he could put right.

As he let himself in at the main door, he noticed a poster on the noticeboard on the lift. 'Questions about God? Come and learn about your personal salvation,' it said, in large white letters on a purple background. Perhaps it was a sign. The lift arrived, and the doors stood open for him, but he let them close again as he leaned in to read the small print on the poster. It listed the times of the weekly service where newcomers were welcomed. It took place at six thirty on Wednesdays – which was tonight. That had to be another sign.

At six twenty-five, he stood under a heavy, grey sky, looking up at an imposing building next to the Old Street roundabout. He must have passed it dozens of times on the bus, but if he had ever noticed it, he would have taken it for a magistrates' court, with its fake Grecian columns. Slung across the front of three of the columns, however, was a huge sign saying GOD IS LOVE in white on purple. Stefano felt his insides turn over at the prospect of going in. Would they be able to smell the sin on him, like a cloud of CK One?

Kevin had not been happy about him taking a night off, but since he had been so sluggish and lethargic lately, it had not been hard to make the case that he was coming down with something.

'We'll just have to manage short-staffed, won't we, sweetheart?' he said. 'But you know I won't be able to pay you for a shift. And strictly speaking you're meant to organise your own cover. If you're not better tomorrow, you'll need to find someone else for me, you understand?'

Stefano had said yes, he understood, and perhaps he would ask Rook, who was always happy to cover a shift on one of his free days. In his present mood, however, he felt like never going back to the Edward, in which case Kevin would have to pull his own finger out and find a new barman himself.

As far as Adam was concerned, he was at work, as normal. It could be awkward if Kevin phoned the flat, but he was very unlikely to do so, and in any case, the worst Kevin could do was sack him, and Stefano was by no means certain he cared. He took a deep breath and willed himself up the chipped stone steps.

He had assumed he could slink in unobserved and sit

somewhere at the back. But there were greeters in the doorway. As he approached, he found a hand extended towards him. It belonged to a mousy blond steward of about his own age, in a cheap suit and a nerdy haircut. He told Stefano he was welcome and then passed him on to a matronly black woman who led him into the church.

It was actually a large, undecorated hall with plain, whitewashed walls, galleries at the back and sides, and a lectern on a stage. The only thing that made it look like a church was the rows of austere wooden pews. These were mostly full already, with more men than women. Stefano noted a lot of hair with a just-washed look, and mismatched shirts and jumpers.

His usher escorted him down the centre aisle and showed him to the end of one of the rows about halfway back. So much for unobtrusive: he was at the dead centre of the auditorium. He imagined dozens of pairs of eyes staring down at him from the upper galleries, wondering why he was there, what his particular sin was, whether he had truly repented of it. What would they say if they knew he lived with Adam, that he spent his working life behind the bar of a gay pub? That he was beyond salvation? Was there really such a thing?

He expected organ music – even at his primary school they had managed Mrs Macpherson's piano – but there was nothing to announce the start of the service other than dead silence falling, as a smart-suited preacher with too-black hair slicked down his forehead strode onto the platform and took his place behind the lectern.

He surveyed the hall and Stefano was afraid to look

away. The preacher seemed to hold his gaze for a second then opened his mouth.

'The subject before us today, friends, is the superiority of the Gospel,' he said.

In these austere surroundings, Stefano had been expecting some kind of full-throated harangue. But this was a soft voice, almost whispery. Amplified from every corner of the hall, it had the effect of enveloping the audience in a seductive whisper.

'It is the power of God unto salvation for everyone that believeth,' the preacher continued. 'St Paul's letter to the Romans, chapter one, verse sixteen.'

Hands reached for Bibles, and Stefano hastened to do the same. He had once known the order of the books of the New Testament off by heart, but he had forgotten even that, and he panicked when he could not see St Paul at all.

'Let me help you,' whispered a voice closer to hand. The elderly Caribbean woman beside him took his Bible off him, flicked expertly to the right place, and handed it back. It was under Romans, not St Paul. How could he have forgotten that?

'God has unlimited power and he can do anything he wishes,' the preacher whispered.

Stefano had found the right bit, but he could not see that phrase anywhere.

'He could work in any number of ways. He chooses to work through the gospel.'

He looked at his neighbour, saw that she was looking straight ahead, and realised this was the preacher using his own words, not reading. Again, he should have known that.

'As we all know, my friends, the world is an evil place where terrible things happen. This is because of sin! The good news is that God has a plan, and this is the plan of salvation. It began with the incarnation of Christ in human form. God poured out his anger against sin in the punishment he visited on Christ, so he would not have to visit it on the rest of humanity, and to the rest of the world, he promised eternal life. And eternal life, my friends, can be achieved through repentance, when a poor lost sinner comes to God in prayer and says that he believes in Christ. But we all know that many people do not want to hear the message of the gospel.'

The preacher's voice had gradually become harder. It now had a less seductive, more gravelly tone. This was turning into a harangue after all.

'We all know about the many disagreeable traits of character which God's children show. We all know about atheistic teaching which deliberately takes people away from the word of God and his wonderful offer of grace. We all know about the people who rebel against him, running away from him, people who are more proud than we can imagine, so arrogant, so unteachable they ought to go down on their knees and long for his pardon.'

Stefano swallowed. It was as if the preacher had known he was coming.

'Then there are people who are dirty. There are people who are sensual, there are people who are unclean. There are people who are so bad they are perverted!'

This time the preacher was surely looking right at him.

Eventually the sermon ended and there was a hymn, although not one with a tune that Stefano could remotely follow. Before they sang it, the preacher announced that the stewards would take up their offering for the Lord's work. It took Stefano a moment to grasp that this meant money. Panicking again, he realised he only had a twenty-pound note. Doing his best to mime the words for the sake of appearances, he went through the motions with a velvet pouch that was carefully sewn at the neck to deter light fingers. Nobody would notice that he did not put anything in. After the pouch moved on, however, he realised that God might notice, and he could have kicked himself. Twenty quid would have been a bargain if it meant avoiding eternal damnation.

At the end of the service he returned his Bible and hymn-book and made for the exit. He felt more exposed than ever and was eager for his own company. But the phalanx of eager greeters who had guarded the entrance now had the exits covered with equal vigilance. An older man, also in a dark suit, had Stefano's hand in a ferocious grip before he knew he had even offered it. The suit was flecked white around the collar.

'I'm Frank, one of the pastor's assistants,' he said, standing a couple of inches too close for comfort. 'Did you enjoy the service?'

'I didn't really come to enjoy it,' said Stefano, attempting to back away those couple of inches, and finding there was a door jamb in the way.

Frank put his head on one side.

'So what brought you to us today?'

Stefano hesitated. He was resigned to having this conversation, especially now that he was trapped, but he was unsure how much of himself to reveal. Before the accident on the beach, he would have crossed the road to avoid people like this. Now, however, he had a need for answers.

'I'm here because…because I think I've had a conversion. Well, I know I have, because I didn't believe in God before and I do now. Probably. But the thing is… You see, I've had quite a…well…sinful life so far. Before I knew they were sins, because that's when I thought God didn't exist, you know? But I'm sure they still count, as sins I mean. And I need to know what my chances are.'

'Your chances?'

Frank tilted his head, in polite puzzlement.

'Of getting into heaven,' said Stefano. 'I mean, I didn't believe it existed until a few weeks ago, so it's not like I've always wanted to go. It's more that I don't…'

It was suddenly hard to continue.

'You don't…?'

Stefano took a deep breath.

'I don't want to go to hell.'

His eyes pooled.

Frank was standing even closer now and, through his distress, Stefano caught the distinct smell of tuna on his breath.

Frank gripped his arm.

'Anyone can repent, however great their sin, provided they are sincere.'

138

'Yes, I get that bit,' said Stefano. 'But how many times will I need to come to make it certain?'

'How many times?'

'How many services, I mean. How many do you think it will take before I'm saved?'

Frank coughed into a fist.

'Salvation isn't like a course of antibiotics. You have to long for forgiveness, to want it so badly that you run to the Gospel. After rebelling against God, after running away from him, you must want to beg for his pardon.'

'You can't give me a rough idea of how many times I'd need to come before I knew I was in the clear?'

'I think you're misunderstanding the process. That's not how it works. You have to believe. If you don't, it doesn't matter how many times you come. But if you do, you will want to come, because believing in the glory of the Gospel and the plan of God's salvation means you will want to share in it and take it out to other sinners.'

Frank cast his eyes around the room as if he was looking for support. The vestibule was full of small groups talking, like themselves.

'Perhaps you'd like to come and talk to the pastor personally? I can take you to meet him now. I'm sure he can explain it better than me.'

Stefano felt suddenly claustrophobic. Frank had taken a step back to look for the preacher, and he saw the chance to extricate himself.

'I really need to get going,' he said.

'Are you sure? You will come back next week? Can we take your number, or your address? The pastor can visit you at home to pray with you.'

Stefano sensed that he was a fish, slipping out of Frank's grasp and about to escape back into a vast, untrawlable sea.

'No, that's fine, thanks. I'll come back, honestly. But I need to go now. Sorry.'

This was all too much, too soon. He had volunteered that he was a serious sinner, but he remained reluctant to go into more detail and reveal that he was one of those who were dirty, sensual and unclean. These people thought his whole life was sick. A voice in his head objected that that was the whole point of conversion: he was supposed to leave his old ways gladly behind and achieve salvation, and he would never reach it if he secretly hankered after the paths of sin. Nevertheless, he was suddenly certain that he did not want the likes of Frank and the pastor judging his years with Adam. He might allow God to do so, but not them. He was not ready for that.

He almost ran down the steps, which were now glossy with rain. He turned up the collar of his jacket as he made for the bus stop.

13

GOD WILLED HIMSELF not to panic, but he was not sure it was working. All his efforts to dislodge his seeing-tube had confirmed that it was trapped in the window of the Special Hominid's dwelling. He tried to assure himself that there must be a solution to the problem, and he had simply not found it yet, but he was not sure he really believed it.

He tried to free the tube discreetly at first, for fear of drawing attention to himself. When the Special Hominid did not look up from the volume of pictures that he was so closely inspecting, the creator agitated it with greater confidence. This produced no greater effect – not of a helpful kind, at any rate. The tube quivered frenetically across the cosmos all the way down to Earth but, crucially, it did not budge at the bottom end. God pulled again, even harder this time, but still it did not release. Once more he stared down the device, trying to fathom what might be done, but all he saw was the Special Hominid bent over his book, and there was no inspiration for him in that. In frustration, he shook the tube again, giving it more of a jiggle than a tug this time. It danced around all the way down to Earth, in giant, flailing oscillations, creating an immense spectacle right across the universe. At the crucial point, however, it remained stuck as fast as ever.

It took the creator a while to realise that he was not the only one having a tough time. In a break from his efforts, he noticed that the Special Hominid had curled himself up and was rocking back and forth, with one clenched hand crammed into his mouth. This state appeared, even to a spectator of God's inexperience, to be a form of anguish. The Special Hominid's eyes were red and glistened with moisture. The volume of pictures seemed to have upset him.

The Special Hominid eventually got up from his seat and disappeared into another room within the dwelling. The creator heard the sound of running liquid. He emerged again after a short while, then disappeared into the room to which the Other Hominid had retired. The room where the seeing-tube was trapped went dark as he did so, as the Special Hominid extinguished the light that had been burning there.

In the absence of anything to see, the creator listened hard for any other interesting sounds within the dwelling. There was nothing from the hominids. As he listened, however, he heard a familiar noise in the extreme distance: the mysterious oscillating murmur. As before, it was very soft, so far at the background of everything that God might never have noticed it if he had not been straining to listen to the hominids. Once again, it seemed to bounce from one side of him to the other. Momentarily forgetting his predicament, he grabbed his tube and gave it the usual pull to retract it. Naturally, it was still stuck fast at the crucial point. Infuriated, he gripped it more firmly, telling himself that the time for gentleness was past. It was getting to the point where he was prepared to pull the whole dwelling tower off its base, if that was what it took. As he pulled again, however, he heard a faint, metallic crack from his device itself. Frightened of breaking it, he let go immediately. Causing further damage to his tube was the last thing he could afford to do. One distinctive aspect of being a sole deity in the cosmos was that there was no one to call if any of his possessions needed repairing.

It was clear there was nothing more to be done for the moment. He needed to be patient, he told himself. If he went away and did something else, distracting himself properly, and not getting too fixated, the hominids would complete their nocturnal rest. Then, at some stage, they were bound to open the window once more. All God had to do was keep a fairly regular check, so that he could extract his device as soon as it was free and make sure he never did anything so daft again.

The trouble was, anything else he might want to look at tended to involve his tube. Granted, he could watch galaxies spin, young stars rotate around one another, old ones fade away and even witness the disappearance of big chunks of solid matter into one of the empty pits of blackness that he had learned to treat with a healthy degree of respect. These were the big-picture distractions of his universe, and they were all well and good if he was in the mood for entertainment on that scale. However, the true riches of his cosmos were mainly to be found on a much smaller level, on the surface of the rocks. He had always relied on his facility for close-up observation in order to examine and acquaint himself properly with the full, ever-changing detail of these natural wonders. Deprived of his device for the first time ever, it was a shock to discover how much he had come to depend on it. Being without it, even for a few Earth-hours, was a form of torture.

As the Earth turned slowly on its axis and the hominids' dwelling place fell once more under the light of the local star, God waited impatiently for any signs of movement. Eventually, they emerged. The first to appear was the not-so-special one. He went into the room with the flowing water, where he remained for some time, then clattered about in the main room, shaking some kind of foodstuff out of a box into a receptacle and drenching it with white liquid, then sitting to eat it. There seemed to be another individual in the room whom God could not see but who was doing a lot of talking. It took him a while to grasp that this voice was coming from a device which the Other Hominid turned on and then off again when he had finished his food and was ready to leave the dwelling.

After an interval, the Special Hominid emerged in much the same way, going through the same manoeuvres, which were evidently a sort of start-the-day ritual. The only difference was that he did not turn on the same voice box, but a different one. This was a large black machine that stood directly in front of the creator's window. When the Special Hominid approached it, God felt a great surge of excitement: the boy was going to open the pane, the tube would be released, and the problem would be solved with calm, as he had promised himself. His hopes were dashed, however, when the Special Hominid picked up a small wand from the top of the machine, returned to his seat and pointed the wand at the machine. The latter duly emitted a voice – several voices, in fact, supplemented by sounds with a pleasant tonal arrangement which seemed not to come from a hominid mouth – and it now commanded the Special Hominid's full attention as he ate. Unlike his companion, he did not seem to be in any hurry to leave the dwelling.

In the next few rotations of the Earth, God fell into a pattern: trying to distract himself with big-picture amusements for as long as he could manage, before returning to his tube to see if anything had changed that would release him from his predicament. Time and again, he was disappointed. The occasion when all the windows had been opened wide seemed to have been an aberration. All were now kept tight shut.

Only once was there a real glimmer of hope. The Special Hominid had been sitting in the dwelling, as he did all through the daylight periods, while the Other Hominid was out. As he had done on many previous occasions, he sat hunched over the volume of pictures, breaking off only to put his head in his hands. His shoulders vibrated when he did this, which God had identified as a sign of emotional upheaval. Sometimes he lowered himself to the floor, hingeing his legs at the knee and pressing the flats of his hands together. He muttered some form of incantation as he did so, which was of course meaningless to God, and looked upwards. He also burned and inhaled the smoke of a large quantity of white sticks, sometimes lighting one off the end of the last, and the atmosphere became murky, impeding God's view of the room.

The creator was not the only one to notice this: when the Other Hominid returned from his daytime pursuit, he appeared upset by the smoky atmosphere. He waved his arms around, as if to waft the fug away, and began to go around the room opening the panes.

God's spirits leapt once more. Finally, liberation was at hand. Again, they crashed back down. For as the Other Hominid moved from window to window releasing the fastenings that held the panes shut, he pointedly omitted the one that mattered most. He made a movement in that direction, but the Special Hominid intervened, shaking his head from side to side. The Other Hominid duly desisted and that, to the creator's dismay, was the end of it. So there it was: by some freak misfortune, it seemed that his tube was stuck fast in the one window that was destined never to be opened again. It was a catastrophe, and he could not think what he could possibly do about it.

In that moment of despair, the creator had an idea. It came out of nowhere, surprising him with its simplicity. It was bold, ambitious, quite unlike anything he had ever done before, and he was not sure he could pull it off. But desperate times called for desperate remedies, and it might well be his only option.

The more he thought about it, the more sense it made, and his mood finally began to lift. It really was a good idea, and he should be proud of himself for thinking of it. All he had to do now was work out the details.

14

I<small>T WAS ONLY A FEW</small> weeks since Adam had presented Stefano with a book of medieval paintings, but it seemed like much longer That day, he had been optimistic that they might begin to communicate properly again and confront whatever problem it was that seemed to have come between them, following Stefano's accident on the beach. His optimism had been short-lived. The book had disappeared, but Stefano's mood had noticeably worsened. He was morose and withdrawn, and seemed to be testing Kevin's patience to the limit with the number of times he had cried off work.

'Try and get him out of the flat, darl,' Rook had suggested, when they ran into each other in the street and Adam had confided his worries. 'He had a traumatic experience, and he's clearly having trouble getting over it. Hiding himself away indoors isn't good for him.'

There was no point in suggesting a night out. Adam did not want to get Stefano in more trouble with Kevin and, in any case, he had a good inkling how any proposal to go out on the town would be received. A better option, he reckoned, might be to do something more obviously wholesome, with plenty of fresh air.

'Let's do some tourism,' he proposed. 'We live in

this amazing city and we never see half the things that visitors come from all over the world to look at. Why not Greenwich? We've never been, and it feels kind of appropriate, with the millennium coming up. You know, the place where time begins? What do you say?'

Stefano pulled a face at first, but Adam was determined to get his way, and eventually he wore him down. He took a day off work to use up the last of his holiday, and they went on a blustery Monday in November.

Dogs gambolled in the park below them as they toiled up the hill to the Observatory. It was steeper than either of them expected, so they stopped for a moment to watch the squirrels tunnelling in the dead leaves beside the path. It was good to see an innocent smile on Stefano's face as he put his hand through the railings to try and feed one of them a piece of biscuit.

'Watch your fingers. You know they're basically rats with tails?'

The little creature cocked its head to examine the extended hand with its bright black eyes. It stayed frozen in that position for a few seconds, then approached on all fours and froze again. Once more it weighed up the risks, then it made its decision, rising up on its back legs to grab the piece of biscuit in its mouth before scampering away, using its front paws to steady the prize. Stefano seemed mesmerised.

'What?' said he, as he looked up to see Adam smiling at him.

'It's good to see you happy for a change.'

It was clearly not a good thing to say. Whatever his

nameless burden was, Adam had merely reminded him of it, and a cloud came over Stefano's face once more.

Adam sighed.

'Come on, let's carry on up,' he said.

From a distance, the red-brick Observatory building had seemed like a stately monument on its parkland promontory. Up close, it was much smaller, looking more like what it actually was: a lonely house on a hill for a solitary star-gazer. They stood in front of the bullet-pocked statue of General Wolfe and gazed at London laid out below them. Although the clouds were grey, the air was clear. Away to the west they could see the towers of the City. Directly in front of them, where the river meandered elaborately to create the Isle of Dogs peninsula, stood the sole tower of Canary Wharf, a white elephant monument to over-ambitious Thatcherite folly. Perhaps, now that a brand-new Tube station was about to open underneath it, the place would become less of a ghost area.

Stefano cheered up a little as he recognised the view.

'Doof, doof, doof,' he said softly, miming a slow drum roll.

It was true: these loops of the river were the aerial view from the opening credits of *EastEnders*, which they watched on Sunday afternoons if Stefano was not on shift.

Over to their right, on an opposite meander of the Thames, sat the much newer national folly: a huge white marquee, like an upturned saucer, with vast yellow poles sticking up from it.

'There it is,' pointed Adam. 'That's what all the fuss is about.'

The scandal of the Millennium Dome had been all over the national newspapers for weeks now. Adam had visited the site early on, but he had not viewed it properly like this, and Stefano was interested too, because he had seen it on TV.

'It looks like a spaceship,' he said. 'I bet they don't finish it in time.'

Adam was usually loyal to the construction industry, disliking this popular mythology of failure. But in this case, it was true, the deadline was fast approaching, and he would not put money on the building being ready in time.

'Let's wait and see. They may still pull it off. Hey, we haven't settled what we're doing yet. It's not long to go now.'

'What we're doing?'

'On the night of the Millennium.'

Stefano always had to work on New Year's Eve, but they often went clubbing afterwards. Now, however, his face darkened.

'That's ages off,' he said.

'Not really. Six weeks.'

'That's still ages.' Stefano turned away from the view and back to the Observatory. 'Are we going inside or not?'

They bought tickets at the kiosk and joined the few unseasonal tourists idling through the exhibition rooms. On the walls, various explanatory panels told the story of the terrible shipwrecks that had happened because navigators needed to know the right time to calculate longitude, which had led to the long-standing quest for a clock that could still work at sea. To Adam's disappointment, Stefano was in no mood to try and understand any of this. He raced through the rooms, glancing only cursorily at the displays. Adam wanted to linger over them, but was conscious that he was being rushed. He was relieved when he found Stefano stopping to examine the huge old telescopes that the original astronomers had used. Two or three of them were still in place, vast instruments which each reached up from the floor through a hole in the roof.

'Do you remember making telescopes the night we met?' said Adam.

'I remember you being geeky about the stars.'

'You were interested! You said you were, anyway.'

Stefano smiled, but there was a sadness in his eyes that worried Adam. Was it really so painful to remember their first night together?

There was a sign next to one of the instruments telling its history, under the heading 'Studying the heavens'.

'Why do they call it that?' said Stefano. 'They're not studying actual heaven, are they?'

'I think it's just an expression. You can't study actual heaven, because it doesn't exist.'

He knew it was provocative, and he regretted saying it as Stefano turned wordlessly and made for the exit.

In the courtyard at the front of the Observatory, a stainless-steel strip emerged from the wall behind them and ran along the ground to mark the position of the zero meridian. A pair of French girls were taking each other's picture in turn as they straddled it, with one foot in each hemisphere.

'Come on, I'll take yours,' said Adam.

'At least there's a proper line this time, not like on that stupid island,' said Stefano.

The French girls moved on, and Stefano positioned himself where they had been standing.

'Come on, pretend you're enjoying yourself,' said Adam.

He took two or three pictures, then held the camera out, saying, 'OK, my turn,' so they could swap places.

A well-dressed woman in a long coat and sunglasses was smiling at them.

'Hey guys, would you like me to take you both together?' she said. She sounded American.

'That's kind of you, thank you,' said Adam, handing the camera over. 'It's all ready, you just press that one.' To Stefano, he said: 'Which side do you want, east or west?'

They stood on either side of the line. Adam put on his best photo face and hoped that Stefano was making some kind of an effort.

The woman was not satisfied.

'Come on guys!' she called. 'You could at least hold hands across the divide, or put your arms around each other. Don't be bashful!'

Adam laughed and slung his arm around Stefano's neck. But Stefano pulled away just as the shutter clicked.

'Hey, you moved!' said the woman. 'Hold on, I'll take another one.'

But Stefano had already moved away, heading for the

main gate.

'Sorry, was I out of line?' the woman said. 'I just assumed you were a couple. I didn't mean to offend him.'

'Don't worry,' said Adam, taking the camera back. 'He's in a funny mood. It really doesn't matter.'

He checked the picture, which showed him lunging at Stefano, and Stefano doing his best to resist. It was a hurtful sight, now frozen in time. Adam felt his eyes fill with tears. Aside from anything else, the public rejection was humiliating. He pressed the button to delete the image, and watched the pixels crumble away. If only their own problems could vanish as quickly.

'Wait for me,' he called, his voice sounding thin and frail on the wind.

He quickened his pace to catch up with Stefano, who was already on the path back down the hill.

15

KATIE CARTER had spent half her life looking for her brother. As a child, she had been shocked and hurt by his departure, which was never properly explained. There were whispered conferences in the days and weeks afterwards, with raised voices and tearful recriminations, but nobody ever sat her down and talked to her about where he had gone or when he would return.

'But when is he coming home?' she would ask, and she would be told to finish her tea or get on with her homework.

Her hopes were raised when a white envelope arrived, in Steven's handwriting, on her twelfth birthday, three months after his disappearance. She saw it before her parents did, and she opened it excitedly, hoping for news, but it was just a card and all he had written was: *Sorry I didn't say goodbye, Happy Birthday, love Stee xxx.*

'That's more than we got,' said his mother. 'Not even a note.'

'At least we know the lad's alive,' she heard her father saying, when they thought she was out of earshot. 'And we were right about where we thought he'd gone.'

She had seen them examining the postmark, as she had also done before she even showed it them. It was from London EC1.

That made it clear that they cared. Perhaps refusing to discuss it with her was easier than admitting they had no idea where her brother was. Nevertheless, it often seemed to her as if they were trying to pretend that Steven had never existed, so it became her responsibility to keep his memory alive. Hidden at the back of her wardrobe, she kept a shoebox full of pictures of him at various ages, a postcard he had sent her from school camp in Anglesey, his old camouflage hat with badges sewn around it. The birthday cards continued to come for the first five years, until she was eighteen, mainly postmarked London EC1, but some years, London NW1. She kept them on permanent display on the shelf above her bed. When she was old enough, she vowed, she would go to London EC1, and London NW1, to find him herself.

The first Christmas, she could feel her parents making an effort for her sake, but the atmosphere was tense. She was convinced that Steven would make a surprise entry, and her parents must have been too. Her mother made a birthday cake for Christmas Eve and there was a present wrapped for him, but both had disappeared by Christmas morning. That set a pattern for the years to come: the cake would always be made, but they would never eat it, and one year she found it at the bottom of the dustbin, candles and everything. For the next few hours they would have to creep around her mother as she did her annual battle with the turkey, and with anyone else who came too close.

Her father never revealed much of what he was thinking,

but she once found him watching a documentary about teenage runaways, with tears running down his face. She sat next to him on the couch, and he let her hold his hand, but when the programme finished, he refused to ring the number they put on the screen. He just shook his head and went off to the garage to work on the car. She had memorised the number and she wrote it down herself. After a couple of days she plucked up the courage to dial it, but a woman told her they could only record her brother as a missing person on the authority of her parents.

She resolved to talk to Auntie Jill, rehearsing for months the questions to ask when she and Uncle Richard next visited.

'Do you know where our Stee's gone?' she pleaded, when they finally did come.

She had sat in wait on the top stair while Auntie Jill spent a penny.

Her aunt looked at her, reached out a hand to brush a strand of hair from Katie's face, and said loudly for the benefit of anyone downstairs: 'Why don't you show me your bedroom, love? It's ages since I've seen it.'

They huddled on Katie's bed underneath her poster of Wham! in leather jackets and no shirts.

'Poor poppet,' murmured Auntie Jill. 'It must be very hard for you. You miss your brother, don't you?'

And Katie nodded and burst into tears, because nobody had ever asked her that before.

Auntie Jill put her arm around her and Katie let herself go, until she realised she was getting drool on her aunt's cashmere.

'Where is he?' she wailed. 'I know he's in London somewhere, because he sends me cards. But why didn't he tell me where he was going? And why is nobody looking for him?'

Auntie Jill squeezed her hand. 'I expect he had his reasons for not saying goodbye. But he does care about you. And he'll come back when he's ready. Your mum and dad have done all they can, but Steven's a grown-up now. If he doesn't want to come home, nobody can force him.'

Her brother had always liked Auntie Jill and Uncle Richard too. A sudden thought shocked and excited her.

'You live in London! Have you seen him? You would tell me?'

'I wish I had seen him, love, and I would tell you. But no, he hasn't been in touch with us. London's a very big place, and anyway we don't live in London, just nearby.' She gave Katie another squeeze. 'In a sense it's good news that we haven't heard from him. I always say to Uncle Richard, he'll get in touch when he needs us, and so far he hasn't. He knows where we are, so he must be fine.'

'Why did he go there?'

'He was always so interested. He wanted to know about the Underground, and the shops, and the names of the streets, right from when he was small. If only your mother had taken him, then maybe…'

She did not finish the sentence, but Katie understood. It was her parents' fault that her brother had gone. That reinforced her conviction that they could not be relied upon to get him back, so it was up to her.

She stayed on at school to do her A-levels, and when she applied to universities, they were all in London. By then, six years had elapsed since she had seen her brother, and the sense of urgency had faded. She and her father had become closer, and her mother spent most of her time up at the hospital, where she organised the volunteer visitors. Katie was realistic enough to know that Steven would have left home by this time anyway, so it was not a question of getting him to come back. Nevertheless, she had made the promise to herself, and fulfilling it had become part of her future. Her father understood, and discreetly wished her well, but she had the impression that her mother took her move to London personally. She blamed the place for taking her son away, and now her daughter was going there too.

She got a place on a media studies course at the University of Westminster, living out at Harrow, which felt vaguely comforting, because if she got on the A41 at Edgware, she could in principle follow it all the way to her parents' house. She learned her way around, so that she knew the difference between EC1 and NW1, and she gradually came to realise that these sorting offices represented vast posting areas – her own letters home were postmarked NW1, even though she lived miles away – so they were no guide to where Steven actually was. Over the next three years, she sought him all over the city. She made her initial assault on the West End, which was where she was convinced he would be. She started with the snooty tailors in Jermyn Street and Savile Row, then the menswear sections of the smart department stores, followed by the high-street chains. She wondered how long you needed to live in a city of eight million people to walk past everyone at least once. She even started looking into the faces of the homeless in shop doorways, occasionally seeking information for the price of a cup of tea. But the photograph she had was so old, she was not surprised when she always drew a blank.

She stayed on in London for a couple of years after getting her degree, working for a PR agency on the Fulham Road. She still scanned the oncoming faces, partly out of habit, then in desperation when tragedy struck and her brother needed urgently to be found. Deep down, though, she had given up hope, especially when the birthday cards stopped coming. After so many years, he could have gone anywhere, which was a better option than her other, darker fear, based on an unguarded remark that her mother had once made. She needed no reminding that a lot of young men who did not fit in properly at home had died of an unspeakable plague in the time he had been gone.

When she got the chance of a job back up north, working in the communications department of the borough council, she was more than ready to return to her roots. The big city had never really felt like home, and her mother needed her support. She had been promised that the job would involve occasional trips back to London for training courses and other meetings, which was reassuring. It was clear that she was likely to be volunteered for these occasions because she knew the capital well and nobody else on the team had much desire to go there.

That was three years ago, and she had been up and down five or six times since then. She enjoyed the change of scene as much as anything else, as well as going for drinks with some of her mates from uni days, if they were around. Sometimes she crashed on their floors, but on the Wednesday afternoon in mid-November when she arrived for a conference for local government comms professionals, her boss had allocated budget for a hotel. The conference was due to begin at nine the following morning in an old church hall in Shoreditch, and she had been booked into a place somewhere on City Road.

It was already dark by the time she emerged from Old Street Tube station. It was not a part of town she knew well, and the station, built under a busy roundabout, seemed designed to confuse, with eight different exits. She took a moment, when she reached the top of the steps taking her to street level, to get her bearings. The roundabout was a giant poster-site surrounded by vans, lorries and rush-hour buses. Cyclists wove between them with death-defying fearlessness, as if it were perfectly normal to navigate on two wheels through three lanes of traffic thundering in from all directions. London really was another country.

To her right, a single concrete lift shaft soared upwards from an enclosure of construction-site hoardings, the naked spine of some soon-to-be-fleshed out tower. In front of her, a parade of Grecian columns announced some grand temple of something or other: commerce, learning, or public edification. The yellow stone of its façade was floodlit and she saw now that it was a church – a sign slung across the columns proclaimed that GOD IS LOVE in huge white letters.

She looked down to check the printed map she held in her hand. She studied it carefully, making absolutely sure she knew which route she needed to take from this bewildering intersection. When she looked up again, time suddenly slowed down. A young man stood in front of her on the pavement, with short hair and a woollen scarf inside an upturned coat collar. He looked to be in his early thirties, and he had freckles and long eyelashes. He must be exactly twice the age he was when she had last seen him, but to her, he had not changed a bit.

'Stee?' she said, her voice trembling. 'Steven Carter?'

He turned sharply towards her, and she thought she saw panic in his eyes. But they softened when they saw her, looking her up and down to take her in, and now he was standing right in front of her.

'Hello Katie,' he said, and burst into tears.

They went to a café for a cup of tea, where he told her he preferred Stef to Stee these days. She was struck by how southern he sounded. She had so much to ask him, so much to tell him, but he was subdued, and all he would say was that there were heavy things going on his life and he was a bit of a mess. That was when she suggested he come back up north with her the next night, not really expecting him to say yes. To her amazement, he agreed straight away.

She barely slept, or paid attention to the next day's

proceedings at the conference. Her main preoccupation was whether or not he would come, and the whole thing was so unexpected and improbable that she was resigned to the inevitable disappointment when he failed to turn up. To her surprise and relief, however, he was on the Euston concourse at precisely the time he said he would be, with a couple of large hold-alls.

They went into the ticket hall to get his ticket, which cost a small fortune because he had not booked in advance. She said they could go halves if necessary, but he scarcely quibbled. He was nervous, though, fumbling with his wallet and dropping his payment card.

'Stefano Cartwright?' she read, as she picked it up off the floor for him. 'No wonder we couldn't find you. Why Stefano? Why Cartwright?'

'Stefano because… Well, I was given it by a good friend. Or he used to be a good friend. Maybe I can't be close to him any more, I don't really know.'

There was something vague about him, confused. She wondered if he was on drugs.

'And Cartwright?'

He shrugged. 'I preferred it. I never really felt like a Carter.'

'Is that why you ran away, because you never really felt like a Carter?'

'I guess.'

'Don't tell Mum.'

'I think she knows.'

She used her mobile to call ahead from the train to warn her mother not to go to bed, because she was coming over. She did not go into any further detail, because she wanted to make her brother's return a surprise. She had pictured just such an occasion for years: the kind where people fell into each other's arms in an explosion of joy that made all that pain seem, just for a moment, to be worth it. Her mother deserved to enjoy that moment, after all she had been through.

Steven – or Stef, whatever she was meant to call him – did not seem in much of a mood to talk, and Katie felt inhibited by the presence of the two strangers with whom they were sharing a table. In any case, she was exhausted after not getting any sleep the previous night, so she dozed for most of the way.

It was past ten when they arrived at Lime Street. She found herself looking at it through his eyes. Before she left for uni, this had always been such a dazzlingly cosmopolitan place, the gateway to adventure. Now, however, she could see that to him it was just a dwarf version of the London stations.

They took a taxi because it was late, and a special occasion. She was excited now, hugging herself with anticipation at how happy her mother was going to be.

'The tunnel,' he said softly, as they descended beneath the river.

'What about it?'

'It's weird seeing places I'd forgotten about.'

'How could you forget the Mersey Tunnel?'

She was laughing about it. But, as she saw him shrug in the dark, she began to understand how he had forgotten. For all these years, while she had been consumed with

163

the need to find him, he must barely have given them a thought.

When they emerged on the other side of the river, she thought once more how small it must all seem to him: a parade of shops, the sign for the shipyard, a Tudorbethan terrace on the edge of Lord Hulme's famous model village. Nothing went higher than two storeys round here.

'The Close,' he said, as they neared the turning.

'I don't think anything much has changed here.'

'The Jeavonses have got solar panels.'

'That's true. And an extension. But it's not the Jeavonses' any more. She left him for an osteopath from West Kirby, and he moved over to Liverpool, quite a while ago now.'

The hall was dark as they walked up the flagstone path, and the lights only came on through the frosted glass when Katie rang the bell. They heard the clunk of the security bolt being drawn back. She glanced at her brother, but his expression was unreadable.

'Look who I've found!' she cried, as the door opened.

Their mother peered out, small and grey in the yellow light of the hall. She looked from Katie to her brother, then gave a sharp cry and turned and fled, leaving the door open.

'Oh God,' said Katie, following her inside. 'Sorry, this is my fault. I should have known that surprising her was a stupid idea.'

Why had she not thought this through? She had not for a moment considered that it might go badly. She knew how much her mother must have missed Steven over all these years, so it stood to reason that she would be overjoyed. However, Katie ought to have remembered that joy did not suit her family. It might be a nice idea in principle, but was something that, in practice, the Carters did not do.

They found their mother in the sitting room, perched on the edge of the old brown Parker Knoll sofa, sobbing into her hand. Katie sat down beside her and put an arm around her quaking shoulders, while her brother hung back in the doorway.

'Come in, Stee. I mean Stef. Sit yourself down,' said Katie. 'Don't cry, Mum. I'm really sorry, I should have told you. I didn't think. I just thought it would be a nice surprise. Can't you say hello to him?'

Her mother pulled a ball of pink tissue from the sleeve of her cardigan and looked up, eyes glistening behind thick lenses.

'No, it's me who should be sorry. It's no way to welcome someone home after all these years. Hello, son. Aren't you going to give your old mum a kiss?'

16

THE CREATOR HAD lost count of the number of spins of Earth for which his tube had been stuck fast in the Special Hominid's window, twisting around through the cosmos at the mercy of the planet's orbit. Nobody had come to open the window, in line with his own, gloomy prediction, and no amount of tugging or coaxing would dislodge the tube itself. In other words, nothing in his predicament had changed. He did, however, have a plan, which was simple to describe, even if it might prove complicated to execute.

He would go to Earth and free his tube himself.

It was dangerous and daunting, but the more the idea grew in his imagination, the more he liked it, and not just because he could not see any other option. Having thought it through very carefully, he was also excited by the prospect.

His recent escapade in the Greater Multiverse had disturbed and frightened him, but it had been a thrill as well. That feeling of urgency and danger, followed by the surge of relief when everything turned out to be all right, was something he never experienced in his normal existence. He would not want it all the time; far from it. But was it so wrong to yearn for a little stimulation every so often? Now that the idea of going down to Earth had presented itself, it seemed the perfect opportunity for another adventure. It would give him a change of scene, a break from his normal routine. Above all, he would get the chance to do something for once, after so many aeons of simply watching.

The logistics needed careful thought. Since he could hardly go as himself, there were three options, as he saw it.

The first involved turning into a non-hominid creature, such as a quadruped or something airborne. It would give him an interesting perspective, and perhaps the odd useful skill that most hominids did not possess. As a way of getting inside a hominid dwelling to free his tube, however, it did not seem particularly suitable.

The second option was to attempt to produce some offspring of his own, which would then appear in hominid form, as his representative. But this was obviously problematic. Aside from being complicated to organise, it would be a lengthy process, involving a wait not just for the creature to hatch, but to grow up enough to be of any use. He could not do without his tube for that long.

No, there was only one serious option, and that was to inhabit an existing adult body.

Whether it was even possible remained to be seen. Nothing in his existence to date suggested he could tele-transport around the universe into different creatures' bodies. On the other hand, he had never tried. In the general scheme of things, entering the body of one single creature was a modest project. It was not asking a lot: it was just a temporary shape-shift, a change of perspective, the kind of thing that by rights should come with the creatorial territory, and it was something any deity worth the name ought to be able to do. In fact the more God thought about it, the more irritated he became at the notion of not being able to.

Perhaps the fact that he could conceive of it was enough: as creator, thinking that something was within his powers would be enough to make it so. That approach had certainly worked well for him when it came to pointing his tube to locate the Special Hominid. It was a good example of the kind of thing he had been able to do all along but had simply never attempted, and it encouraged him to think that there might be many more.

So he would work on the assumption that it was possible. The other key question was whether he would be able to get back again afterwards. It seemed likely that, if he could go one way, he could go the other way as well. It was a gamble, however, and one that made him queasy when he thought about it. If it all went wrong, could he really spend eternity in hominid guise on the hominid rock? It seemed unlikely that he would be able to, given that hominids were mortals. So what happened if he were trapped in the hominid body when the hominid died? That was a sobering thought – but it was also preposterous to think that such a thing could ever happen. Of course he would be able to get back. He was God, who was eternally present in his own universe, and if some mortal host was doomed to die, it stood to reason that God could leave that host behind whenever he chose. He really ought to have more faith in his own divinity. Aside from all that, he had no other option if he wanted to get his tube back, and he was not sure his existence was worth living without it.

So the only remaining question was, which hominid body to inhabit? The obvious candidate was the Special Hominid himself, but there had been no sign of him through the seeing-tube for several spins of the Earth. That left the Other Hominid, who did not seem to be there so much either. In the apparent absence of his companion, he was spending longer and longer periods away from the dwelling. He departed shortly after the light of the sun first illuminated the tower, and returned long after the Earth had turned away from the light. When he arrived, he spent next to no time on the wide sitting unit directly in the sightline of the tube; instead he hid himself away in the room where he passed the rest of the darkness period, until it was time to emerge and leave the dwelling again. Based on God's observation of the two hominids' normal habits, this was unusual behaviour, and it seemed to correlate to a degree of emotional distress, which even the creator was able to read in the Other Hominid's face and anguished demeanour.

None of this was any reason to reject the Other Hominid as the body to inhabit. While going to Earth would undoubtedly be an adventure, it was also a mission with a clearly defined objective, and the Other Hominid appeared to be the only candidate with direct access to the room where God's seeing-tube was trapped. Nevertheless, it did present the creator with a significant difficulty. Despite his complete lack of prior experience in the business of tele-transportation into a terrestrial habitat, it seemed obvious to him that the venture was only likely to work if he could actually see the hominid he was trying to cast himself into – or, at least, had a very good idea where it was. The mere fact that the Other Hominid had greatly reduced the amount of time he spent in God's direct eyeline narrowed the aperture of opportunity rather alarmingly.

It would be all right if the creator acted quickly, making his decision as soon as he saw the Other Hominid appear through the door of the dwelling and then setting immediately about the operation. But the truth was, God was dithering. The enterprise suddenly all seemed rather daunting, and a daunted adventurer was not best-suited to grabbing the necessary opportunity as soon as it presented itself.

It occurred to him, by way of compromise, that it might be a sensible first step to move closer, in order to position himself directly above the hominid rock. That would surely offer all kinds of practical advantages as he prepared for his expedition.

He had become very used to his vantage point at the mid-point of his heavens, and his initial concern was that he might get lost, mistaking this galaxy for that, or losing his bearings once he got away from the centre. In the event, finding his way to the vicinity of Earth was not difficult. Since he had never had cause to leave his tube extended before, he had never seen it side-on, arcing across the cosmos with its faint, luminescent glow. It guided his way perfectly, and all he needed to do was follow it to the other end. He set out while it was still dark on the part of the Earth where his tube was caught. He glided past galaxies, hundreds upon thousands of them, paying none of them any heed as he went. As he approached the hominid rock, which glowed pleasantly in the light of its star, with the liquid elements laid out in deep blue and the solid parts arranged in their island chunks of green, brown and yellow, his tube still pointed all the way down, sparing him the bother even of trying to remember which point on the surface of the planet he was looking for.

Slowing to a gentle hover, he took his own end of the tube, which he had been carefully holding throughout his journey, and peered down it to see if the Other Hominid was stirring yet.

To his surprise, there was nothing to see. At least, he could no longer see the hominid dwelling. Instead, he found himself looking at the bright, white sides of the tube interior. He turned back to look in the direction he had come – and realised with dismay that, instead of retracting as he progressed across the cosmos, the device had remained fully extended and now flailed back in a wild, glowing loop across half the universe. It looked messy and unkempt, but far more serious was the fact that the bend in the tube completely obstructed his vision down it: he was effectively staring at the magnified sides of his device halfway back the way he had come.

God sighed. Why must everything be so difficult?

He looked down towards Earth, but it was no good:

without the assistance of his tube, he would not be able to see the body into which he was hoping to tele-transport, which needlessly increased the chances of it all going disastrously wrong. There was nothing to be done but return the way he had come, back to the centre of the cosmos, where he would at least be able to see all the way back down his tube.

Back he travelled, past the hundreds upon thousands of galaxies, with the tube trailing behind him in his wake and gradually straightening up as he approached the bridge of the universe. When he finally arrived, he was tired and irritable. His journey had been wasted, and he had half a mind to abandon all thought of his tube for the time being. Now that it was more or less straight again, however, he made himself look down it, just to check it worked properly. It would be just his luck if bending it in half had somehow damaged its internal mechanism and put it out of action completely. To his relief, it was working precisely as it should, and he had a full view of the hominid dwelling room, which was just as he had left it, only now it was bathed in the full light of the shining star. As he looked, he saw the Other Hominid directly in his line of vision, emerging from the inner room and throwing some feeding materials together in what appeared to be a great hurry. By this time, in the daily spin cycle of the planet, he was usually long departed. Something had clearly delayed him, and he was in a state of disarray, fastening garments even as he fed, and attempting to flatten down the hair on his head, which seemed unusually tangled and matted today.

In an unprecedented burst of impetuosity, God made his decision. He would go now! The Other Hominid was in his sight line, everything was illuminated, and there was no time like the present, particularly given the creator's own recent capacity for messing things up. The time for dithering was past. He was ready to take the leap into the unknown which, if it worked out, would allow him to retrieve his tube. If it did not, well... there was only one way to find out.

Summoning all the courage he possessed, he took a final glance at his own familiar surroundings in this cosy spot at the centre of all creation, then turned back to face his adventure. Focus, that was the key to it. Concentrating harder than he could ever remember doing, he thought, to the exclusion of all else, about the hominid body he was aiming for, tuning out all the sights and sounds around him.

At first, nothing happened. But gradually, little by little, he felt himself begin to slip and then to slide. He seemed to be spinning, although it was peculiar, because he could not tell for sure if this was physically happening to him, or whether it just felt like it was. Either way, it was dizzying, a sensation he could choose either to hate or enjoy, depending on whether he resisted or allowed himself to lose control. It was certainly unlike anything he had ever known.

Now he had the sense that he was rushing Earthwards, with the vaguely familiar outline of its land masses surging up at him. On he spun, his surroundings blurred with the speed of it, but dimly identifiable as the large hominid settlement and the tower. And now he was tele-transporting into the tower itself. The Other Hominid must have left the dwelling already, because the creator found himself in some kind of tall internal well, with steps descending all the way to ground level. Propelled by whatever force was carrying him, he plunged down this well as far as the bottom level, where his dizzied senses were just able to make out the shape of the Other Hominid exiting through the main front door of the tower. Now there was someone else in the doorway too, a female, just behind the Other Hominid, also going out of the same door. The spinning accelerated still further and everything went black for a moment or two. And then suddenly it was clear again, and God was looking at the world from the height of a hominid head, through two hominid eyes.

He had made it. He had arrived on Earth in hominid form.

But something was not right. Through these two new eyes, he saw a sight he ought not to be able to see, namely the rear view of the Other Hominid departing in haste along the carriageway outside.

Damn and blast.

The creator had transported himself into a hominid body, all right. To that extent, his mission was a triumph. The problem was that he had landed in the wrong one, and he did not have the foggiest idea to whom it belonged.

17

TODAY WAS TURNING out to be a good day, Irene Probert thought to herself as she ran a comb through her hair in front of her hall mirror. She even caught herself smiling, although she was embarrassed to see how lop-sided that smile came out. She had noticed it in photographs, and she really must try and stop doing it. To the extent that it was conscious, she imagined it would give her a raffish, sardonic air; but the truth was, she just looked a bit daft.

The occasion for her good mood was a letter in the morning post from James, who had been her son Ollie's best friend since their first term at secondary school. The stamps were marked Botswana where, the letter explained, James had been teaching English for the past couple of years. Expressing the hope that her address had not changed after all this time – as if Irene were going anywhere! – it asked after her health, offered a few colourful details about the village where he was living, and then got on to his main reason for writing, namely to apologise for his failure to keep in touch. This, he rightly observed, was a breach of the faithful promise he had made to her the last time they had seen each other.

He had tiny, tight handwriting which was hard to decipher at first, but once she had got used to it, she read:

I was bruised, exhausted and emotionally drained by everything we had been through. Looking back, I reckon it was some kind of post-traumatic comedown, and the only way to cope was to get as far away as possible – first to the west of Scotland for three years, and now here. I can see now that it was very unfair not to explain that to you, especially as I know it must have been so much worse for you. I also should have replied to your letters and cards, which did reach me, and I'm ashamed that I didn't. I hope you can forgive me. My contract is about to end so I should be back in London for good very soon. Can I come and see you? If you don't completely hate me, I'd like to come and say sorry in person.

She would write back to him later to say how delighted she was to have heard from him, and how much his unexpected letter had lifted her spirits. He was right about the need to apologise: his rebuff had hurt her, at a time when she needed all the help she could find, just to get from the beginning to the end of the day. However, the fact that he had done so now, unprompted and out of the blue, wiped away that hurt. Of course she would forgive him.

In the early days, when she had first realised the tragic route that fate had mapped out for her and Ollie, and she felt beleaguered by so much fear and narrow-mindedness, her instinctive reaction had been to harden herself, attempting to turn fury into strength. Later, she had held on to grudges as a kind of compensation for not being able to hold on to her son. But if there was one thing, above all else, that her involvement with St Saviour's had taught her, it was the power of forgiveness – not for the sake of some abstract piety, but for one's own sake, because it helped to let things go and it stopped the hurt festering. That had been the big revelation when she opened herself to Christianity in middle life: it was full of sensible wisdom that made her feel better if she followed it. And really, James' offence was very minor in the general scheme of things. He was just a frightened boy who had tried his best for a while, when life had asked him to grow up too fast, and he had found it all too much. From the tone of his letter, he had more than made up for that now. He sounded very grown-up indeed. Hearing from him out of the blue would be something nice to chat about with Peg this afternoon.

Although Peg was meant to be one of Irene's good deeds – assigned by Sharon, the small, solemn vicar of St Saviour's – she had become a firm friend. Originally from Bethnal Green, all of two miles away, she still regarded herself as an incomer to Hackney, after nigh on fifty years – first in the little two-up, two-down where she had lived with her husband Bert until the street was condemned as a slum, and then in the revolutionary new tower in the sky, in which they were eventually rehoused. As Peg told it, Bert Ross's parents had either been comedians or short on imagination when they gave him the name Albert. He had turned it to his advantage, however, incorporating the joke into his patter. 'They do say you'll never get rid of an Albert Ross around your neck,' had been his early line to Peg, 'but trust me, gorgeous, you'll never want to.' To Irene, that sounded as cheesy as hell, but Bert had clearly been smooth enough and handsome enough to get away with it, and his prediction had been right: they had spent forty-two happy years together, until emphysema carried Bert off. He was only a couple of years into his retirement from the bakery where he had spent his working life breathing flour dust. Peg told Irene she had a lingering suspicion that she could have claimed compensation, but she had never tried. Instead she had settled into an active, childless widowhood, busying herself in the work of St Saviour's until her arthritis confined her to her flat and she became one of the needy rather than the needed.

Irene had started visiting her to keep herself busy, having eased off on her work hours when Ollie was ill, and discovering that it was not so simple to ease back into them when it was all over. For years she had guided tour groups of all nationalities, ages and sizes around London. Now, in more competitive times, she was confined to a specialist beat, escorting interested parties around Highgate Cemetery, or the more obscure courtyards of the Square Mile, in search of hidden Roman heritage. This scaled-down working life suited her, she gradually realised, because it left her more time for enriching pursuits, and one of the most enriching was seeing Peg. She was pushing eighty, and had had only the most basic formal education, but she was nobody's fool, she could make Irene laugh on days when she thought she might never smile again, and she had helped her see that life could still be worth the effort, even if the loss would never stop hurting.

She was fond of fig rolls and sweet sherry, and Irene needed to make a detour via the nearest Tesco Metro to pick up both, even though she was earlier than usual today – it was barely lunchtime – so she was not sure that sherry was appropriate. Better not to open it than arrive without, she decided. It was Peg's only indulgence, and she could always have some later.

As she made her way back down Mare Street, it was starting to rain and she quickened her step. Passing the town hall, she was relieved to see that the appalling hell-fire preacher was not there. She remembered that boy, of about Ollie's age, whom she had seen listening to him a few weeks ago. The poor creature had seemed so aghast, as if he were taking it all personally. That was a strange reaction to have in these parts, where the urban rough and tumble tended to toughen people up and inure them to such slights. That was why she had stopped and spoken to the lad, because he seemed so badly in need of a kind word. That, and because she would hate people to think that the Church was monolithically prejudiced in these matters. She was not sure if any of it had sunk in. Funnily enough, the lad turned out to live in the same block as Peg, and Irene had smiled at him in the lift a couple of weeks later. He seemed to have other things on his mind, though, and she had not tried to speak to him.

As it turned out, Peg was only too happy to start drinking sherry at midday. Irene sliced a plate of fig rolls in half, lengthways, so that Peg could dunk them in her glass. She had previously suggested serving the sherry in a tumbler, into which each biscuit would fit comfortably, but Peg insisted on using her best crystal, because there were standards to be maintained. So the fig rolls had to be served in slender, dippable fingers, like crudités.

'You're going to see this James quite soon, then?' Peg asked, when they were both settled.

'I hope so. He was always a very nice boy. He says he's coming home in the New Year.'

'But he really hurt you by going off like that and not keeping in touch?'

'Well, he did rather. But that's all water under the bridge now.'

'I suppose he's only human. I always found life so much easier if you remember that everyone is. Like my Bert. He was so human sometimes, I could have swung for him, but that's another story.'

She laughed with the nicotine-stained bark that had not diminished, even as her body had begun to turn in on itself, and long after she had given up smoking.

'I expect you still miss him terribly, don't you?' Peg continued.

'Who, James?'

'No, I mean your Ollie. How many years is it now?'

'Coming up seven,' said Irene. Yes, she still missed him, just as she imagined she would always miss her heart if someone gouged it out of her chest.

'Poor soul,' said Peg. 'They can cure it now, can't they?'

'Not quite cure, but there are good treatments,

certainly, that seem to work. I'm delighted about that, obviously, but...'

'But it's not fair, is it, that your Ollie didn't hold out long enough to get the benefit?'

Irene shrugged.

'Life can sometimes seem very cruel,' she sighed. 'But what can we do?'

'Have you got that photograph of him?' said Peg.

'Have I!' she laughed.

Usually it took her forever to find anything in the old tapestry bag she carried everywhere. But her photo of Ollie, in an easy-access zip pocket just inside the neck, was the one thing she could instantly locate. She had shown it to Peg before, but was always delighted to get it out again.

Peg clutched it in an arthritic claw and peered through her thick spectacles.

'Oh Irene, I know I've said it before, but he was lovely, wasn't he?'

It was true – everyone found Ollie lovely. That had been his undoing.

'And he looks so gentle.'

Again, Irene shrugged assent. Even as a small boy, he would cup a daddy long-legs in his bare hands to take it outside, because he would never hurt a living thing.

'Such a beautiful colour, too. You know, I never asked. What was his father? Jamaican?'

'Afghan,' chuckled Irene.

'Oh my word! How did you manage that?'

'It was the Sixties. I did a lot of travelling.'

'You must have. Me and my Bert never got beyond

Tenerife, and we didn't like that much. We were happier in Frinton.'

'I was keen to see the world,' said Irene.

'And he didn't want to be involved with Ollie, this Afghan chappy?'

'I never told him. I didn't know him very well, and I didn't find out I was pregnant until I was back in England, so I didn't see the point in bothering him, even if I had the means to contact him, and I don't think I had an address. They didn't really do addresses, where he lived. Anyway, that seemed the right thing to do in those days, before men made such a clamour about paternity. This was decades before I found the Church, of course.'

'Jesus taught us not to judge, and I don't judge you, my dear, any more than I judge your poor Ollie. You know that. I'm just so deeply sorry that you lost him.'

She passed the picture back and squeezed Irene's hand.

'I know you are, Peg. Thank you,' said Irene, as she tucked the precious photo back in its zip pocket.

Later, as she got in the lift, she could feel the effect of two glasses of sweet sherry with only a couple of fig rolls for ballast. She really ought to have had a bite of something before she arrived – or asked Peg if she could make them both a sandwich.

She pressed the button for the ground floor, but instead of going down when the doors closed, the lift continued upwards. It stopped on the tenth floor, where a young man with hair that looked like he had just got out of bed, which was the fashion these days, and slightly jug ears that glowed pink in the doorway, with the sun behind them, got in with her. He turned away from Irene, with his face to the doors, precluding any kind of contact. He was breathing heavily, and he was clearly in a hurry to get to the bottom, because he jabbed his finger impatiently at the ground floor button when they stopped for no reason, with no one waiting, at the fifth and fourth.

'Kids, I expect,' said Irene, but all she got back was the barest of grunts. Charming, she thought, after she had made a detour to pick him up. Then she reminded herself that he was not to know that.

At the bottom, he sprang out ahead of her. He made a vague attempt not to drop the outside door on her, flinging it deliberately wide so that she would have longer to catch it. In a modern world that seemed in a permanent, bad-tempered hurry, that was a courtesy for which she told herself to be thankful.

As she stepped through the door and out into the street, it was raining much harder than it had been earlier. Under the shelter of the tower's porch, she delved in her bag for the floppy sou'wester hat that she kept in there for just such an occasion. As she did so, she was suddenly aware of a very peculiar sensation. A warm shiver went right through her, which was by no means unpleasant, but it was disconcerting. She was long past hot flushes.

Drinking on an empty stomach at lunchtime really was a terrible idea, she told herself, as she put her head down against the rain and made for the bus stop. Next week she really ought to leave the sherry to Peg, and stick to tea.

18

STEFANO HAD BEEN given his old room, still with the same navy-blue bedding. The walls, once the same shade as the sheets, had been reclaimed by the neutral cream of the rest of the house. He could not blame his parents: he had hated the blue himself, but after making a great fuss to get it, he had never been able to admit his mistake. There was still the same old formica wardrobe, full of what looked like his father's clothes. His own abandoned belongings had been duct-taped into boxes at the back of the cupboard, with 'Steven's stuff' markered in his mother's hand.

'I'll let you sleep in as long as you like. You must be tired after your journey,' she had said after Katie went home. She was polite, as with a stranger visiting for the first time. Had he eaten on the train? Was the carriage full? He could see she was dreading the real questions as much as he was.

He lay in his single bed, looking up at the dark shape of his old flying-saucer light-shade. He heard the lights click off in the hall and listened to his mother's slow tread on the stairs. The top step creaked; he had forgotten that. And the street-lamp still cast the same glow through the curtains, dissolving the intervening years. If the dreaming boy who had last lain here could know what lay ahead, what would he have done differently? It occurred to him that the act of looking back on Steven Carter lying in the same bed all those years before was not so different to looking down on his own pale shape on the black volcanic sand. He wondered if he could pass back into his old self as easily as he had returned to the body on the beach.

In the next few days he began to understand how much hurt he had caused. At first, in London, he had assumed they would force him to go back home if they knew where he was. After a few years, when he was old enough to do what he liked, he convinced himself that they did not care very much where he was, and he put them almost completely out of his mind. His annual birthday card to Katie was a gesture that allowed him to tell himself he was not totally unfeeling. Every year, as he put it in the post, he had imagined the joy it would bring, and the thought made him happy.

It was a pathetic gesture, he could see now, but at the time, something about London itself seemed to make it all right: coddled in the smoggy anonymity of a city that stretched as far as the eye could see, and was so obviously a different country from the world outside, it was possible to forget that anywhere else existed. His attitude was bolstered by the behaviour of virtually everyone he ever met: all his friends, every customer at the Edward, all his casual hook-ups, and Adam, were refugees from an unfriendly, unsympathetic world outside the M25 where none of them had ever belonged, and to which they returned as little as possible. Adam went no more than a couple of times a year. Stefano was simply going two times a year less than that.

His mother's anguished response to his return had been a shock, opening his eyes to the hurt he had caused. When he started to see, it was dizzying. One night many years ago – it could not have been long after he arrived in London – he had dreamed that he was Adolf Hitler in his bunker in the last days of Berlin, suddenly realising that the destruction of Europe was his fault, and understanding that there was nothing he could do to make it better, and he would have to shoot himself. This dream had come back a few times over the years, and now he remembered the sensation, the sudden realisation of great guilt. Perhaps his subconscious had been troubled about his family all along.

He resolved to be a better son and to do what he could to atone. He imagined he might finally be able to bond with his mother, building a solid, adult relationship, using his contrition as the foundation stone. That was his intention, and it was sincere. Achieving it proved harder. With the idealised mother of his high-minded ambitions, he would be relaxed and uninhibited, talking to her as an equal, as she would to him. His actual mother was as uptight and reserved, to Stefano's eyes, as she had been when he was sixteen. Telling her about Adam was the obvious first step towards letting her into his life, but he found he could not bring himself to do that. Before he knew it, he had reverted to the manner of the sulky, reticent teenager he had been when he last lived here. It was the only way he knew how to be when he was under this roof. He wished he could be brighter and more open with her, but the pull of the old pattern of their relationship was too strong.

In the next few days the old battle-lines became clear. He discovered he was unwilling to talk about any of his life in London: not mentioning it might help erase its sinful traces. He therefore planned to hold out under questioning. He had not bargained for his mother's equal determination to ask nothing. As the days went on, he saw this as an affront. He wondered if he should retaliate by telling her everything.

In the end she blinked first.

'Are you going to tell me where you've been all this time, or do I have to guess?'

He had been there three days and was sitting at the kitchen table, flicking idly through the bits of old Christmas card she cut up for shopping lists, while she stood at the stove.

'London.'

She poured corn oil into a frying pan and set a slab of liver to sizzle.

He counted in his head.

'Is that it? London?' she said finally. Twenty-eight.

'I haven't been anywhere else, apart from a few holidays.'

She turned on him and pointed her spatula, shiny with oil.

'Don't get clever with me, young man. London's a big place, and fifteen years is a long time.'

'A place called Hackney. I don't suppose you've heard

of it, so what difference does it make which part of London I was in?'

A distant, nagging voice told him not to be so rude, but the powerful force of deeply ingrained habit drove him on.

'I have heard of it. Hackney carriages, everyone's heard of them. You think you're mighty big because you live in London. But your mother's not so stupid as you presume.'

She turned back to peel an onion.

He had straightened a paper clip and was trying to wrap it round a pencil.

'You don't know where it is though.'

He looked up cautiously and saw the telltale stiffening. But she let the jibe go.

'And do you have your own flat in Hackney?' she said instead, pronouncing the name as if it needed rubber gloves.

'Yes. A council flat.'

'Ah.'

'What does that mean?'

'You don't have a job, then.'

'How do you work that out? People who live in council flats are allowed to have jobs.'

'Do you then?'

'Do I what?'

'Have a job?'

'Yes.'

She tapped her foot, and he told himself to stop baiting her. But it was so hard. He did not know how else to talk to her.

'In a bar,' he pushed himself.

'A barman?' she repeated mockingly, pretending she was impressed.

'Actually I was the manager.'

'A bar manager! Bully for you.'

He glared at the back of her head. If he had returned a millionaire City trader, sweeping her out of Woodville Close and around the world, she would have had to be grateful. That would have been more than she could stand.

'It can't have paid much,' she added, removing the liver from the pan and pouring more oil for the onions.

'What makes you say that?'

She spooned gravy granules into a jug and added water from the kettle. He waited, but this time he only got to eleven.

'Since we didn't hear a peep out of you for fifteen years, not a card at Christmas, nothing to tell us you were alive, you must have been hard up. Couldn't afford the stamp.'

She turned to him and folded her arms.

'You could at least have the guts to look at me and face up to the damage you've done.'

He met her eyes and was shocked to see how steely they were.

'Your sister and I buried your father on our own. We stood in that church and then we stood by that grave, just the two of us. Everyone asked if there was any word from you. What was I supposed to tell them? We didn't know whether you were alive or dead. Very comforting, don't you think, on the day you bury your husband?'

He stared at her, determined not to look away, but her fury had shamed him. For a second he saw the world through her eyes. He swallowed.

'I'm sorry.'

'Finally.'

She wiped her eye with the back of her hand, and her voice was softer.

He held her gaze and cautiously reached out his hand for hers.

'Onions are burning.'

She nodded, letting go his hand and turning to rescue her pan.

He still could not believe the extraordinary stroke of luck that had placed him on the Old Street roundabout just as the little sister he had not seen for fifteen years was emerging from the Tube. It surely could not be entirely an accident.

At first, he had not intended to return to the church with the temple columns, the frightening preacher and the helper with the tuna breath. Everyone there was too weird, and he could not imagine ever wanting to become one of them, talking about salvation and perversion. Having hurried away as fast as he could, he had hoped to put the whole experience behind him and find some other way of alleviating his concerns.

It was difficult, though. Everywhere he looked were reminders of the infernal jeopardy he was facing: not just those horrific Bosch images that he could not get out of his head and which continued to invade his dreams, but also the preacher outside the town hall, who seemed to single him out. And when Adam wanted to hug in public for a photograph on the Greenwich meridian... A few seconds earlier, they had been looking at a giant telescope pointing through the ceiling of the Observatory and up towards the heavens, as the notice specifically said. Stefano kept thinking that if he looked through it, he would see God's eye looking back down at him from the other end. Then Adam made an unwarranted dig about heaven not existing, knowing how provocative that would be, yet barely two minutes later he wanted to be tactile in public. In that moment, all Stefano could think of was God looking down that giant telescope at the pair of them, and judging him. He knew he had hurt Adam by pulling away from him, especially in front of that American woman who had insisted on taking the picture; but when the fate of his immortal soul was at stake, he reckoned he was justified.

He was so rattled by the experience that he resolved to return to the next Wednesday service at the church, a couple of days later. That was where he was going when he saw a vision from his past, all grown up in business clothes, with her blond hair in a ponytail and a dusting of freckles on her forehead. It was weird how she could look so good but also frighteningly like their mother. And what were the chances that the two of them should be in that precise same spot, when a couple of minutes later they would have missed each other entirely? It was surely a sign from on high, confirmation that he was on the right path. That was why, when she suggested he come back home with her, he accepted straight away. If he was being offered the chance to put things right, square his celestial accounts and avoid an eternity of diabolical punishment, there was no way he was going to turn it down.

Katie had told him on the train about their father's series of heart attacks, the third of which had proved fatal. They had put adverts in newspapers and made an appeal on the radio when it happened, hoping that someone who knew him would see or hear. They were not to realise that nobody knew Steven Carter. He was truly sorry for putting them through all that.

Mourning his father was another matter.

After he had been back at Woodville Close for a week, his mother took him to the big municipal cemetery, and Stefano read the inscription where he himself got a mention (or at least Steven did), but it was hard to feel anything. Alan John Carter, 1941–1996, beloved husband of Marion, might have been the father of Katie and Steven, but he did not feel like any relation to Stefano. Katie said she had once found their father sobbing with grief over his photograph, years after he ran away, which he found astonishing. Could the mean-spirited man whose face had contorted with disgust at talk of inside legs or Earl Grey tea, and who made vile jokes about Aids, really have cared about him? Staring down at the stone, he made himself think of the Ten Commandments and tried to please God by honouring his father. When nothing came, he tried picturing the heart attack, with Alan clutching his chest over breakfast in bed on Father's Day (a detail that Katie had left out, but which his mother had not spared him). This time he was rewarded with a lump in his throat. At least God would know he was making an effort.

He had wanted to buy the flowers, but his mother rejected his choice – 'Don't be soft, your dad could never abide chrysanths' – and dismissed his attempt to pay, embarrassing him in front of the girl in the shop. Now she commanded him to hold open a plastic bag for the dead blooms they were replacing, which she pulled from the brass vase and held out for him to take without turning round. He did his best to suppress his irritation, telling himself he did not deserve much more. As she continued to bark her orders, however, pulling weeds from around the stone and wanting to know where he was with that bag, he wondered what it would be like if he really were grieving. He surely deserved some consideration.

'Bring the scissors. Where have you got to?'

No wonder he could not feel anything. He looked down at the small grey head and the wilful back bent over its labours, and a wave of dislike passed through him. He winced as he realised that would put him further out of favour with God, and he blamed her all the more.

It was a relief to get back to the claustrophobia of the Close.

She had always liked to ambush him over breakfast when he was still half-asleep and she had been up for hours. One morning, she asked: 'How long are you intending to honour us with your presence? Only I've got meals to plan, and I never keep much in stock now it's just me. I'm not complaining, but I will need to know.'

'I wasn't planning on going back. I thought you realised.'

She sat down heavily.

'Hey? But...your flat? And your job... Won't they be expecting you?'

'Not really. None of that matters very much.'

He carried on smearing his toast with jam.

She started to reply, but her head slumped and she brought her hand to her face.

Stefano put his knife down.

'Don't you want me to stay?'

When he had agreed to come back to the North West with Katie, he had not envisaged staying for good. In his distressed state, he was thinking in the moment, and anything beyond next week was too hard to think about. The longer he was away from London, however, the harder it became to see himself ever returning there. So the idea of staying for good had gradually taken shape in his own mind, as the most natural thing in the world, and he had assumed he would be welcome: it simply had not occurred to him that he might not be. Now he saw that he could have handled this better: he should have broached the question sooner, asking his mother if she minded. It was her house, after all, and at the moment he was living off her. Why was it such a struggle? With a stranger or a friend it would be easy to do the right thing, to know his place and show the required degree of politeness, gratitude and sensitivity. For some reason, though, it was so much harder with family. More immediately, there was the problem of what he would do if his mother did not want him at Woodville Close. The idea of going back to his old life now filled him with such terror, it felt like an absolute impossibility. He raced through his other options. Katie had a spare room where he could probably stay for a week or two, but any longer was bound to be tricky. They had been getting on well, and he had found it much easier to open up to her about his life with Adam, which she had agreed to keep secret from their mother. Nevertheless, she lived with her boyfriend and they were meant to be getting married in the spring, so he would only be in the way. And that was where his options seemed to run out.

His mother continued to sob angrily.

'Why are you crying? I don't know what I've done wrong now.'

She snapped her head up.

'Yes, you do. Whatever you've done, you know all about it. We're the ones who are in the dark, as usual. You're in some kind of mess that means you've had to run away. Oh, I wish your father was here.'

She buried her face again and he got up and went to her, putting an awkward hand on her shoulder and moving it from side to side in a way that he hoped was soothing.

'It's not like that. Honestly, I'm not in trouble.'

She looked up.

'Not...drugs? You hear such stories.'

'Not drugs. Nobody's after me, and I'm not in any trouble. Not the way you mean.'

'I knew it! What have you done?'

'Nothing.'

She eyed him suspiciously.

'What about your flat, all your stuff?'

He shrugged. He would need to sort something out with Adam eventually, either to sub-let the place to him or to transfer the name on the tenancy. For the moment, there was no need to tell his mother any of that.

'And it's not the police?' she continued. 'If you've done anything wrong, you must tell me.'

'I haven't done anything wrong.'

Once more he thought, 'Not in the way you mean anyway,' but this time he kept it in his head.

Later, when he was helping with her morning dusting, as he had done as a child, she said: 'It must be a girl. That's the only explanation. I've got to ask – were there children involved? Are you married, Steven?'

Her eyes seemed larger than ever behind her glasses.

Once he would have laughed at the absurdity of it, but now her wideness from the mark merely emphasised his plight. To save himself from crying, he took refuge in defiance.

'My name is Stefano. I changed it by deed poll.'

'Not in this house, it isn't. Never mind any deed poll, under this roof you'll answer to the name your father and I gave you. And don't reply to my question if it pains you so much. But just you ask yourself, my lad: how many mothers have to beg their own sons to tell them if they're married? Just you ask yourself that.'

She slammed the door, leaving him to her trinkets. He heard her wrenching the Hoover from its home under the stairs, followed by the scream of the motor.

He followed her, shouting above the machine: 'Is that all you care about, whether you've got grandchildren? You're not bothered about me at all.'

It was an arms race of victimhood. At least he was good at this.

'Well the answer's no,' he added, as she turned the motor off.

'I suppose it's a relief really,' she said, digesting it.

'Why's that?'

'I couldn't bear to think your father had gone to his rest with flesh and blood he had never seen.'

'Yes, that must be a great relief.'

'So you've not been married or anything?'

'No. You can also comfort yourself that my father didn't miss out on a nice wedding.'

He did not see the slap coming. It was surprisingly painful. He turned his back with all the dignity he could muster and went to his room.

19

NOTHING IN THE creator's aeons of existence had prepared him for the shock of life as a terrestrial biped. How did these creatures cope? For billions of years he had taken for granted his cosmic vantage point with its view of anything he wanted. Now he found himself trapped in a single hominid shell, where his roaming attention could go nowhere without the body he was confined within. At a stroke, his picture of the universe had shrunk to the microscopic portion visible through this mystery hominid's eyes. Even that was obstructed by the brim of some head-cover that had been pulled down low to shield his host's face from falling liquid.

This liquid was forming broad pools on the flat grey walkway, which the Mystery Hominid was taking measures to avoid. As his host looked down, God noticed two large bulges under his host's garments, at chest level. At least he now knew one thing about the body he had landed in: the Mystery Hominid was a female of the species. She sidestepped one of the broad pools and jumped across another, but the slab on which she landed was loose and it dipped under her weight, splashing liquid onto her feet. As it did so, a tall red vehicle bearing rows of seated hominids passed alongside, through another pool of liquid, which now rose in a wave, drenching his hostess' lower garment.

'Oh for crying out loud,' she said.

Here was another discovery: God could understand her thoughts and words. He was not sure who was meant to cry out and why, but he had a clear comprehension of all the various words and phrases swirling around his hostess' head. He knew that the falling liquid was called rain, that the tall red craft were buses, and that the pools of rain were puddles. Other names remained a mystery he would no doubt find out what sherry, Peg and Ollie were in due course – but it was good to know that he would be able to follow hominid language.

The other revelation was physical sensation.

When the rain fell from the sky, he felt it, tingling and unwelcome, on his hostess' face. When the puddle soaked her trousers, as he now discovered her lower garments were called, he felt them clammy against her limbs, clinging uncomfortably to them as she walked. And he became aware of a dull, nagging sensation in her feet, not particularly noticeable at first, but harder to ignore once he had identified it, which was called an ache. He had no idea hominids suffered so much as they went about their regular activities. It had certainly not occurred to him that coming to Earth meant he would suffer these torments too.

His hostess kept thinking how much she wanted to get home. This was a bad sign, considering she was getting further away from the grey tower all the time: it implied that her home was not in the place where God most needed to be. Meanwhile, their journey was becoming more trying. It had been bad enough when they were proceeding on foot, but now she squeezed with various other hominids into a small road-side shelter where they watched several buses go past until the one she wanted appeared. She showed some kind of document, which seemed to be a requirement for entry, to the hominid at the controls – another female – and found a seat deep in the interior, pushing past a lot of other passengers to do so. Collapsing onto the seat provided a welcome respite from the ache, but this was tempered by God's ever-growing dismay at how rapidly they were now moving away from the place where his tube was trapped. Not rapid in cosmic terms, of course, considering how far he himself had travelled from the centre of the universe that very day, and not even rapid relative to the other hominid craft on the road, most of which easily outpaced them. But it was faster than walking, and God had no idea how he was going to find his way back to the tower to fulfil his mission.

The bus stopped frequently for hominids to get on and off, but his hostess remained where she was. Now she was thinking about someone called James, and something called the spare room. It was all meaningless to God, and he let her get on with it. Eventually she reached forward to press a signal-button which, the creator had worked out from observing other passengers, required the driver to stop. She squeezed back through the little crowd of hominids clustered around the doorway and finally managed to get down from the bus. At least the rain had stopped.

He wanted to look around at everything, because it was such a novelty to view a planet from this level, but it was difficult because he was seeing it through her eyes and her head was fixed in the direction they were going. As best he could tell, there were no towers in this new landscape. Instead, they were in a region of lower-lying dwellings laid out in long rows. Each one had a window bulging out at ground level, and another one directly above it. Each dwelling also had a coloured door and a patch of vegetation in front, in various states of cultivation. They walked past a long series of these dwellings, then turned into another, similar street, and then another one. It was bewildering, and he was not sure he would ever find his way if he had to do this on his own. Finally they stood in front of a blue door behind a particularly unkempt section of vegetation.

His hostess looked down into the bag she had been carrying and started searching through it. It contained all manner of baffling artefacts, but none of them seemed to be the one she wanted.

'Don't say I've come without...' she muttered audibly, accompanying it with a woeful mental picture of herself sitting outside the entrance, unable to gain access to the dwelling. This in turn made the creator panic: he had no wish to stay out here, when the rain could resume at any moment. Now she was holding the bag against her ear and giving it a shake. A faint rattle inside seemed to give her encouragement and, after another fumble, he felt a flood of exultation surge through her as she pulled out a small fluffy effigy, from which trailed a variety of jagged metallic objects. One of these she now directed at a small hole in the door. Despite the irregular shape of this object, it fitted snugly. When she twisted it, the door swung open.

'Hello Emmie,' she called, as she stepped inside.

They were in a long, thin chamber. Directly ahead, a set of steps seemed to give access to the upper part of the dwelling, while on one wall hung an array of images, mainly of hominid faces.

From the corner of his hostess' eye, God noticed that they were not alone in the chamber: there was another hominid alongside them. His hostess now turned towards this figure, who was wearing a bright yellow head-cover and also turned to greet her. This must be Emmie. But neither creature acknowledged the other. Instead, he felt his hostess raise her hands above her head and remove something. As she did so, the other hominid – who was also female – removed her yellow head-cover and patted her grey hair. Still not speaking to the other party, his hostess leaned towards Emmie, and Emmie did exactly the same, and the creator braced for the impact of their two heads smacking together. The bump did not come, however, as both females fiddled to tuck their hair behind their ears.

As he understood, God wanted to laugh out loud at his own mistake. What an extraordinary invention this image-reflecting device was! And how come he did not have one of his own?

The diversion was only temporary, however, as he

remembered the grim reality of his situation. This dwelling was clearly his hostess' home, and it was a dauntingly long distance from the tower, where he needed to be if he was to free his tube. He really had made a terrible blunder. The question was, what should he do about it? Staying put would mean suffering all the discomforts of hominid existence, without any obvious means of fulfilling the mission he had come to achieve. The most rational course of action would be to get himself out of his hostess' body as soon as possible and back to where he had started, so that he could make a second, more accurate stab at landing himself in the right dwelling. It was tiresome to have to go through the whole process all over again, but it was hard to see any viable alternative.

Having removed her outer garment, his hostess opened a door into a room at the back of the dwelling.

'Hello Emmie,' she said again, and a small black-and-white quadruped jumped down from a narrow platform beside a window and rubbed itself against her leg, purring gently. 'Are you hungry, my darling?'

She opened the door of a storage unit from which God felt an immediate blast of cold air, and took out a small container. From it, she scraped some gelatinous stuff into a shallow dish and placed it on the floor. The creature ate greedily from it.

Now his hostess opened the storage unit again, bringing out various items which she set down on a flat surface. She began slicing and spreading to assemble something which the creator gathered was called a sandwich. When it was done to her satisfaction, she put it on a flat dish and cut it in half crossways. At the same time, she took down a container called a mug, dropped into it a small pouch full of some aromatic substance, and pressed a button on another receptacle, which promptly lit up at the base and began to make a low, roaring noise, like a very distant supernova, which gradually increased in intensity until steam gushed from the top of the receptacle. There was a click and the light on the base went out, leaving a cloud of vapour. His hostess picked up the receptacle and poured clear, steaming liquid from it onto the aromatic pouch, then squeezed the pouch after a few moments, so that the clear liquid turned brown. She added a drop of Emmie's liquid, then picked up the mug and flat dish, and carried them both into a room at the front of the dwelling, where she sank into a deep, soft seat with rests for her arms and head. There was another soft rest for her feet, and God felt suddenly soothed by these comforts, pleasantly surprised to discover that hominid physical sensations could be good as well as bad. Perhaps he would defer his return for an Earth-hour or two.

She picked up the sandwich and bit off a piece, telling herself how hungry she was. Hunger was a sensation the creator had never known, but now he discovered that satisfying it was very enjoyable. It was also fascinating how the food itself produced sensations of its own, and he fancied he could identify the different elements she had put in there: the part she called the bread; the element called cheese; a cooler, wetter part called tomato; and a zingy, exciting chunk of what he guessed must be the pickle. Between each bite, she would lift the mug of hot, aromatic liquid, which was called 'a nice cup of tea', and suck a small amount of it into her mouth. It became cooler quite quickly, so that she could take larger mouthfuls, and it was agreeably refreshing after the drier, solid food. How strange to think that hominids had been doing all this for hundreds of thousands of their years, and it had never occurred to God that it might be enjoyable.

She finished the sandwich and they continued to sit there – the creator was beginning to think of the two of them as a kind of item – in comfortable silence, only disturbed by the quadruped Emmie jumping onto his hostess' lower limbs. She ran her digits through the creature's fur, and Emmie looked back up at her through slitted eyes. What could the animal see, God wondered. Did it detect anything different about its mistress? It would not matter if it could. He was the master of the universe, and he could take up residence wherever he pleased without having to be furtive about it. All the same, he rather liked the idea of going incognito, and was genuinely intrigued to know whether his presence was detectable to any of these Earth creatures. In this case, it seemed not. The animal simply settled into its position and closed its eyes in an unconcerned fashion.

God was still idly contemplating this creature when, without warning, his hostess' eyes began to close too. Her head lolled back against the top part of their seat, and waves of black oblivion threatened to engulf him. Alarmed, he tried to fight back, but the waves were too strong. A moment or two later, he realised with a start that his thoughts had been on some crazy detour. He was on the point of panicking when it occurred to him that this slipping away of consciousness was not unpleasant. His hostess seemed to be submitting to it willingly, and perhaps he should just follow her example. Noting blearily that this planet really was one surprise after another, he gave himself up to a delicious, gloopy blankness.

He had no idea how long it lasted. Emmie was lying in the same position when consciousness returned, so it could not have been that long. The strange thing was that he felt so refreshed – sated and content in a way he could not remember ever having known.

His hostess twisted one of her arms towards her and consulted a device strapped below the base of her hand.

'Oh Emmie,' she said. 'That sherry has done me in. Remind me: next week when I go back to see Peg, it's strictly tea for me.'

She addressed Emmie as if she could understand, but the animal did not seem to talk back. It merely blinked, signalling either agreement or incomprehension. Either way, this seemed to satisfy her, as she settled back into her chair to rest her eyes once more.

God was now relaxed enough to join in without a qualm. She had just said she was going back to the tower next week. He was not certain how long that was but, from the way she said it, it did not sound as if he would have long to wait. It meant that his mission was not a complete disaster after all. In the meantime, he might as well enjoy a few more of these simple hominid pleasures.

20

AT FIRST ADAM was just upset. Although it had been obvious for weeks that something was very wrong, Stefano's abrupt departure – announced in a note he found when he got home from work – was a devastating blow. He spent a lot of time crying, mired in misery and disbelief, as he contemplated the destruction of his comfortable domesticity, and the disappearance at a stroke of everything he had thought was assured about his future.

He and Stefano had become such a settled item that he had neglected his old friendships, and he now found he had few, if any, natural confidants to fall back on. He looked for solace in anonymous encounters, spending too many late nights in a bar in Dalston where fumbles could be in dark corners behind draped camouflage netting. He was ashamed of the neediness with which he angled to be invited back to other people's places, for the companionship more than anything else, and to avoid going home. None of it made him happy, just tired and occasionally very late for work the next day.

He was too embarrassed to contact any of their mutual friends – more accurately, those of Stefano's friends whom he also regarded as his own by default. He was particularly nervous of approaching Rook, who he feared might instinctively take Stefano's side: he was feeling too fragile to lay himself open to critical dissection. So it was a surprise to hear a familiar Aussie voice crackling though the intercom one evening.

'Hey, darl, you're finally there. Can I come up?'

Adam buzzed him in.

'So where's Stef? What's been happening with him?' Rook wanted to know, before he had even sat down. It must be serious if he was using male pronouns. 'I've been calling his phone, but it always goes straight to voicemail and he's ignored all my messages. What the hell's been going on?'

'Your guess is as good as mine,' said Adam gloomily. 'To be honest, I thought you might be more able to tell me. I think he tuned me out of his life a while ago now. I didn't realise he had done it to you too.'

'You and me both, darl. And Kevin too. By the way, she said she's been calling here, as well as the mobile, and can't get hold of anyone. She's hopping mad about it.'

It was true, there had been a string of increasingly testy messages from Stefano's boss on the answerphone. Adam had not had the energy to respond to any of them.

'I couldn't face talking to him,' he said.

'She'll survive, I guess. So anyway, this whole thing with Stef is because of what happened on that beach, his near-death thingo?'

'He seems to have got God,' said Adam. 'And yes, it all started with his accident.'

He contemplated for a moment how much had changed

since that moment, and how none of this nightmare would now be happening if Stefano had been a couple of steps closer to the beach when the wave broke. That thought brought tears to his eyes, which he did his best to blink away as he continued: 'You know I found a Bible under his side of the bed, along with that stupid Hieronymus Bosch book that I bought him?' he said. That discovery, a few days before their visit to Greenwich, had shocked him. He had not realised how far all this stuff had gone. 'He took both of them with him.'

'And where do you reckon he's gone?'

'His note said he was going back home. But the stupid thing is, I don't even know where that is. Can you believe that? He was so secretive about his background, not only have I never met a single member of his family, I haven't even any idea where he grew up. I know he was born in Rome, but he told me he grew up in this country, because his father was English. I just have no idea where.'

'He was born in Rome? And what, you're saying his mum's Italian?'

'Didn't you know? That's how he got his name.'

Rook was looking at him strangely.

'Darl, he got his name from me. His real name's Steven. I called him Stefanie the first day we met, and he hated that, so we compromised on Stefano. It kind of stuck, and he's been Stefano ever since. He changed it by deed poll years ago, so it's on his passport. I thought you knew.'

Adam's eyes brimmed with tears again, but this time of humiliation, not regret. Their entire five years together had already begun to turn into a distant memory. Now the relationship seemed more like an illusion, something that had never really existed at all, because it had been built on a lie.

So Rook's visit left him furious as well as upset, which proved to be a debilitating combination.

An obvious focus for his anger was the manner of Stefano's departure. He had clearly been suffering from some private turmoil, fed by the credulity and the capriciousness which Adam had always found maddening and beguiling in equal measure. But he had done his utmost to understand that turmoil, and to help him through it, and he did not deserve to be treated with such callous indifference. He had been discarded, their time together binned without so much as a backward glance. He had spent so much time and effort attempting to see the problem through Stefano's eyes, to understand how he might be hurting, that he had forgotten to fight his own corner, even in his own mind. Now, as dismay gave way to resentment and outright rage, he saw that he had been treated unpardonably.

His fury was not reserved for Stefano alone, because the gullibility that had destroyed their domestic harmony did not exist in a vacuum. It had been cultivated, watered, fertilised by thousands of years of religious superstition, excusable once, when creation myth was the primitive equivalent of scientific hypothesis, but enduring long past the point of no excuse. It took cynical advantage of those, among whom Stefano now undoubtedly numbered, who did not possess the rigour or the mental wherewithal to know that they were being had. They were welcome to believe what they liked, of course they were; but when those beliefs had consequences, such as frightening Stefano into abandoning his own life and ruining other people's, Adam reserved the right to be angry.

The more he thought about it, the more he saw the malign influence of this superstition. A couple of mornings after Rook's visit, his radio alarm clicked on to the sound of a bishop telling him that marriage was a sacrament between a man and a woman for the purpose of producing children, without the interviewer bothering to ask why, in that case, everyone over child-bearing age was not also banned from walking down the aisle. He ate breakfast listening to a different station, but the world seemed to be conspiring to insult him.

'So we're talking to Chris from Crawley,' the presenter was saying. 'Tell me, Chris. What kind of ladies do you like?'

'Well…'

'I hope you do like ladies, by the way.'

'Definitely.'

'Just checking. You never can be too sure these…'

Adam hit the off switch, smashing the radio into silence.

On the Tube, he sought refuge in a novel, but his eye was drawn to a headline in his neighbour's newspaper about Baroness Winch, the Tory peer who was fighting to keep the clutch of anti-gay laws which had remained on the statute books since Victorian times. 'The doughty peer who wants to keep our children safe', read the banner across the top of the story. There was no respite in the office. Barry, a pony-tailed designer from the seventh floor, stopped to pass the time of day with Adam's editor, George. The latter made a trademark of novelty waistcoats, and happened today to be wearing a bright pink one, which became the focus of Barry's satire.

'Is there something you haven't been telling us, Georgie boy?' he rasped.

George chuckled indulgently.

'Grow a moustache and then we'll really start to worry.'

George chuckled even more.

Adam hunched over his desk. He looked up when Barry had gone, expecting some acknowledgement of the obvious offence. But George was tapping away at his keyboard, still smiling.

His journey home was another occasion for anger. He had taken to counting the discarded cans, plastic bottles, fast food wrappers and newspaper spreads in the respective gutters of Westminster and Hackney, in order to quantify the difference. He had begun it as an interesting pursuit that would pass the time as he walked the same streets day after day, and might produce a social good if he wrote his findings up and sent them to the local paper. The findings, however, made him seethe with discontent, all the more now, when he thought of that flat in some leafy part of Zone Three that he might have bought if he had not moved in with Stefano. Tonight there were nine cans and seven bottles on the little stretch of main road between the bus stop and home, and a soiled nappy outside the door of the flats. He wished he could find the culprit so he could smear it in their face.

In his flat, the downstairs neighbour's music was thumping through the floor, a reminder that he could never shut the world out, however much he wanted to. He tried to watch the news. A cardinal had died, famous chiefly for his denunciations of gay sin, and Tony Blair had sent a message of condolence praising his wisdom and humanity. He switched channel, just in time to see an advert for yoghurt in which consumers were invited to laugh at the plight of a fat straight man being pursued down an aeroplane aisle by an amorous male steward.

With a strangulated shout, he turned the TV off, flung the remote into a corner of the room and fled to the bedroom, where he threw himself onto the bed and pressed the pillow over his head. Silently he screamed into the dark cotton, which smelled of sweat, hair gel and, faintly, of Stefano. It was still only seven o'clock but he yearned to sleep so that the world would go away until the morning. He began to wonder what he had in the bathroom cupboard that might make it go away forever. It was not a real prospect, but the fantasy took him away from his misery and gave him some peace.

He must have dozed off, because he was woken by a loud knocking on the door. He and Stefano had little contact with their neighbours, and usually the only people knocking on the door itself, rather than ringing the downstairs buzzer, were Jehovah's Witnesses or election canvassers who had persuaded someone to let them in and were working the building, floor by floor. They usually went away if no one answered, but now the knock came again, more insistently. No doubt they could see that the living room lights were on.

He dragged himself off the bed and back into the main room. Peering through the spy-hole, he saw what looked to be a middle-aged woman, without any obvious rosette, clipboard or other paraphernalia to identify a hawker of politics or religion.

He opened the door.

'Hello?' he scowled.

'Hello,' the woman said. She smiled, in a peculiar, lopsided way. She had a cross pinned to the lapel of her raincoat, Adam now saw.

He waited, but she did not say anything else.

'What can I do for you?' he said impatiently.

The woman looked uncertain, as if she was not clear why she was there either. Adam wondered if she had some kind of dementia, although she did not look old enough. He did not remember seeing her in the block before, although he did not always pay much attention.

Suddenly the set of her face changed, as if she had made a decision.

'The green-eyed one isn't here, is he?' she said. 'It's just you, isn't it?'

'Sorry?'

'It doesn't matter which one of you, really. I just need to come in.'

She put her foot forward to step into the flat.

'Sorry, but who are you?' said Adam, closing the door far enough to prevent her coming any further.

She looked harmless enough, but she was definitely strange, and he was not in the mood for some weirdo to barge into his flat, even if she did have some mental health condition she could not help.

'I don't really have a name,' she said. 'Well, she does. She's called Irene. But that's not important.'

'Who are you talking about?'

There was no one else there. Was she a schizophrenic? If so, was she dangerous? Maybe that was just a stereotype. Either way, this was far too weird for comfort.

'I'm sorry,' he said. 'I really can't help you.'

He closed the door and leaned against it, breathing heavily, then turned and softly double-locked it. He was still middle-class enough not to want to give offence to weirdos that he was shutting out of the flat.

He sneaked a look back through the spy-hole. She had not moved, and now she knocked again.

Go away, he mouthed desperately.

There was no sound, and he thought perhaps she had gone. He was about to turn and look through the spy-hole again when there was another, louder knock.

'Go away or I'll call the police,' he shouted.

This time, to his surprise, she did turn away. Having watched her move in the direction of the lift, he went around the flat switching all the lights off, and shut himself in the bedroom. He contemplated calling Rook to help try and calm himself down, but after a while his breathing returned to normal and he felt the sense of crisis pass. At least he had dealt with it unaided.

He sat for a long time in the dark, wondering who the hell she was. And why had she called Stefano 'the green-eyed one'?

21

ALTHOUGH HE HAD recovered from the immediate shock of finding himself in a hominid body, God still could not get over how complicated life on Earth was.

His hostess' dwelling was controlled by all kinds of knobs and buttons: switches on the walls to light up rooms; dials to turn to prepare food; a button-filled wand to change the pictures on the tee-vee. It was all so bewildering, and he was full of new-found admiration for these creatures, for managing to navigate their way through it all.

The tee-vee itself was a remarkable contraption. It brought a never-ending succession of hominids into the dwelling. Some of them talked directly at his hostess and the creator, telling them about the important events of the day. Others showed them objects, activities or locations elsewhere on the planet which were presumably designed to divert or inform them. Others still ignored them altogether, talking to each other – and sometimes running after one another, fighting or coupling – with no apparent inkling that anyone else might be watching. God wondered how these encounters were captured. It no doubt involved even more of the clever gadgetry that these hominids seemed so fond of.

His hostess liked programmes, as the creator learned to call them, in which a group of people had a short amount of time to dig holes in the ground, searching for obscure evidence of previous generations of hominids. It occurred to God that he must have witnessed some of these long-gone creatures, or he could have done, if he had been looking in the right direction at the time. It was strange how these present-day hominids were so fascinated by them, while he himself had not been fussed one way or the other. His hostess also liked programmes where teams of hominids took a room in a dwelling and made it look completely different in a small space of time. This process was called a makeover, and it was often carried out in a way that even God, as a newcomer to the planet with very little feeling for terrestrial aesthetics, could see was unsuccessful. These pursuits were entertaining enough, and certainly a good deal easier for the creator to understand than the other kind of programmes, the ones where random hominids harangued each other and threatened to murder each other in their own dwellings, without anyone addressing their observers directly or explaining what was going on.

His hostess did not like these programmes much either.

'Why must they always shout, Emmie?' she asked the quadruped. 'Can't anyone ever be happy in Albert Square, even for five minutes?'

The creator noticed that she still carried on watching.

The entertainments he liked best involved a game called football, where two bands of hominids competed to propel a small spherical object into a confined space called a goal, using only their feet – or maybe sometimes their bodies or their heads, but never their hands. This game could induce real emotional turmoil, especially if you decided you wanted one particular side to win. God noticed that he could get more out of it if he watched the way the hominids organised themselves to co-ordinate their group effort, rather than just focusing on whoever was kicking the ball. He decided he liked football a lot. Unfortunately, his hostess did not. The only reason the creator discovered the game in the first place was because someone happened to call her on the long-distance communications device called the telephone while the football was on, giving him the chance to watch it uninterrupted. Otherwise, she changed the programme at the first sign of it. It was very frustrating.

After watching the tee-vee for a while, it was time to go somewhere called bed, which was on the upper level of the dwelling. First they went into a room called the bathroom, where his hostess carried out all manner of strange procedures on her own person: rubbing in potions and poking around in her mouth with a variety of implements. When she was finished with all that, she went into a room at the front of the house where a low, cushioned platform, large enough for at least two hominids to lie down, lay decked in soft, coloured fineries, so inviting that the creator wanted to sink into them as soon as his hostess peeled back the top covering, creating an even more inviting soft pocket to slip into.

Before she did that, however, there were more rituals to be completed. She removed all the garments she had

218

been wearing, placed them in a pile on a chair, and then put on a different set, which she pulled from under some of the padded finery on the bed (as he now identified the platform). Even then, she was still not ready. Having extinguished all the lights in the room except the one nearest the bed, she now dropped to her knees and turned her face upwards, towards the top surface of the room, in the way that he had also seen the Special Hominid do while the creator was watching through his seeing-tube.

'Dear God,' she said. 'I am thankful for all I have.'

The first time he heard it, this took him completely by surprise. What was she saying? Did she know he was there?

'My body aches, but I know that's just part of getting old. I am blessed to have my health, and I am thankful for all that I have. Even when I struggle – and you know I do struggle from time to time, God, because I tell you about it – I am blessed to have faith.'

Mention it? When? What was she talking about?

'May I know the power of your love and the wisdom of your word, and thank you for making me aware of the love that surrounds me. Please watch over Ollie, wherever he is, and let him know that I think of him every hour of every day. And thank you for bringing James back to me, as well as for opening my heart to the possibility of forgiveness. Amen.'

With that, she got up off her knees, climbed into bed and turned the light out, leaving God to try and work out what the hell had just happened.

His ability to do so, however, was severely restricted.

His hostess was evidently in need of sleep, and now it began rapidly to descend on her, whether the creator liked it or not. There was nothing he could do but succumb. He would have to leave his puzzle until the Earth turned back towards the sun, or 'tomorrow', as the hominids would put it.

Aside from this ongoing conundrum, he continued to discover the plusses and minuses of terrestrial existence. On the debit side was an unpleasant business called going to work. The experience began with an alarming thing called the Tube. When his hostess first thought the word, it made him think of his own stricken seeing-tube. He was not prepared for a moving-staircase plunge into the depths of the Earth, being bashed and shoved by a herd of other hominids, then being forced into an ever-smaller space in a long, narrow cavern with a black maw at each end, and worst of all squeezing uncomfortably into the serpentine conveyance that emerged from one of those maws in a rush of hot air and a blaze of lights. The discomfort eased when a young male hominid vacated his own seat and offered it to the creator's hostess, but this was unsettling too: God wondered if this benefactor had some special insight that enabled him to detect the divine presence. But the young man evinced none of the nervousness or awe that God might have expected in such circumstances; he just stood gripping a bar suspended from the ceiling, engrossed in something his hostess also liked to read, called the *Guardian*.

Work itself consisted of conducting groups of visitors around parts of the settlement, or 'city', that would interest them. This ought to have been good news: the creator himself was a visitor, and he was not averse to sight-seeing. The problem, as he soon discovered, was that his hostess' idea of interesting was not his. On the first of these days, the tour focused on a small section of the city called, bafflingly, 'the City'. The creator was beginning to realise that it was easier to accept these quirks than to waste time looking for an explanation. The neighbourhood was full of towers like the Special Hominid's. Unlike that one, which was dull and grey, these structures gleamed as they soared upwards. Some had sharp edges, some were rounded, and one of them was shaped rather like the canisters in which God had watched hominid travellers leave their planet; they all jostled for a piece of the sky. He wondered what went on inside them, how the hominids had managed to build them, and what would happen if one of them fell over. But his hostess acted as if they did not exist. Instead she pointed at the flat grey earth, while her little group of followers peered and fired their flashing devices in the direction she indicated. This seemed to be because something else had once stood on the same site, which they all thought was fascinating. Finally they gained entrance to one of the towers. Ushered through a beeping arched portal, they were given shiny insignia which they had to attach to their garments. They then descended a set of stairs leading below ground level. Their destination turned out to be a pile of earth – brown not grey this time – and a few rounded stones, preserved behind a window, to which the group once more pressed their flashing devices. The stones had been put there by some people called the Romans. Again, God must once have seen them going about their business, and he did not quite see why all the fuss.

At the end of every day, just before his hostess got into bed, came the ritual he had previously observed. She would make a kind of speech addressed to God, in which she thanked him for all manner of things he had not been aware of doing, and made various requests, large and small, that he could not see he was in any position to grant. Every time she did it, the creator had far less time than he would have liked to puzzle it over, because she fell asleep almost as soon as she closed her eyes.

Whenever he tried to make sense of it the following day, he pondered his initial assumption, namely that she had somehow worked out he was there. Instinctively, he had assumed that this would be a bad thing. But when he thought about it some more, he could not find any real justification for that reaction: it would only be a bad thing if she were stricken by terror, or if she found some way to obstruct his aim in coming to Earth. There was no sign of the former, and he could not see how she could do the latter.

On further reflection, however, the assumption was not really sustainable. If she really believed he had taken up residence inside her body, would she not be asking why, or making some mention of it in her thoughts? The fact remained that, every time she made these speeches, she looked upwards, at the ceiling of her bedroom, which was also roughly the direction of the creator's usual place at the centre of the heavens. The unavoidable conclusion was that she was addressing God, day in, day out, as a normal part of her routine, and for some reason she thought they already knew each other.

The picture became a good deal weirder a few days later, when she did not have to go to work and spent a little longer than usual in bed. When she did finally get up, she chose her garments with marginally more care than normal, spending a little longer adjusting her hair in the reflecting glass, which God now knew was called a mirror. After eating breakfast, drinking a dose of the potion called coffee which always made God feel more lively, and giving some food to Emmie, she let herself out of the house and started walking up the street rather than down, in a direction the creator had never been before. After ten minutes or so – God was interested to see that he was acquiring a hominid understanding of time – they arrived outside a large building made of red stone blocks. It consisted of a square tower on one side, with no windows at all for most of the way up, but some tall, arched ones right at the top; next to it was another large structure with a steep, peaked roof. This second part of the building presented a red-stone face to the road, in the centre of which was a much bigger arched window.

In his few days on Earth, God had already been in several large buildings with his hostess, but this one took him completely by surprise when they walked in. The other structures he had visited were divided into different levels on the inside, but this one had been built as one, vast chamber, with a vaulted ceiling and a colonnade of pillars on either side, all topped with arches. At the far end was another arched window, which glowed bright with colours now that the light was behind it, and seemed to show images of hominids doing various things. Below was a low table with some kind of golden ornament on it; from this distance it looked like two wands, one pointing straight up, the other attached to it crosswise. In the intervening space, rows of hominids sat in hard little chairs, looking smaller than ever in this vast interior. The creator's hostess accepted a plain-covered book from an elderly female just inside the entrance, and then joined a loose procession of other hominids filing down the centre of the space looking for somewhere to sit. His hostess found a place, somewhere in the middle, having smiled at and greeted several hominids around her.

No sooner had she sat down than she sank to her knees. She did not speak, but the creator received her thought as clearly as if she had done.

'God in heaven, receive our prayers this day. I pray that we, and all who worship you, will remain faithful and true to your word brought to life in your son, Jesus Christ, who is alive and reigns with you, in the unity of the Holy Spirit, one God, now and for ever. Amen.'

What on earth was she talking about? Had the poor creature lost her mind? What was 'worship' when it was at home? And what was that about a son?

Now she was lifting herself up off her knees and settling back into her seat. From what God could see, nobody else seemed to consider this little display peculiar. They, unlike him, could not hear what she was thinking, of course. Already, though, a nagging suspicion was creeping into his mind. He had a feeling that this building had something to do with the weird stuff she was saying, and that she had come here to be among like-minded hominids. If he could hear all the rest of their thoughts, what were the chances that they were all thinking much the same thing? And if so, what the hell was he meant to make of it?

An hour later, when the gathering broke up, he was a good deal clearer – although clarity was not necessarily an improvement. God was gobsmacked.

His hostess was by no means alone in the relationship she imagined she had with him. The conversations she held with her bedroom ceiling before going to sleep every night, and the thoughts she had just expressed while on her knees in this place, corresponded more or less exactly in tone and content with the sentiments voiced by the small female hominid in floor-length white robe who had officiated over whatever it was that God had just witnessed. That meant there were at least a hundred hominids, by his rough count, who shared his hostess' strange notions. It was conceivable that the only creatures on the whole planet who entertained these beliefs were gathered in this echoing hall, united in a discreet, tight confraternity by their bizarre illusions. But God had an ominous suspicion that the truth was otherwise. He had struggled to follow everything he had just heard – there was so much extraordinary stuff flying at him that it was impossible to process all of it at once – but the presiding hominid, whose name was Reverend Sharon, had said enough about 'worldwide fellowships' and 'millions of followers for generation on generation' to point him towards one, increasingly unavoidable conclusion. Whether he liked it or not, the whole damn species was convinced of this guff.

He remained sketchy about the details, but the headlines seemed to be these: he, God, had such a special regard for the hominids of planet Earth that he spent his whole time devising rules for them, which he had somehow passed down to them via particular hominids who claimed to know his mind; he watched their every move, however many billions of them there were, all at the same time, and he knew not just their deeds, but also their thoughts; and (this was the best bit) when they expired he magicked them off to his realm in the sky where the deserving ones shared eternity with him.

Who did they think was meant to run the place, not to mention all that sitting in judgement and weighing evidence he was meant to have collected throughout their lives? It would all be very well if he had an army of administrative helpers, but he was on his own; always had been. If these hominids only knew. He had his work cut out just trying to get his one lousy seeing-tube back.

It made him peevish for a while, because it was such a presumption, with such little regard for the practicalities at his end. Then he realised that it was absurd to get defensive about a fantasy that clearly had everything to do with their own need to make sense of their fleeting hominid existences. God had only spent six days in his hostess' body, but seeing everything through her eyes – feeling every sensation, witnessing every emotion – had already given him some notion of the inescapable hugeness of existing, from their own point of view, no matter how ineffably tiny they each might be in terrestrial terms, let alone cosmic ones. He had experienced at first hand the ache of separation his hostess felt for her offspring, who had expired prematurely, as well as the consolation she derived from convincing herself that he was in a 'better place', and that she would be reunited with him one day. He had been dimly aware already that she entertained these notions, but only now that he properly focused on them did he grasp the full extent of her expectations. And just as he, God, could not meaningfully contemplate a time when he would no longer exist, he could see that they must experience much the same difficulty. Their solution was entirely wishful thinking, of course; but he could see how they had got there.

And, the more he thought about it, he had to admit that it was nice to get some credit at long last. True, he was being credited for all kinds of things that he had not done, could not possibly have done, and had no intention of ever attempting to do. But they were also recognising his undeniable achievement in creating the universe. It had all happened such a long time ago that he had could barely remember what he had done, and most of the more interesting developments had happened entirely of their own accord once the whole thing was up and running. Nevertheless, recognition of any kind was gratifying, and long overdue. He had never received it from any other part of his cosmos – although, to be fair, it had never occurred to him until now to look closely enough to know whether it was there or not. Perhaps there were other places with similar ideas about him, in other galaxies. He would have to investigate, if ever he managed to free his damned seeing-tube and return to his own proper place.

On that note, he had another couple of days, if he had counted correctly, before they were due to return to the Special Hominid's tower, where they were due to visit an infirm hominid called Peg.

These plans were almost scuppered when his hostess received a call on her telephone telling her that she would have to work at precisely the time she had been planning to pay this visit. After receiving this news, she pressed a series of buttons on the device, and God heard a disembodied hominid voice saying 'hello' as his hostess held the implement to her ear.

'Hello Peg, it's Irene,' she said.

God was getting the hang of the idea that they all had names to identify them, and he had already gathered from previous conversations of this sort that this was hers.

'Hello, my darling,' said the disembodied voice. 'I'm looking forward to seeing you tomorrow. Don't tell me you're calling because you can't come.'

'Oh Peg, I'm sorry. I'm going to have to work. It's a last-minute booking, and I'm afraid I can't afford to turn it down.'

'Well, why don't you come round after?'

'What, in the evening?'

'Whenever you're finished. You complained last time

that it was too early to drink sherry. If you come at five or six o'clock, it won't be, will it?'

Irene made the heh-heh sound that indicated merriment.

'Right you are,' she said. 'I'll see you after work.'

'God bless you, my dear. You know how much I appreciate it.'

'I do, Peg, but the pleasure is also mine. Especially if it's at a more suitable time for sherry.'

Throughout the next two days, the creator found himself anxious and unsettled. A lot depended on this visit to the tower, but it was not obvious what he was meant to do when they got there. He had no idea how he was going to gain access to the Special Hominid's dwelling. Come to think of it, he did not even know how he would find it. There were many levels in the tower, and he knew the one he wanted was nearer the top than the bottom. Beyond that, he was not sure.

These worries preoccupied him so much that he effectively tuned himself out of a repeat tour of Roman remains in the City, and another the following day of a hominid burial ground, where Irene explained to her charges which celebrated characters from terrestrial history lay under which stones. In one sense it was a mercy that God's attention was elsewhere, otherwise he would have been mutinously bored.

Afterwards, they took a couple of buses across what felt like a great swathe of the city to the tower where Peg and the Special Hominid lived. Again, God wondered how all these hominids ever found their way about. He would have had no idea where to get down from the bus, and it was lucky Irene knew.

Ahead of them was the tower. The Special Hominid's dwelling was up there somewhere. But where was the luminous arc of God's seeing tube? For a moment, he allowed himself to entertain the hope that it might have come free of its own accord, rendering this whole mission unnecessary. But he knew that was not really it. The tube was still there, all right; it was just that he could no longer see it now that he had the vision of a hominid. He hoped that was not going to be a problem when he finally got close enough to free it.

Irene pressed a button to tell Peg she had arrived, and they passed through the doorway where, seven days earlier, God had bungled his arrival on Earth. At least, that was how he had seen it at the time: the thought made him feel oddly disloyal now. She might not have been his chosen hominid host, but he had developed an affection for Irene in this time he had spent in her body and her life.

To reach Peg's dwelling, she pressed another button next to two silver doors which, after a certain interlude, amid the sound of a machine whirring somewhere within, now slid apart to reveal a small compartment. There was a further panel of buttons mounted on the wall, arranged in two vertical columns, each one marked with a symbol representing a number. God had not yet learned to read these symbols, but he watched as Irene pressed the one that correlated to where they wanted to go. The doors started to close behind them. As they did so, a hominid foot inserted itself between them. This was enough to persuade whatever mechanism controlled them to change direction and open them again. The body attached to the foot now followed it into the compartment. God could hear Irene expressing silent surprise and disapproval that this interloper had not so much as acknowledged her presence, which was called being rude. Especially since it was not the first time, she was thinking. The creator's own reaction, however, was much more upbeat, because he recognised the Other Hominid. A week earlier, chance had placed Irene in close proximity to this very creature just as God was attempting to tele-transport into his body. Now luck had once more brought them into close contact.

Oblivious to either of them, the Other Hominid now pressed a button of his own, and the doors slid closed again. God might not be able to read the symbol on the button, but he could remember its position well enough: third from the top, on the right-hand column.

Through the next couple of hours, the creator struggled to suppress his impatience as they visited Peg. He felt bad for this, because she seemed a nice old creature who had gone to the trouble of making them sandwiches, squares of thin pink stuff called ham carefully arranged between identically sized squares of thin white stuff. He could see it must have been an effort for her to make them, since she was twisted over by her infirmity.

The only thing that quelled his sense of urgency to visit the Other Hominid's dwelling was the appearance of the famous sherry. This was a rich, bronze-coloured beverage, and it tasted very sweet, in a way that he found most appealing. What was remarkable about it, however, was that it also came with a soothing warmth that seemed to suffuse the whole of Irene's body. It numbed her senses too, which God would have regarded as cause for alarm, had she herself not been so utterly calm about the phenomenon.

'It certainly hits the spot,' she said to Peg after her first sip.

After a while, God decided that he liked the spot being hit. He made a mental note to look out for this sherry again.

Irene had consumed two largish glasses of this potion by the time they took their leave. This meant she was more pliable, and God was emboldened, for the dramatic action which he had been mulling over while he waited for the two hominid females to finish talking, and which he had now resolved to take.

Irene and Peg said their goodbyes, and his hostess walked back towards the set of sliding silver doors, pressing the button beside them to summon the mechanical compartment. It arrived, they got in and she raised her hand to press one of the lower buttons that would take them back to ground level. God saw his chance. Taking control of her limb, he nudged it further upwards, so that she was actually pressing the third from the top, on the right-hand side. It really was possible to override her. It was a risk, he realised: if she felt him doing it, he was effectively giving his presence away, and she might be terrified. However, she remained blissfully unaware that anything out of the ordinary had happened. That gave him more options for whatever came next.

As with Peg's level, there were four blue doors off the main hallway on the Other Hominid's floor. God had no idea which was the dwelling he wanted. The door nearest them had a notice attached to it, bearing an inscription which he supposed must be the name of the occupant. That was no help, even if he could read the script, because he did not know even know what the Special Hominid or the Other Hominid were called. The door also had a button mounted on the frame. Deciding that this was as good a place to start as any, God induced Irene to press it. It set off a metallic chime within, as well as the loud, repetitive bow-wow-wow call of some quadruped that seemed to be scratching against the inside of the door.

'Shut it, Benjy, and get out the way!' said a female voice as the door opened. 'Whatever you're hawkin', I don't want it and I don't want to borrow money off you neither. Didn't you see the sign? Though to be fair you don't look like a shark. What is it, darlin', Jehovah's Witnesses? Speak up.'

But God and Irene had already turned away, because this was not the place.

'Don't mind me, darlin', will you?' shouted the female hominid. 'Honestly, the nerve of some people!'

She slammed her door shut as she carried on cursing behind it.

The creator could see a light underneath the next door. There was no button to press but, emboldened by the sense that his mission was so close to being accomplished, he brought her hand down on the door twice, making a sharp retort which echoed around the hall. There was no response from within so, after a minute or two, he did it again. This time he heard someone moving about inside. There was a rattling on the other side of the door. It opened a crack, and then a bit wider, to reveal the Other Hominid.

At last – success!

'Hello?' the Other Hominid said.

God had seen and heard enough Earthly communications by now to realise that the face looking at him was not friendly. Perhaps he should let Irene take over now – she at least knew what to say to other hominids.

'Hello,' he let her say.

'What can I do for you?' said the Other Hominid, staring hard.

God realised that Irene had nothing to say at this point. He therefore had no option but to take over. He really should have thought this through.

'The green-eyed one isn't here, is he?' he said in her voice. 'It's just you, isn't it?'

'Sorry?'

'It doesn't matter which one of you, really. I just need to come in.'

He raised Irene's foot to step into the flat.

After that, it all went badly. The Other Hominid closed the door to an even narrower slit, and then slammed it completely, refusing to open it again, even when God knocked some more. He eventually gave up when he heard mention of something called the police, which sounded alarming, even if he was not precisely sure what it meant.

It was ridiculous. He was the creator of the universe, yet he could not manage to enter a simple hominid dwelling, and he was no closer to achieving his quest than he had been a week ago.

If he was back in his own proper place at the centre of the heavens, he would have kicked an asteroid in frustration. Here, he could not even do that.

22

Irene could honestly say she had never felt so close to God.

Her discovery of a strong Christian faith, where previously she had had none, had alarmed some of her friends, who had viewed it as a sign of her collapsing mental health after the loss of Ollie. They tended to be the friends who had not been present enough to witness the various changes that had brought her to St Saviour's, so she did not pay much heed to their concerns or miss them when they faded from her life. Since then, she had drawn strength from her new community, from the counsel and friendship of Rev Sharon, and also from the intimate personal relationship she felt she had formed with her maker, by way of their nightly chats.

She was aware that these conversations were one-sided: other members of the congregation, and her nice Nigerian neighbour two doors down, confided details of the messages God had given them directly, but Irene could not say, hand on heart, that she had had such an experience herself. This did not diminish her faith; if God was going to talk to her, he would do it in his own time. And when all was said and done, she could not have gone completely barmy, as her former friends supposed, if she was not even hearing voices.

Lately, however, if felt like something had changed. It was hard to describe but, if pressed, she would say the idea of God had grown within her, quietly and without fanfare, making her feel more weighted, that she was somehow carrying divine ballast, and was therefore more stable, better equipped for life's journey. It was not something she had talked to anyone about, even Rev Sharon, but that was fine. Whatever had changed, it felt deeply personal, and there was no great need to boast to the world about it.

The other recent development was a little more disturbing. It was the kind of thing she would have to tell someone about, sooner or later, if it got any worse. She was worried about taking that step, however, for fear of where it might lead. If something really was wrong, she preferred to defer for as long as possible the need to put a name to it.

She had been having episodes. That was all she was prepared to call them for the moment. Anything more than that was too frightening.

First, there was the football. This was a game she had always disliked. She associated it with tattooed, beer-bellied thugs running amok in blameless European cities, and she was always relieved to see from the headlines in the tabloids at the corner shop that England had been knocked out of the World Cup, or the Euros, or whatever competition was on. She made no secret of this antipathy to Ray, her next-door neighbour of thirty-odd years, and he occasionally goaded her on the subject by pretending he had forgotten she loathed the game. She assumed he was doing so again when she passed him on his way back from the shops with his pint of milk and his rolling tobacco.

'Enjoy the game last night, did you?' he said.

'Ha very ha, Ray,' said Irene. 'The old ones are the best, eh?'

He looked nonplussed, and a little hurt.

'No, I meant it,' he said. 'I could hear you watching it through the wall. You'd turned the sound right up and I could hear you cheering. I was worried you might have squatters or something, and I came halfway round to check. But I saw through the window that it was just you, and you seemed to be having a high old time, so I thought I'd best leave you to it. Next time, though, let me know, and I'll bring some cans round.'

She let him continue on his way without replying, because she had no idea what to say. Was he pulling her leg? He seemed to be dead serious, but she had no recall of so much as glimpsing a televised football match the previous night, never mind turning the volume up and cheering for England, or Arsenal, or whoever she was meant to have been supporting. She wondered – indeed, rather uncharitably, hoped – that it might be Ray's mind playing tricks on him, but something held her back from believing that. She could have told Ray he was talking nonsense, that she had been watching *Time Team*, which was always her midweek highlight, and she had planned her supper around it accordingly. Now she came to think of it, however, she had no memory of that episode. It was meant to be about Hadrian's Wall, which she knew because she had seen the trailer the previous week. But she could not for the life of her picture any of it.

Then there was the matter of the sherry. She had seen Harvey's Bristol Cream on offer in Sainsbury's, and bought a bottle for her next visit to Peg – that much she remembered clearly. She also remembered unpacking it with the rest of her shopping and putting it in the larder cupboard next to the fridge. What she did not remember was getting it out again, opening the seal and drinking the best part of half a bottle, but that seemed to be what she had done a few days after the football episode. Her first, panicky assumption when she saw the open bottle on the kitchen counter was that she had had an intruder – some kind of wino burglar with a very sweet tooth. She had embarked on a cautious, room-by-room inspection of the house, armed with an umbrella that she imagined she might be able to use as a truncheon. However, she had very quickly abandoned this search on discovering one of her crystal glasses, all sticky on the inside and with a definite whiff of sherry fumes, next to the chair she had been sitting in for the past couple of hours. The headache she suffered the next day provided further corroboration that she herself had been the tippler. Once again, she had zero recall of touching a drop.

What was she supposed to make of these developments? You could have blackouts without realising it, she knew – like mini-strokes, that were so mild, you did not even notice you were having them. But this was not a fainting fit or a momentary loss of consciousness. If she was right, it was more like sleep-walking when she was wide awake. Or was she developing a split personality? That was a seriously worrying prospect, and she ought to tell someone – but who? If she went to the doctor, it would get flagged in her notes, whether it turned out to be something or nothing. Maybe she would save it for Rev Sharon, or for Peg the next time she went round. Or perhaps she would just wait and see if anything else happened, then definitely mention it.

To her relief, nothing did – not as far as she was aware, anyway. Thus, when she next called on Peg, she was able to restrict the conversation in good conscience to less alarming topics, such as the hundreds of millions of pounds being spent on a plastic tent on some wasteland on the lower reaches of the Thames, which Peg had been following in great detail.

'It's typical Tony Blair,' she pronounced. 'It'll be gleaming and shiny on the outside, but empty inside. As for that other one, Mandelson, I wouldn't trust him as far as I could spit on him. They say it's going to be like the Festival of Britain. More like Festival of Backhanders.'

Irene felt she ought to mount some kind of defence against this slanderous diatribe, which she imagined came more or less directly from the *Daily Mail*. The extravagance was not easy to defend, though. After the relief of getting rid of the Conservatives at long last, the new political dawn was fast losing its rosy glow, and it was becoming depressingly harder to give the country's new masters the benefit of the doubt, especially where this blessed Dome was concerned.

'Let's wait and see,' she said. 'They've promised us something spectacular, and they wouldn't have done that if they didn't know what they were doing. I can't believe they'd go to all the trouble and expense of building it unless they had some good things to put inside it.'

'It's the Queen I feel sorry for,' said Peg. 'You know they're making her go and open it? At her age, they should let her put her feet up and watch the telly on New Year's Eve, like the rest of us oldies.'

'Yes, but what's she supposed to watch?' said Irene. 'The rest of you will be watching her, and if she was at home too, there'd be nothing for anyone to see.'

'Oh, get away with you and pour us some more sherry,' said Peg.

Irene was pleased to have made her laugh. Trapped in her flat all day, in her poor, contorted body, the old girl did not have much else to smile about.

On the way to the bus stop afterwards, she felt a hand on her arm.

'Excuse me...'

'Yes?'

She turned to see a young man in a fawn mac with the collar up, and a tartan bag slung over his shoulder. About the same age as Ollie would be, and with slightly jug ears, he looked vaguely familiar, but she could not place him.

'You came to my flat, didn't you?' he said. 'Look, I'm sorry I was rude to you and slammed the door. And I wasn't really going to call the police. It was just that I was having a really bad day, and I wasn't coping very well. I'm still not, actually. But...well...you asked about Stefano. I

241

need to know how you know him.'

Irene listened to this speech with a sinking feeling. She realised where she had seen him. He lived in Peg's building and she had seen him twice, now, in the lift, and he had been surly on both occasions. She also had the dimmest of memories of his face in a doorway, but it was only fleeting, more like a déjà vu than something real. She certainly had no recall of any conversation, any rudeness, or mention of the police. In ordinary circumstances, she would assume the fault was his, that it was a clear case of mistaken identity. But given the strange things that had been happening to her lately, and that nagging sense that she had seen him before, she could not say with any confidence that she had not knocked on the door of his flat and asked for a Stefano, whoever that might be.

'Where do you live?' she asked cautiously.

'Lumley House,' said the young man.

That was Peg's building all right.

'I'm sorry to ask,' she continued. 'But when did I knock on your door?'

The young man had the same puzzled look as her neighbour Ray had given her.

'About three weeks ago.'

'And do you remember what day of the week it was?'

He was growing impatient.

'I can't remember. It was three weeks ago.'

'Do try,' she said. 'It really is important.'

'A Monday or a Tuesday, I suppose. No, I'd got off early, so it must have been press day, Tuesday.'

'Oh dear,' said Irene quietly.

'So…it was you, wasn't it?'

'I think it must have been. But I'm afraid I don't remember you slamming the door in my face, so there's honestly no need to apologise.'

'All right,' the young man said cautiously. 'You were quite strange at the time, and that's still strange. But about Stefano?'

'I'm afraid I've no idea. Are you sure I said I know him?'

'Yes. Well…actually you didn't ask for him by name. You said you wanted to see the green-eyed one.'

'Who?'

'He's got green eyes.'

'I see. And…I'm sorry to ask, but who is he to you?'

The young man blinked.

'He's my…or he was my…' he struggled, and then his face crumpled. His mouth turned down at the corners and now contorted into a silent wail, a string of drool dangling towards his woollen scarf.

'Oh dear,' said Irene again, conscious that they were on a busy high street, cluttering up the pavement as well as creating a spectacle that was in danger of robbing the distressed young man of his dignity.

'Look, you're clearly having a difficult time, and you and I seem to have met before, which I can't remember, so that's quite hard for me too. This isn't the place to discuss any of it, so would you like to come to my house? It's only a few stops on the 106, and I do have half a bottle of Bristol Cream, if that's any inducement. Otherwise, I make a good, strong cup of tea. Then you can tell me all about it. What do you say?'

23

It was Millennium Eve, and Adam was throwing a party for himself and two women of a certain age – one old enough to be his mother, the other closer to his grandmother's vintage.

This was not the celebration with which he had envisaged ushering in the new, modern epoch. Ordinarily on New Year's Eve, Stefano would arrange for Rook and a bunch of their friends to come to the Prince Edward, which usually had a late licence until one or two in the morning. There they would see in the New Year against the backdrop of whatever drag show Kevin had booked in. This was always a hit-and-miss affair; last year a group of male nuns called the Sisters of Perpetual Indulgence had performed what was intended to be a comedy version of a Victorian poem called 'The Wreck of the Deutschland', which constituted a spectacular miss. Nevertheless, Stefano could be relied upon to slip Adam free drinks whenever Kevin was not looking. Afterwards, if they were in the mood and had been able to get some pills, they would go to Heaven or Trade, where they could jump the queue because Stefano could always get them on the guest list. It was at times frustrating not to have any other options, but as long as Stefano worked at the Edward, that was his place, and Adam's was always beside him.

This year, he could theoretically go back there for old times' sake. That was what Rook and his friends were planning to do, and the latter had been at pains to stress that Adam was welcome to tag along. But it was the last thing Adam wanted to do: propping up the bar which his lover had abandoned, along with everything else, was not his idea of a good time. He was in no mood for any kind of joviality, and standing watching other people whoop it up was the worst of all worlds. Nevertheless, the evening had to be got through somehow. Stefano had already ruined his life, but Adam was damned if he was going to let him also ruin an event that only happened once every thousand years. Spending it with his strange new friend Irene and the elderly downstairs neighbour in Lumley House whom she visited every week was a suitably offbeat solution that summed up the bizarre state of his life since Stefano's disappearance.

After his breakdown in the street, he had taken up Irene's suggestion and returned with her to her home. She had told him her name as they waited for the bus, and he was feeling comfortable in her company by the time they walked up the path to her front door. Gone was all the alarming weirdness she had displayed when she had asked for Stefano as 'the green-eyed one'. Now she just seemed warm and friendly, as if it were a completely different person who had knocked on his door. If she really did have some kind of split personality disorder, that was perhaps not so surprising. All his instincts, however, told him that this was a kind, receptive person

245

who was just what he needed at the present time. If he were wrong about that, time would just have to tell. At least he would only have himself to blame.

Her house was chaotic and eccentric, but comfortable. Large by the standards of his own flat, rambling and smelling faintly musty, like a second-hand bookshop, it was the kind of place that she had no doubt bought for a song before he was even born. The living room was lined with panelling that had clearly been salvaged from somewhere older and grander: it did not fit well at the corners, and screw heads jutted crookedly from its smooth surfaces. A sofa had been assembled from a brass bedstead, and a threadbare chaise longue was piled high with old copies of the *Guardian* at one end and the *Lady* at the other. Above and around the fireplace were stiff portraits of dour-faced grandees glaring out of dark, cracked canvases, each one labelled in an archaic, gilded hand with a name: Johannes Probert, Thos Proberte, Cath'rin Probertt.

'Are they really your ancestors?' said Adam, awed by the splendour, however incongruous it was.

'They are now,' said Irene, with a loud laugh.

She gave him sherry and dry-roasted peanuts, and he told her the whole story of Stefano's accident, apparent breakdown and abrupt departure. He related it haltingly at first, but expanded into full detail, without reserve, as he discovered that she was a good listener.

'I really did think it would all somehow go away and he'd get over it. I wasn't expecting him to walk out, so it's knocked me sideways,' he said, as he got to the end.

'Apart from anything else, I'm so angry at this stupid superstition we're surrounded by that has put the fear of hell-fire into him and has now destroyed two people's lives.'

He had noticed she must be a Christian from the cross she wore on her lapel, but he was too upset to worry about offending her.

'Don't you blame him for any of it?' she asked.

'Of course I do. I blame him for not resisting, for not listening to reason, for being so weak.'

'Perhaps you'll just have to be stronger than he was.'

'Maybe. I don't feel like it at the moment.' Emboldened by the sherry, he added: 'Are you sure you've never met him? You honestly did come to my door and ask for him, you know.'

Irene ran her hand through her hair.

'I really don't know what to say about that. Certain things have been, well, happening. It's rather worrying, I don't mind admitting. I don't recognise the name Stefano. But you say I didn't use it? Do you have a photograph of him? Then I can tell you if I know him.'

'Not on me. But I can bring one round, if you like. If you don't mind me coming again, that is.'

'Of course not. I'd love to see you. But I've got an idea. Don't come here, come to my friend Peg's flat. She lives two floors below you, and I'd like you to meet her. I can't always go as often as I'd like, and it would be marvellous to have someone else to call on in emergencies. I think you'll like her. Why don't you bring the photograph along when I see her next week?'

And so he had done just that. Irene was right: he did like Peg. It shamed him that he knew so few of his neighbours, and he enjoyed hearing stories about the estate, and some of the people who had lived there, from an original resident.

'Although I never really think of it as home,' she said wistfully. 'I do miss my Bethnal Green.'

Adam laughed, because Bethnal Green was only two miles away and he assumed she was joking. It was not until he saw the rebuke in Irene's eye that he realised his mistake.

'I brought you the photograph of Stef,' he said to her, changing the subject.

'Oh good,' said Irene. 'Let's have a look.'

She tilted her head back to peer through her bifocals at the picture he handed her.

'I do know him from somewhere,' she frowned. 'Now where…? I know! He was listening to the preacher. That makes a lot of sense now. I tried to talk to him, to tell him that true Christianity isn't about fear and rejection. Oh, I'm sorry Adam. I wish I'd tried harder now. If only I'd made him listen, you could have avoided all this heartache.'

'If Stef doesn't want to hear, he doesn't hear,' he said. 'There's nothing you could have done. Anyway, you didn't even know him.'

'And at least you tried,' put in Peg. 'Most people wouldn't of. Where is he now, anyway, this Stef?'

'He's gone back to his mother's, I think, but I don't have an address.'

'What part of the country does she live in?'

'I don't even know that.'

'Isn't that a bit strange? How long did you live together? Five years? And you never met his mum?'

This was still a sore point after Rook's revelations that Stef's mother had never been anywhere near Rome, and that Stefano himself was actually called Steven. If Adam ever caught up with Stef, he would like some answers on those points too, but he had not brought himself to tell Irene all that yet. The hurt was too recent, and he was still not sure what to make of it himself.

'Well, it's different for us,' was all he said. 'You know, lots of parents don't want to know.'

'Or lots of children think their parents won't want to know, so they don't make the effort to tell them,' said Irene.

After that, he did visit Peg, on a Sunday afternoon when he was feeling particularly lonely. She was effusively grateful that he had taken the trouble. He tried to tell her that she was doing him as much of a favour as he was doing her, but she seemed not to believe him.

It was she who brought up the Millennium. As someone who had lived through a good three-quarters of the twentieth century, Adam expected her to be at least mildly intrigued at the prospect of seeing in the twenty-first. However, she seemed more concerned about the construction of the Dome. He attempted to impress her by telling her that he had been to the site, and he knew how much concrete had gone into the foundations, but she was interested only in the profligacy of Tony Blair and the shiftiness of Peter Mandelson.

'What will you do on New Year's Eve?' Adam asked, to try to shift her off that subject.

'I shall have an early night,' she said firmly.

'You can't do that. You've got to welcome the new millennium. It won't happen for another thousand years.'

'It's no fun on your own, dear, is it?' she said. 'And the new millennium will still be there in the morning.'

It occurred to Adam that his father, convinced that the Millennium Bug would bring civilised life to a halt on the stroke of midnight, might dispute that, but he thought it best not to concern Peg with all that.

She was certainly right that New Year celebrations were no fun on your own. It made him think about his own plans, and it gave him an idea. Later, he telephoned Irene with his suggestion.

'Both of you could come to my place,' he said. 'It's higher up than Peg's, so we may be able to see this River of Fire they keep talking about in the papers. It's going to be amazing, apparently: a wall of fireworks all the way down the Thames. You're meant to be able to see it from space. The three of us could have a drink and watch it together. Don't worry if you've got something else planned, though.'

She said she did not, and she was all for his idea.

It was a great weight off his mind. It would not be the wildest of New Year festivities, but it put an end to the dread of being alone, which had been making him physically queasy every time he thought about it.

It also enabled him to go back to Suffolk in relatively good heart for his birthday and a family Christmas. His father had stockpiled the cellar with enough tinned food and bottled water to last a year, to the profound embarrassment of his mother, who said she hated sardines anyway and would rather starve if the Millennium Bug brought the country to a standstill, but there were no major arguments. Adam did not even mind that nobody mentioned Stefano. It was better than having to give them a version of what had happened.

So now he was cleaning the toilet, hoovering and dusting for the first time in weeks, and making room in the fridge for the bottles of cava he had bought. His guests were coming for a late supper before seeing in the New Year, and he had managed not to burn a big dish of sausages and onions, with a gravy made from a bottle of cider, which he thought would appeal to both Peg and Irene, with their taste for sweet, sticky alcohol. The potatoes were peeled and ready to boil for mash. Apart from Rook's visit, it was the first time anyone had been over since Stefano had left.

The flat was still showing signs of his disorderly lifestyle when the pair of them arrived. Irene stooped to pick up a pile of mail that Adam had left lying on the doormat.

'Thanks, but it's probably just bills or junk,' he said as she handed him the stack of envelopes and flyers.

The writing on the topmost envelope, however, made his chest tighten. He stared at the letter without opening it, so that Irene immediately noticed.

'Is it from him?' she asked quietly.

Adam nodded.

'Where is he? What does the postmark say?'

'Wirral,' read Adam, and shrugged.

'And are you going to open it? Go on, you read it, and I'll take Peg's coat and find us a drink. By the way, I hope you don't mind but there may be someone else coming...'

He was not listening. The letter which he pulled out of the envelope consisted of two sides of writing paper, scrawled in a large, messy hand, and it did not say much. It read:

Dear Adam

I'm sorry I left in such a rush and I only wrote you such a short note, but I needed to go. It's for the best, believe me. I've been all over the place since what happened on the beach, and coming back here was what I needed. At first I thought it would just be for a few days, but I really can't face coming back to London. I don't think we can be together any more, because I'm so frightened about being punished. I'm really, really sorry, but maybe it will stop you from being punished too.

Things are quite hard here, but maybe that's my penance from God, if there is a God. Better to suffer it now than in the next world, anyway. I know all this must be incredibly tough on you, and I hope that you may one day be able to understand and forgive me. I don't want you to hate me.

If it's not too much to ask, could you do me a favour and send me some clothes? I need a warm jacket – my thick grey woollen one, not the bomber jacket. And maybe some T-shirts – nothing with writing on, and not the Fred Perrys, but anything else is fine. And my Calvin Klein jeans. I've put in a fiver for postage.

What are you doing for Millennium Eve? Are you going to the Edward? If you do, say hi to Kevin from me, although he probably hates me too. If it makes you feel any better, our Millennium night up here will probably be pretty dismal.

Love Stef x

PS I'm sure it's OK for you to stay on at the flat until we get something more permanent sorted, so don't worry about that for now. But you won't have my half of the rent.

Adam pulled out the crumpled five-pound note that was also tucked into the envelope and blinked back tears of hurt and rage. So this was how their five years together came to an end. It was OK for him to stay on at the flat until they got something sorted. Nice.

He was glad to have Irene there. He looked up to show her the letter and noticed that, having settled Peg in a chair by the radiator, she had gone to the other side of the room and was fiddling with something behind the

TV. She seemed to be trying to open the window. Having opened the catch and pushed the window wide, she stood there for a couple of seconds, gesturing at thin air as if she were feeding some unseen object through the gap. Then she closed the window again.

'Is it too hot in here?' said Adam. 'It's usually easier to go on the balcony if you want some air.'

'Mm?' she said. 'Hot? No, it's lovely, thank you. Just right.'

She seemed not to have any idea what he was talking about. It brought back a memory of that first time they had met, on his doorstep.

'Anyway, tell me what's in it,' she said, bringing Adam's attention back to the letter in his hand. 'What does he have to say for himself?'

'He's not coming back, but he wants some clothes sending,' he said, holding out the letter for her to read. 'He sent me a fiver for the postage.'

'Has he now?' she said, taking it off him and reading it through. 'What a little charmer he is.' She sighed. 'I'm sorry, Adam, really I am. It really is too cruel. I've half a mind to…'

She was interrupted by a ring at the buzzer.

'Oh, that'll be…'

Adam had already picked up the entry-phone.

'It's James,' said a crackly voice.

'Who?'

'Irene invited me. I have got the right flat?'

'Buzz him up,' Irene urged. 'I'll explain.'

Adam shrugged again.

'Tenth floor,' he told the voice.

'I hope you don't mind,' said Irene. 'He's Ollie's oldest friend and he's only just got back to London. He's been away for a few years and he's lost touch with a lot of people, so I thought it might be nice to include him.'

James was tall, slim and deeply tanned, having just returned from southern Africa, with sun-bleached hair and an array of tribal beads around his neck.

'Hey, it's brilliant up here,' he said, striding to the balcony. 'You can see all the stars. Can you recognise the constellations? They're completely different in Africa, you know – you see a totally different sky. Not that I know what I'm looking at in either hemisphere. I never knew which one the Plough was, for example, because it looked nothing like a plough, and also because it seems to depend on a completely arbitrary group of stars. You could draw the dividing line in a different place and then come up with an entirely new collection of objects to name them after, like the Great Rabbit, or the Spatula, or the Reliant Robin. Sorry, I'm gabbling, aren't I? Thanks for having me, by the way. I really appreciate it.'

Adam noticed Peg and Irene exchanging smiles.

'Let's eat,' he said, remembering that he had a saucepan of boiled potatoes that needed mashing. 'And are we going to watch the fireworks in real life or on TV?'

'Both, I say,' said Irene. 'Then we can choose whichever is better.'

As it turned out, there was not much in it. The River of Fire was a great let-down, which at first they blamed on their own distant vantage point, but it was clear from the television commentary that everyone else watching it was underwhelmed too.

As the bongs of Big Ben chimed the millennium in, they clinked glasses and embraced. When it came to embracing James, Adam was not quite sure what was appropriate, but they each entered into the spirit of the moment and no harm seemed to have been done. Any embarrassment was swiftly dissipated by the sight of the Queen and the Duke of Edinburgh on the box, attempting to join in with 'Auld Lang Syne'. Not only did neither of them know the words, they also had no idea they were meant to cross their arms before linking hands with their neighbours'.

'Bless!' said Irene. 'She's never done it before.'

'It's a liberty,' complained Peg. 'Look at that Tony Blair, grabbing her hand like that. She's the Queen, for heaven's sake. Has the man no shame?'

'Off with his head!' said James.

They carried on watching the televised celebrations for a while. They all agreed that they would far rather be where they were than stuck in the Dome. The commentator said that the VIP guests had had to queue for hours just to get in, and nobody looked as if they were having much of a time.

'They're all worried about how they're going to get home,' said Peg. 'I don't blame them, stuck down there in the back end of nowhere.'

'Wasn't the whole country meant to have ground to a halt by now?' said Irene.

Adam had forgotten all about that, but it was true:

the Millennium Bug catastrophe seemed not to have happened. He could imagine his father being made to eat sardines on toast for lunch every day for the rest of the year, as his mother's revenge.

As they were all eventually leaving, Irene took Adam to one side.

'Those clothes,' she said. 'Can you parcel them up, but don't put them in the post.'

'Why?'

'Because I've got an idea. Give me a ring tomorrow, and I'll tell you about it.'

24

LYING ON HIS OLD single bed in his self-imposed exile, Stefano tried to work out why it was all going so badly. He was not honouring his mother, that was for sure – except by his presence, in her own withering phrase. That meant he must also be making things worse with God.

He put his hands together and tried to pray. Back in his days of childhood devotion, when he was taken to church by his mother or crouched with his eyes closed in school assembly, he had never thought to ask for anything for himself. Hard as it was to imagine from his present perspective, he had been blissfully free of any worries that he needed to take to God in the form of specific requests, and praying had been a passive business in which he merely listened to the solemn voice of the vicar or headmaster. Now, he had very specific concerns on his mind, but he was not entirely sure how to raise them. Was he just meant to ask for things, or did he have to make commitments in return? If so, how would he know what was a fair exchange? If Almighty God could see his way to not sending him to hell, he would do his level best in return to honour his mother. But if God could also make his mother a little easier to honour, that might make everything go more smoothly.

There were times when he wanted to blurt it all out about Adam, just to see her face. He hated her knee-jerk rejection of anything that did not fit the neat attitudes of her own small world, and he wanted to push against her narrow-mindedness. But it was no longer that simple. By freezing Adam out of his life and turning his back on London, he had swapped sides. If he had really repented, he ought to be able to look his mother in the eye, tell her he was sorry and own up to his mistake in rejecting the values she had tried to instill in him. So why could he not? He stared up at the Artex swirls on his ceiling and felt the walls crowd in, just as they had when he was sixteen. It went against the grain to tell his mother she was right. If, however, he could not do so, where did that leave his immortal soul?

Eventually he sat up. He could start the way he meant to go on, by going downstairs and being nicer to her.

She was in the sitting room with a cup of tea.

'This is the first sit-down I've had all day. I didn't offer you a cup. I thought you'd come down when you were ready for one.'

'I'll make one now.'

'Help yourself to a chocolate biscuit. You know where they are.'

He made himself tea, squeezing out the bag and putting it in a plastic dish in the shape of a teapot where it could be used again, and found a silver-wrapped biscuit in the tin that was older than he was. Somehow she even managed to buy the same brands from his childhood.

He returned to the sitting room and sat down opposite

her, in his father's chair.

She gazed at him sadly. 'You look like him. It's one of the reasons I had such a shock that night when you arrived.'

'I should have warned you I was coming,' he said.

'That's over and done with now.'

He was grateful to her for that. She was being conciliatory. However, the question of whether he could remain indefinitely had still not been resolved.

'Is it all right if I stay here? I can go to Katie's for a bit if it isn't, and then I can get my own place.'

It had occurred to him that he might try a council swap. It would be rough on Adam, who would have to move out of the flat in Hackney, but it would enable Stefano to make a fresh start near his mother and sister.

'Of course you can stop here,' she said. 'This house is too big for me. It'll be nice to have the company.'

'OK. Good. Thanks.'

'But I'm not calling you that stupid name.'

He smiled.

'Call me Stee. That's short for Stefano and Steven.'

She shrugged and they drank their tea, but something was still clearly bothering her.

'What are you going to do?' she said eventually. 'There's nothing for you here. You've lost touch with your friends from school, and most of them have gone away themselves. You don't know a soul, apart from Katie, and she's away half the time, not to speak of the wedding to plan. And what will you do for work? You'll have to get a job.'

'I'll be all right. There's always pub work going.'

But one month became two, and he did not get a job. He had lost his confidence, and the idea of walking into a pub to ask for work filled him with trepidation. He seldom ventured out of the house at all. He walked over to Katie's one evening a week, and she told him about her life in the years he had missed, which was easier than him talking about his own. Dale, her boyfriend, always welcomed him effusively and then made himself scarce. He was a maths teacher and always seemed to be marking or preparing lessons, and his principal diversion was watching sport on the box. Once it had been established that Stefano had nothing to say on that subject, there was an awkwardness between them, but it was embarrassed rather than hostile. Stefano reminded himself that he had never known how to talk to straight men, which set him worrying again about how he was going to manage in his new life. He would be useless behind an ordinary bar.

One Saturday afternoon, he noticed that *The Ten Commandments* was on TV, and he and Katie spent the best part of four hours watching it. Katie was loudly excited, as their mother had once been, by the sight of Charlton Heston in a short tunic. Stefano recalled the strange stirrings he had once felt for Yul Brynner and the sweating Hebrews, but only as a memory. He had not confided his religious worries to his sister but, for him, watching the film was a revision course in Bible studies. It prompted him to think about tackling the real thing once he got back to the sanctuary of his bare bedroom.

Considering it was meant to be the greatest story ever told, he was surprised at how rambling and repetitive the narrative was. Parts of it were also alarming. To his relief, the part of *The Ten Commandments* where Moses killed Edward G Robinson with the tablets bearing the inscription 'Thou shalt not kill' turned out to be Hollywood invention. Unfortunately the scriptwriters had also airbrushed out some far more disturbing material. In the actual Bible, he discovered, Moses commanded his supporters to kill their brothers, friends and neighbours simply for having a party, and he seemed to do it with God's blessing. Stefano did not remember being told about that by Mr Romsey or Tommy Tosspot. It was shocking behaviour, and it had implications for his own future. If that was how God and his servants reacted to a bit of music and dancing, how would they feel about Stefano's old lifestyle in London? Rook had taught him to be safe as far as his health was concerned, but in terms of licentiousness, some of his exploits before meeting Adam would have trumped all of Moses' party-loving followers put together. That thought made him feel sick with dread, but it reinforced his conviction that he was right to have abandoned London.

His mother was wrong-footed to find the Bible by his bedside. He hoped she would be pleased to find it, and perhaps she was, but she found it hard to say so. Instead she tried to use it to spur him into getting out of his torpor and leaving the house.

'Would you like to go to church?' she suggested. 'I haven't been since your dad's funeral, and it would upset me to go now. But I can always ask Sue Throup, that lives in the Jeavonses' old house. She goes to St Andrew's. I think she may even be a churchwarden. I'm sure she'd be more than happy for you to go together, if you don't want to walk in on your own. Would you like me to ask her next time I see her? Or I could call round there. It's no trouble at all.'

Stefano had no desire to go to church with the neighbours. It would be obvious that he was new to it all, and he might have to explain why. That would get back to his mother and he did not want her knowing his business. It was simpler to go through his own form of rudimentary devotions in the privacy of his room and hope for the best. He had no real way of expressing any of that to his mother, other than by telling her that he did not feel like going to church with Sue Throup. He did so more forcefully the second or third time she suggested it, and before he knew it, the Church had become a new front in their battle, with his refusal to go providing further evidence of his indolence.

'You don't go either, so get off my back!' he reminded her at one point. She had no reply, but he later regretted the taunt, because he could see from her face that it had stung her.

He attempted to make himself useful around the house, such as by helping with the cooking, but he reckoned without his mother's resistance.

'I managed quite well before you decided to show your face, and I can manage quite well now,' she would say, apart from on the days when she was tired of cooking, when she berated him for expecting to be waited on hand and foot. He had blotted this part of his childhood out, but now he remembered very well: you could never win with her, whatever you did.

Dusting was the safest bet. Every day he picked up and put back the framed photographs that crowded the mantelpiece: himself as a child; Katie on a roller-coaster and at her graduation; his parents on holiday in the caravan, and surrounded by extended family (but not their son, of course) at their silver wedding. He thought of the framed pictures in his own flat, and wondered if Adam had taken them down yet.

His mother made a cake for his birthday, and went to the trouble of putting thirty-one candles in it. He did his best to make himself nice, and the next day for Christmas, and he could see how pleased his mother was to have him there. On New Year's Eve, they watched the Queen at the Dome, and Katie and Dale thought it was hilarious that the monarch did not know what to do during 'Auld Lang Syne'. They were right; it was, and he tried to enter into the spirit. At this time of year, however, it was hard not to miss his old life. He had to sneak back to his bedroom to look at some of his paintings of hell, in order to remind himself why it had been so crucial to turn his back on it.

Tensions with his mother were never far from the surface, and it all finally came to a head in the first week of the New Year, when Katie had joined them for lunch.

'You promised me you'd get a job and you've done nothing,' his mother started.

'I've got some savings. I can pay you rent.'

'It's not about the money. I'm concerned about you

frittering away your life doing nothing.'

'Well, you needn't be. It's my life.'

'Sitting around all day, never any fresh air, never seeing anyone; it can't be healthy. Tell him, Katie.'

'Don't drag me into it, Mum. I can't make him look for work if he doesn't want to.'

'He's your brother. Talk to him. Maybe you can get through to him, because I certainly can't.'

'I am here, you know.'

'Oh, we know that, my lad. No danger of missing that.'

'Go easy on him, Mum.'

But she was fired up.

'I've been going easy for two months while he's been sat in this house, bone idle. I'm glad your father isn't here to see it. For all those years when we didn't know if he was alive or dead, we hoped and dreamed he'd made something of himself, even if he didn't want to know us. Now he comes back and what do we find? He's spent fifteen years working in a bar.'

'It was a very successful bar.'

'Keep it shut. I wasn't talking to you.'

'You were talking about me.'

'Because it has to be all about you, doesn't it? You've no consideration for anyone else. You'll barely tell us a thing about your life, what you've done all these years, like you're looking down your nose at us.'

'All right, I'll tell you. I managed a very successful bar called the Prince Edward, which was a gold mine for its owner because it was always packed out, because it was one of the biggest gay bars in North London. I was good at the job because I understood the customers, because I'm gay too, always had been, always was, in my fifteen years in London. And for the past five years I lived with a man called Adam, and yes, he was also gay, and yes, we used to do it up the bum. Happy now?'

He knew he was throwing caution to the winds as far as his immortal soul was concerned. But really, what difference could it make? God must know about all this stuff anyway.

His mother clutched her chest and for a moment Stefano thought it must be her heart. She rose from the table, scraping back her stool, and fled the room, dropping her starched napkin by the door.

'What the heck do you think you're playing at?'

His sister's fury took him by surprise. Her cheeks were pink and her mouth had narrowed to a point.

'Do you have any idea what she's been through, first with you and then with Dad? I'm sure you had your reasons for walking out, though frankly, when most people yearn to see the bright lights, they go for the weekend and then come home again. At the very least they send a postcard. It's too late for you to make your peace with Dad, who loved you more than you will ever know, and never stopped blaming himself after you ran away. But Mum's still with us, and now you're back, you can damn well treat her with respect. God knows she can be difficult, but nobody's forcing you to stay here. She's trying her best to adjust and all you can do is mock her, throwing things in her face that you know she can't deal with. Just what is your problem, anyway? What are you doing here?'

He was stung by her bitterness.

'I thought you wanted me here. You said you were pleased to see me. You asked me to come back.'

'I did, but I don't want you here like this, as a shadow of a person. For weeks I've been waiting for you to tell me what's going on. I wondered if maybe you've got Aids and you'd come home to, well...'

'It's called HIV these days and you don't really die of it any more. But no, I haven't.'

'That's brilliant, really it is. But if it's not that, what is it? Are you depressed? Maybe they can give you tablets for that. You've got to do something, because I will not stand back and watch you destroy that woman all over again. Read my lips, Stee, or Stef, or whatever the heck your name is, I will not let you do it.'

He could hear his heart pounding. Being read the riot act by his little sister was a rite of passage he had not ever anticipated.

Out in the hall, the doorbell went and Katie started to get up. But they heard their mother's step, followed by the front door opening and the sound of voices.

'You don't know what it's like,' he said, closing his eyes as he felt tears press forward. 'It's not easy for me either, coming back here after all this time.'

'I'm sure it isn't.' Her tone was gentler. 'But why have you come back? That's what I don't understand.'

'It's complicated. I don't know how to explain.'

'Try. I've got plenty of time. But I've waited long enough, so you'd better start talking.'

He opened his mouth to reply, not sure what was going to come out, but he was spared the need. Their mother appeared in the doorway, her face blotchy and drawn. Stefano braced himself for a bruising, knowing he deserved it and would have to apologise – and that was not counting how much more trouble he had got into with God in the past half-hour. However, she merely said: 'There's someone to see you, Stee.'

A woman followed her into the kitchen. She looked about sixty, with messy hair and a comical, lop-sided smile.

'I'm sorry to interrupt your meal. It's ghastly timing and I should have called ahead, but I only had the address, not the number. You're Stefano, aren't you? We've met briefly before, in the street, but I don't suppose you remember. My name's Irene Probert, and I've got some of your clothes in the car. We also need a little talk. I've driven more than two hundred miles specially, so I hope you'll hear me out.'

25

'I STILL DON'T understand who you are or what you want,' said Stefano, as Irene slowed to negotiate a circular junction. It was the third time he had said it since getting in her craft.

'All in good time. Do you think it's the first or the second exit?'

'How should I know? I don't even know where we're meant to be heading.'

'I keep telling you, we're going to the beach.' She did a full circuit then opted for the first exit after all. 'Do I get the impression that paying attention isn't your strong suit?'

'The beaches round here are all horrible. They're like mud flats. We used to come when I was a kid and I always hated it. Anyway, it's the middle of winter. Nobody goes to the beach in January.'

'The mud flats are the best bit. You wouldn't know it, for all the notice it gets, but we're going to one of the most exciting Iron Age sites in the country. I do hope the tide's all the way out. I meant to check but it slipped my mind.'

'Why do I get the impression that your idea of exciting won't be mine?'

From what he could see through the window, as well as from past experience, God was on Stefano's side. Now they were passing a row of low-lying dwellings and shops. The sky was heavy and grey.

'I've always been curious to see this place,' his hostess continued, ignoring her passenger's complaints. 'And if I have to drive for five hours on your account, I think I'm allowed an indulgence of my own.'

'I didn't ask you to come.'

'Maybe not, but I brought your clothes and I'm here for your benefit.' She turned to look at him, then turned hurriedly back to the controls to stop the craft veering onto the wrong side of the trail. 'To judge from the atmosphere in your mother's house, I'm doing you a favour getting you out of there.'

Through his own rather impressive quick-wittedness, the creator had managed to free his seeing-tube on Millennium Eve, as he had learned to call it. He had been intrigued to learn, via a remark of Peg's, that this occasion was special to the hominids because it was meant to be two thousand Earth-years since the creator's own son had arrived on the planet. There was an agreeable symmetry in his completing his own terrestrial mission on this day, even if the events it commemorated were complete news to him.

Having unsnagged his device and cast it adrift from the tower, where he could retract it later, he was now free to return to his proper place. However, he was not ready to go home quite yet, especially once it became clear that Irene planned to pay this visit. He could not pass up the chance to meet the Special Hominid, who had unwittingly been responsible for this entire adventure. Squeezing into Irene's vehicle and suffering the horrors of the thundering grey trail out of the city were the price of staying.

From the short journeys they had made in this machine, he was familiar with the stop-start way of moving, where any progress was made in short hops between red lights on poles. But now, as they joined the flow of traffic, left the buildings behind and steadily increased in speed, God felt smaller and more vulnerable than at any time since his arrival on Earth. The mechanism of the vehicle sounded suspect even to his untrained sense, and he wished he had more confidence in Irene's ability to drive it. Her own anxiety was obvious, as her hands trembled and she shouted rebukes at other drivers, even though they could not possibly hear her. It occurred to the creator that the experience might be less alarming if he did not have to look at the road ahead. But his hostess had to keep her eyes open, so he had no choice.

After four hours on the road and a stop at a place called Services, where the creator exploited his powers to follow an entrancing smell and made Irene buy something called a Happy Meal, they left the thundering trail for smaller roads. Several times Irene stopped to consult one of her maps. She turned it every which way before selecting her route, and navigation seemed to get harder the further they progressed. She also began to get agitated about the purpose of the journey itself. God could hear her internally rehearsing various opening lines for when they arrived, and her state of nerves was in danger of rubbing off on him. At one point, having taken a wrong road in a neighbourhood full of small houses with gardens around them, she had to turn the vehicle around, a complicated manoeuvre in which the creator's own name was invoked in a disrespectful tone. He began to think he would have to find some way of chastising her, but this was neither the time nor the place, and at long last they found the inscription she was looking for.

W-O-O-D-V-I-L-L-E C-L-O-S-E, made out the creator, who had been doing his best to learn the alphabet.

'Thank God for that,' she said, and he decided to overlook her earlier blasphemy.

The female hominid who opened the door had a sagging, used-up look and her eyes were moist behind their magnifiers. Nevertheless, as Irene crossed the threshold in response to the female hominid's resigned invitation, the creator instantly preferred the place to their own residence. Unlike Irene's floors, which were hard and bare, these were covered with thick fabric, soft underfoot and adorned with pictures of bright flowers. The ceiling was carved in recurrent swirls, like a cosmos in miniature, while the windows that had appeared completely draped from the outside were nothing of the kind: the fabric let in a silvery light and allowed anyone inside to see out. It was a fascinating trick, and the whole place was an unexpected delight. God would have liked the leisure to enjoy it, but that was not part of Irene's agenda. After the briefest of exchanges with the moist-eyed female, they were shown into a room at the rear and the creator found himself looking at the Special Hominid.

He had a moment of anxiety that Stefano might see through his disguise and remember him from the seeing-tube, which would have taken a lot of explaining to Irene. But his apprehension was needless. While God recognised all too well the green eyes that looked up at him from the table, there was no sign of any recognition back.

Irene was set on getting Stefano out of the house

'There's somewhere not too far away that I'd like to visit,' she said. 'We can have our talk there and kill two birds with one stone.'

So now they were back in her vehicle, crossing a featureless patch of straggly vegetation. They entered another belt of dwellings and, when Irene turned her head to the right, God caught a glimpse of something shiny at the end of one of the side roads. She put her foot hard on the brake and spun the steering-rotor to thrust them onto the smaller road, crossing the path of another vehicle which flashed its eyes in rebuke. At the end of this side-road, they emerged onto a long, broad expanse of grey road, running along what looked like it ought to be the sea, but was actually just wet sediment. The sea itself was a distant silver thread on the horizon. A trio of young hominids were amusing themselves by jumping on and off narrow boards on wheels down a flat incline onto the sediment. One or two older specimens made their way along the walkway, accompanied by quadrupeds on strings. On the sediment itself, abandoned marine conveyances sprawled uselessly. This was no more God's idea of exciting than it was Stefano's, but Irene seemed delighted. She slowed her vehicle to look over the low parapet at the sediment.

'The tide's perfect! Can you see any darker patches on the sand? That's what I really want to see.'

'Oil slicks? Lovely. If you want, I can look out for dog muck on the pavement too. Or some nice graffiti? There's some. "Spaz is a poof". Fabulous, isn't it?'

'You really are the most infuriating creature.'

'At least I don't kidnap people and take them to beaches from hell.'

'Ah yes, hell. We need to talk about that.'

She glanced at Stefano in time for the creator to see his face change colour, darkening from the normal pinkish cream into a redder shade.

'It's just an expression,' he said.

'Look!' she cried, slamming her foot hard down on the brake, making a large vehicle with blacked-out windows hoot angrily as it swerved past. 'See that patch over there, where the sand is darker, just beyond the red boat? That's part of the ancient forest. The dark bits are the remains of trees that were cut down five thousand years ago. Doesn't that make you tingle?'

The creator could not see Stefano's facial expression, because Irene was still looking out towards the sediment, but he could imagine it.

'The place I really want is further along,' she continued. 'I think we can park there and walk onto the beach. And look, the rain has stopped. Everything is turning out beautifully.'

'It looks exactly the same as the rest of this horrible prom to me,' said Stefano, as they stopped a little further down the trail.

She continued to ignore him, and they all got out of the vehicle – two out of three of them with great reluctance, and one of them sighing audibly. But Irene was impervious to Stefano's protests.

'You must explain to me what it's like to have no poetry in your soul,' she said, turning the key to secure the vehicle doors. 'What do you do for happiness?'

He opened his mouth to say something, but nothing came out.

She touched him on the arm.

'Sorry, that was below the belt. Happiness is in pretty short supply for you at the moment, isn't it? Believe it or not, I am here to help.'

She marched across the trail, making for a gap in the parapet where steps led down to the sediment. Behind her, God could hear Stefano hastening to catch up.

'What do you mean? Why exactly are you here?'

'Do you realise that without this wall, none of this land would be here?'

'Very interesting.'

'Oh, but it is. You wouldn't believe how fascinating. At the start of the nineteenth century, when Liverpool was beginning to develop as a port, they dredged the Mersey estuary. It messed up the currents and the tide started washing away the dunes of the shoreline. They used to go much further out. If these defences weren't here, the sea would have washed away the land we're standing on as well.'

'As far as I'm concerned, it's welcome to it. This place has always been depressing.'

Again, the creator could see his point. The entire vista was flat, grey and bleak.

Irene ignored him.

'When the dunes were swept out to sea, they found all sorts underneath,' she said. 'Flint arrows, gold brooches, the foundations of houses. Some of it was from the Stone Age. There had been serious traders here long before the Romans arrived, yet nobody knew about them. If the dredging had never happened, we would never have been any the wiser. Can you honestly say you don't find that just a little exciting?'

'OK, if you're into that kind of stuff, I guess so. I just don't see what it's got to do with me.'

'Ah, the sweet self-obsession! I've already told you this little expedition has nothing to do with you, my pet. I simply wanted a chat, and this is as good a place as any. Go and wait in the car if you want. I'm going to spend ten minutes satisfying my inner mudlark.'

She threw him the device to open the door of the craft, called the key, which he only just caught, then turned her back and walked onto the sediment, her shoes making sticky imprints and a faint squelch.

God was bemused. What was the point of bringing the boy here if she was prepared to abandon him?

'Hey wait!' shouted Stefano behind them. 'Since you've dragged me here, you may as well tell me what you came to say.'

Irene relaxed the two fingers which God realised she had held tightly crossed inside the pocket of her coat. From the relief flowing through her, he inferred that she had no real desire to leave him behind.

'I think that direction, don't you?'

She jumped across one of the liquid channels that flowed away from the parapet. Stopping to let Stefano catch up, she bent to examine a small coil of damp sediment.

'I want to talk about your beliefs,' she said.

'Hey?'

'You heard.'

'What have they got to do with you?'

'Absolutely nothing, my dear. But they have had a big impact on your boyfriend – or your ex-boyfriend, whatever he's meant to be.'

'I still don't understand how you know Adam. Where did you meet him?'

She paused for a moment.

'Do you know, that's a moot point. But never mind about that for now. We were talking about you and your beliefs. Actually, I don't really know what they are. All I know is what Adam told me, and I don't think you discussed them much with him.'

Stefano lowered his eyes.

'I suppose you know what happened on that other beach in the summer. What I saw?'

'You had a nasty fight with a wave, you swallowed half the sea, and while you were having the kiss of life, you imagined you were looking up a long, white tunnel of light. This came with a lovely ecstatic rush, and you thought you saw yourself from above. That's pretty much it, isn't it? Unlike you, you see, I do pay attention.'

'Not everyone takes it seriously.'

'I take it very seriously and I attend to the details.'

She stopped, and a winged biped that had been trotting ahead of them stopped too.

'It's a sandpiper,' she whispered, pointing.

God remembered the two birds she had talked about killing with a stone, and wondered if this was one of them. She put a finger to her mouth to indicate that Stefano should be quiet. When she resumed walking, the creature did the same, always keeping the same distance ahead.

Stefano showed no interest in the bird.

'I bet Adam didn't tell you I saw an eye,' he said. 'That's the part he really refused to accept.'

Now Irene gave up on the winged creature too. She was not even armed with a stone, the creator realised.

'Actually he did tell me that. Or, more accurately, he told me you thought you saw an eye. As far as I'm concerned, if you say you did, then that's what you saw.'

'Really? Thank you.'

'You're welcome,' she said. 'But what I still don't understand is why you had to abandon your life, your home and your job because you saw God.'

The creator was interested to hear this too. Without meaning to be, he had clearly been involved in this story from the very beginning, and he knew that something connected with that event on the sedimentary strip had profoundly unsettled the Special Hominid. He was still not clear what the problem was.

'Because I didn't think he existed before. Now I know he does, I'm frightened he'll punish me for all the things I did when I didn't believe in him.'

'What things?'

'You know. To do with my...lifestyle.'

'Being gay, you mean?'

He nodded, with an expression that even the creator could identify as dismal, and God sensed a surge of emotion within Irene's body, as if this information had moved her profoundly.

'And you think God will send you to hell for it?'

He nodded again.

The creator was finding this fascinating. He had no idea he wielded such influence, even if it was predicated on entirely imaginary things that he had no intention of doing.

Irene continued: 'Why would a God of love do that?'

'Because he says it. It's in the Bible. He told Moses. Everyone says it, everyone knows it. The bishops, the preachers in the street. Where have you been? And anyway, why do you care so much? I still don't understand why you've come here. And don't tell me it's to see this soggy patch of mud.'

Irene stopped on the damp sediment, and God could feel she was composing her thoughts.

'Two reasons,' she said at length. 'I had a son, Ollie. He'd be a bit older than you, if he were still here. He didn't make it. We still called it Aids back then. He died in great discomfort and fear, and it was a rotten waste of a beautiful young person with all his life ahead of him. So I hate to see other people, who still have that life ahead of them, throwing it away, through stupidity or fear or refusal to face up to what they need to do.'

Stefano's face crinkled.

'Believe me, I'm really sorry about your son. I lived through some of that too, and I can imagine how terrible it must have been for you. But you know, I also really hate it when people call me stupid.'

'I wasn't doing that. But you are afraid, and the reason for that is partly the stupidity of other people who have made you afraid. Look, I said there were two reasons. The second reason is that I believe in God, and I can tell you with utter certainty – as I once tried to tell you before, in the street in Hackney, only you don't remember – that he doesn't give a flying flip about you being gay. What he does want is for you to stop being so bloody beastly to your mother, your sister and whoever else's life you've ruined, notably Adam.'

God could see Stefano's face going red again.

'Before we left the house I had a chat with your sister,' Irene continued. She carried on walking now, towards the thin line of sea that was growing gradually thicker. 'A nice young woman, I thought, and obviously at her wits' end.'

Stefano hurried to catch up.

'Is she?'

'You know she is. You've turned up out of nowhere,

after goodness knows how long, and imposed yourself uninvited, mooching about the place without a smile or a nice word for anyone, like a black cloud that won't go away.'

'I know. But I hate it here. I always have.'

'So why did you come back? There's nothing keeping you here. If you hate it so much, go home.'

'I can't. I just can't.'

'Because London is such a hotbed of sin?'

'Because of who I am when I'm there.'

'But don't you see? That's who you are everywhere. It's why you're so miserable here, if only you'd realise it. You can't change who you are just by forcing yourself to stay somewhere you think you don't belong. At least you understood that when you were sixteen and you ran away from home – yes, your sister told me – even if you did treat your family appallingly in the process.'

She bent to retrieve something half-buried in the sediment but, whatever it was, it was not what she had hoped. She threw it away and another bird swooped, hoping to eat it, before flying off in disappointment. Perhaps Irene would kill this one, God thought, but the hominids just stood watching it go. Their back-and-forth dispute seemed temporarily forgotten, and even the creator was contented for as long as the moment lasted, contemplating the shiny expanse. It seemed less bleak now he had become used to his surroundings. There was a strange beauty to it all, and he felt almost at home with this small-scale, human version of infinity.

Irene broke the silence.

'It's getting pretty wet, isn't it?' she said. 'Maybe we ought to turn round.'

The shoreline parapet now seemed as distant as the sea had been. Irene's vehicle was no more than a red speck.

'But how do you know he doesn't care?' said Stefano abruptly. 'It's all right for you to say that. You're straight: you don't have to worry. You can believe what you want and if you're wrong, it doesn't really matter. To me, it will.'

'Because God is love; that's how I know.'

'That's not knowing, that's just what you want to believe. What if he isn't love? Or he only loves certain kinds of people? I mean, have you read Exodus?'

Irene was about to reply, but the creator himself was reaching the limits of his tolerance. He was cold and wet, they were a long way from the shore, and he was in no mood for any more of this tiresome speculation, in which each of them clung to their own version of wild make-believe.

'Hell's teeth, boy, don't you realise I am God?' he said, wheeling on Stefano. 'Let's just sort this out once and for all. Read my lips. I don't give an asteroid's whistle what any of you do with the things between your legs. Why don't you just go back to your damn boyfriend and give everyone a break? Or don't, I'm honestly not that bothered. Either way, you're not going to hell. Trust me, there's no such place.'

His grasp of idiom really was improving.

Stefano backed away, but his expression spelled more mirth than awe.

282

'You're God? Erm, right. Just as long as we've got that sorted.'

Oh God, thought the creator, for want of a better expression. He should have anticipated this. As far as Stefano was concerned, Irene had just announced her own divinity, and it was hardly surprising if he thought she was mad. God looked over the boy's shoulder at the horizon. A clap of thunder and a flash of lightning would do nicely now, but he was by no means confident he could pull it off.

Stefano was looking at the sky too. 'You're right, though. We'd better get a move on. The tide's coming back, and it's going to chuck it down in a minute.'

He set off at a brisk pace, turning back only when he realised that his companion was not following.

'What's the matter?'

Irene and the creator did not move.

'Look, I'm sorry, all right? You can be God if you want. But can we go back to the car before we get drenched?'

Without waiting for a reply, he resumed his walk.

God closed Irene's eyes and counted to ten. It was galling of his target to have an attack of unshakeable atheism at this precise moment.

'Stefano!' he shouted, in a creatorly voice that made every winged biped on the sediment take flight in unison.

The boy was already trembling when he turned round. Now his mouth fell open at the sight of Irene levitating a foot's length above the beach.

'Oh fuck,' he said, then clapped his hand to his mouth and sank to his knees with a wet thwack.

Worrying that he might have gone too far, God allowed Irene to take control of her own body again.

'Where was I?' she said, looking around at the soggy expanse. 'And what on earth are you doing down there?'

'You were telling me you were God and I didn't believe you. But now I think I do,' said Stefano in a small voice.

'Will you please get up?'

She held out a hand to pull him off the sediment. Having restored him to an upright position, she produced a piece of white fabric from a pouch in her upper garment.

'Here, use this to get the worst off your jeans. What were you thinking?'

Instead of taking it, Stefano just stood there.

'Don't do this to me,' he said in an even tinier voice, barely audible now. 'You're really doing my head in.'

The creator realised this was fun. He was causing havoc, and it could potentially be a hoot.

'My pet, I'm sorry if I've sounded harsh. All I was doing was setting it out logically because I don't want you to wreck your life for no reason. I'm really not trying to play God myself, if that's what you mean – although to be honest you're not making a lot of sense at the moment.'

'Who's talking now – you or her?' whispered Stefano.

God was enjoying himself far too much to let the boy out of his misery, and made no move to override his hostess.

'Are you all right?' she said. 'I'm afraid I may have pushed you too hard.'

'Asteroid's whistle,' said Stefano, making the shape of the words more than uttering them. 'Do asteroids whistle?'

The creator relented.

'She doesn't know I'm here,' he said, using her voice this time, since the divine version was evidently too intimidating for ordinary conversation. To dispel any further doubt, he raised Irene's body a foot's length above the sand once again. This levitation trick was nothing special when he put his mind to it.

'Oh God,' said Stefano.

'The very same,' said the creator, pleased with the witticism.

Stefano was visibly trembling.

'Are you actually inside her?'

'Yes.'

'But…why?'

God hesitated.

'It's complicated,' he said.

'Are you here because of me?'

'In a way,' said God. 'But not the way you think.'

Stefano was pinching a piece of his own skin between his thumb and finger.

'Am I dreaming this?' he said.

'Not unless I am too.'

'So you are real?'

'I'm as real as you are.'

Stefano ran a trembling hand through his hair, leaving a streak of wet sediment.

'What about her? Is she real?'

'Of course she's real.'

'And how long have you been there?'

'A while.'

'All day?'

God chuckled. 'Longer than that. A few weeks.'

'So that means you must know Adam too?'

The creator nodded Irene's head.

'I've even been to the place you live. Twice.'

The creator had a sudden urge to pour out everything about his adventure to Stefano: all his impressions of the past few weeks; his mix-up when he arrived in the wrong body; the strange things he had learned about hominid behaviour; his exciting new discoveries, like sherry, football and Happy Meals. Aside from his brief exchange with Adam on the doorstep of their flat a month or so ago, this was the first conversation he had ever had, not just during his visit to Earth, but in his entire existence.

But Stefano was stuck in his own worries.

'Am I losing my mind?' he whispered, apparently as much to himself as to the creator.

'No, you haven't lost your mind.'

'So what are you doing here? You said it was because of me. Have you come to punish me? You said you couldn't give an asteroid's whistle...'

'I don't.'

'Really? What about the Bible – all that stuff in the Old Testament?'

'Nothing to do with me. I'd never heard of it until a few weeks ago.'

'You're kidding! I thought you wrote it?'

Irene's body made the shrugging gesture.

'And you're serious that hell doesn't exist? I mean, this

isn't some kind of trick, where you're tempting me, and if I say the wrong thing, you send me to hell?'

'It's not a trick. Hell honestly doesn't exist.'

'Wow. So that means…everyone goes to heaven?'

The creator sighed. It was a shame to disappoint these poor, trusting creatures, but he could not in all conscience indulge their fantasies.

'Not really,' he said.

'Oh, so only some people? Where do the others go then?'

'Nobody goes there. Heaven doesn't exist either.'

Stefano's mouth fell open.

'You are shitting me!' he said, then clapped his hand over his mouth. 'Sorry, language. But this is really huge. It doesn't exist for anyone? Not even for Jesus, or, I don't know, Florence Nightingale…or Mother Teresa?'

'Not even for them. I have no idea who they are.'

'You have no idea who Jesus is?'

'Him, yes, just about. But only recently. The other two, no.'

Stefano's eyes were wide.

'But…I mean…how…I mean…this is massive. Why are you telling me this? Do I have to tell the world? Because I don't think they'll be pleased. And they may not believe me.'

'It doesn't bother me,' said the creator. 'Do what you like.'

Stefano's forehead crinkled again.

'So where do you live?' he said at length. 'Isn't that heaven?'

'You can call it that if you want, but I guarantee you, there's no one else there,' said the creator. 'Think about it. There are billions of you, just your species on this planet alone. How is it supposed to work?'

'You don't have to take all of us. Just the ones who deserve it. And only the Christians, obviously. Other religions have got their own gods.'

'Have they?'

Now it was the creator's turn to learn something.

'Yes. Though I think you look after the Jews as well, and maybe the Muslims too. I'm not really sure.'

'These other gods – do they have their own heavens too?'

'I suppose they must do. I don't know much about other religions, though. I'd have thought you might know.'

'Why?'

'Well, you know, you've probably met them.'

God shook Irene's head.

'It's honestly just me up there.'

Even as the creator said it, the thought made him sad. He could not imagine how different his existence might be if there really were other gods to share his heavens with, to whom he could return and have a good laugh about the ludicrous expectations of these Earthling hominids.

'So what do you do all day?' Stefano persisted. 'I mean, if you're not deciding which of us are good and bad?'

God was too embarrassed to tell him the honest truth, which was 'not very much'.

Instead he said: 'You're not the only planet in the

universe, you know. Do you have any idea how many there are?'

Stefano remembered something from a long time ago.

'Actually I do. It's...not a gazillion...a sextillion. Or maybe ten sextillions, I can't remember. No wait, maybe that's stars not planets. Are there more planets than stars, or less?'

The creator realised his own knowledge was in danger of being found wanting, and he had no wish to get bogged down in detail.

'You can take it from me, it's more than you can possibly imagine,' he said. 'You hominids are really very insignificant in cosmic terms.'

'So how come you were looking at me?'

The question took the creator by surprise.

'When?' he said.

'I saw you. I had an accident when I was swimming in the sea, and I looked up this long white tunnel, and I saw an eye at the end. Some people don't believe me, but that was you, wasn't it?'

'I don't really know how that happened,' said God. This conversation had taken a strange turn, so that he was the one who was being interrogated. 'It's never happened before.'

'I knew it! I knew it was you! But wait...' The triumphant smile froze on Stefano's lips. 'If you saw me, and it never happened before, is that why you're here? To silence me?' He sank to his knees and put his hands together in entreaty. 'I won't tell anyone, honestly. We can pretend it never happened.'

'Please get up,' said the creator. 'I'm really not that bothered. In any case, you've told everyone already.'

Stefano seemed unconvinced, because he remained cowering on the damp sediment.

The creator sighed.

'If you must know, I have a tube. It's the way I see everything. Not just here, the whole universe. And one day I looked down and you were looking back at me. This had never happened before, so I was intrigued. I followed you back to your flat, and my tube got stuck in the window. I had to come to Earth to get it out. That's all, nothing more. Will you get up from there now?'

Stefano slowly got back to his feet, looking dazed.

'So…this tube…is it still stuck in my flat?'

'No, I released it.'

'I see. That was when you met Adam.'

'That's right.'

'But he didn't know that you were…well…you?'

'No.'

'And that was the whole reason you came to Earth, that you're here in her body?'

'Yes. But I was also curious to see what it was like.'

'What?'

'This. Everything. What it looked like from down here.'

Stefano looked out across the sediment, and a note of his old disdain returned to his voice.

'Why would you want to see what this looks like?'

'Maybe not precisely here.'

'Oh God.'

The creator was on the verge of repeating one of

290

his witticisms acknowledging his awareness of the use of his own name as an exclamation. Then he saw the look on Stefano's face and turned to follow his gaze, to where the distant line of sea was neither thin nor distant any more. It had become a thick band, and one of the marine conveyances that had been lying on its side had now righted itself. Ahead of them, back towards dry land, channels in the sediment were filling in to leave a shrinking archipelago of islands in the lapping liquid.

'We'd better hurry,' said Stefano. 'Come on. I thought you knew – I mean she knew – what she was doing. We should never have come so far.'

Having taken full control of Irene's motor functions, God now did his best to keep up, following the boy as he tried to plot a course across what remained of the sediment. He wanted to ask what was happening, what bizarre property of the sea made it advance on the land with so little warning. But he sensed that it might undermine his new-won authority to reveal such ignorance. In any case, his guide was too far ahead.

'The tide comes out of nowhere on these beaches because the sand is so flat,' Stefano shouted as he paused to seek out the best way. 'They used to tell us about it at school. I should have thought about it, but she was so busy bossing me around and I just...'

He broke off abruptly, and to God's surprise he started to laugh, smacking his hand against the skin above his eyes.

'What am I thinking?' he said. 'We don't need to hurry, do we? You can just send the tide back!'

God peered back at the encroaching flood. It was a shame to shatter the boy's illusions, but he shook Irene's head.

'I'm not sure I can,' he said, and carried on walking.

Now it was Stefano who hastened to catch up.

'What do you mean?'

The creator decided honesty was the best policy. 'I don't even know what this "tide" is.'

'But...you must know! How can you not? It goes up and down. It's something to do with the moon.'

'Well, there you are. I can't change that. It's not what I do.'

It was true that he had been exploring his powers lately and, little by little, had been discovering he was capable of more than he had thought. Turning back the sea, however, seemed a more complicated business than directing a seeing-tube or rising a few inches off the sand. Especially if it involved moving the moon, which he now knew to be the rock those Earthling travellers had been so keen to reach. Was that perhaps why they wanted to go there, to stop the tides?

'Why not? You flooded the Earth and parted the Red Sea. Surely you can push back a poxy bit of tide!'

'I didn't do those things. I don't know anything about them.'

'In that case what's the point of being God?'

The creator laughed bitterly.

'Sometimes I ask myself the same question.'

A few minutes earlier, the young hominid had cowered before him, but now Stefano's expression spoke more of disappointment.

'If you can't turn the tide back, we need to get a move on,' he said. 'Come on, this way.'

In Irene's body, the creator hurried after him.

The shoreline parapet had been getting gradually closer, but now a widening expanse of water blocked their way. The only way across was over to one side, where one narrowing path of sediment remained.

'Sorry,' called Stefano. 'We're going to have to run.'

God pushed Irene's body into an imitation of his companion's gait.

'This is so ridiculous!' the boy complained, breathing heavily. 'I can't believe I've got God's life in my hands. Haven't you…I mean hasn't she got a phone? You know, a mobile?'

Suffering equally from the exertion, the creator shook his hostess' head. 'She says she doesn't believe in them.'

'Shit!'

'I'm sorry about that.'

'No, I mean…'

Stefano pointed ahead, to where their shrinking path had disappeared altogether. To make matters worse, rain was falling too.

'We're definitely going to get wet,' said Stefano. 'Are you absolutely, totally sure you can't do anything with the tide? You don't need to turn it back. Just hold it off for ten minutes.'

The creator had no wish to put it to the test and then fail. It would do nothing for his dignity.

'Quite sure.'

'This is so stupid! You don't seem to realise – you could drown too!'

God contemplated the suggestion, then shook Irene's head.

'She might, but I wouldn't. I can leave whenever I choose.'

He hoped so, at any rate.

'Oh great. You're all right, then.'

The boy definitely had an attitude problem now.

'So what are you still doing here? Why haven't you gone back already?'

'I'll stay a little longer.'

The creator had never had an adrenaline rush before, and had no way of knowing that was what it was. All he knew was that it felt remarkably good.

'Suit yourself. But you're going to have to wade through that, and I warn you, it's going to be cold. I should take your shoes and socks off. We may as well go the direct way instead of round there. Follow me. Here goes.'

Stefano removed the two layers of protectors from his own feet and ran into the channel. At its deepest, the liquid came halfway up his legs. He turned round to check on the creator.

'Hey, that's not fair!' he protested at the sight that greeted him.

Out of politeness, God did his best to stifle the laugh that was trying to force itself out. He was hovering Irene's body just above the surface of the liquid. He now followed his guide across it without getting her feet wet. Stefano meanwhile stumbled into a dip in the submerged sediment that brought the water to the top of his legs. He shouted in anguish as he tried to hold his own shoes clear. This time the creator could not suppress his open mirth. He tried to rearrange Irene's features into a serious expression as his angry companion righted himself and turned round again.

'This is all your fault! Or her fault,' Stefano shouted, splashing on faster now that he no longer cared about his garments.

He emerged from the channel and resumed his fast gait across the last stretch of sediment that would bring them safely to the parapet. Climbing the slope to regain dry land at last, he tried to squeeze the worst of the liquid from his lower garments. The pair of them stood side by side in the rain for a moment, panting as they tried to get their breath back. Then Stefano, still carrying his shoes, walked awkwardly across the trail back to Irene's craft.

The creator realised he would need to cede control back to his hostess. Bad as she was at driving, he had even less idea of how to do it than she.

'Have you got my car key?' Irene said.

Stefano handed it over, not noticing the change, and she clicked the doors unlocked.

'Just look at that weather,' she said, slamming her door closed. 'Good heavens, I'm wet, but you're absolutely soaked.'

Stefano scrutinised her critically.

'So you're back.'

'What do you mean? I've never been away.'

'I mean, it's Irene now, isn't it?'

'Who else would it be?'

'Believe me, you don't want to know.'

God was shaking so much with mirth he was surprised his hostess could not feel it.

Stefano's eyes blazed.

'And yes, since you come to mention it, my jeans are wet through, because you nearly got us both killed. I thought you knew what you were doing. But you didn't think about the tide, did you?'

'Honestly, I've no idea what you're talking about. You should get those jeans off while I put the heater on. Come on, don't be shy – believe it or not I've seen a man's legs before. But how you can say I nearly killed you…'

'Look!'

He pointed through the rain-spattered window at the sea, which had now come all the way to the parapet.

Irene's mouth dropped open.

'That wasn't there a moment ago.'

'Yes it was.'

She put a hand to her head.

'Do you know, it's an extraordinary thing, but I've no memory of getting back here. Oh dear. I hope I haven't blacked out again.'

'You were fine. If you'd blacked out, you'd have fallen over and you'd have mud all over you. As you may notice, I'm the one with the soaking clothes here.'

'So how come I'm not as wet as you?'

'You…you found a better way to get across.'

'Did I really? I honestly don't remember.'

'I hope you're pleased with yourself,' he said softly.

'Why?' said Irene.

'I wasn't talking to you.'

God was enjoying this joke as much as he could recall ever having enjoyed anything. Stefano was clearly consumed with frustration, but it served him right for his disrespectful attitude.

Irene got the car started and drove forward in search of a place to turn it round. She dealt with the manoeuvre ineptly, going forwards and backwards five times before she accomplished it. The creator expected derision from Stefano, but the boy seemed to have a more pressing concern.

'Have you gone, or can you still hear me?' he said softly.

'What?' said Irene, distracted by having to cross a line of oncoming vehicles to turn right.

Stefano would not be deterred by God's lack of response.

'Just send a sign if you're still there,' he pleaded.

'I still can't hear when you mumble,' said Irene, peering into her mirror as she finally accomplished the turn.

The creator relented. He could not carry on appearing and disappearing at a moment's notice, but he could at least put the boy out of his misery. As they re-entered the featureless patch of straggly vegetation which they had passed through on their way, he gave the steering-rotor a nudge so the craft wobbled suddenly.

Irene gripped the rotor in alarm.

'Sorry, I don't know what happened there.'

Stefano made no attempt to stifle a triumphant laugh of his own.

'It's not funny,' said Irene. 'At least I'm not one of the eighty percent of men who think they're above average behind the wheel. Anyway, you'll have to forgive my senior moment, but I can't quite remember where we'd got to in our discussion.'

She turned and looked inquiringly at Stefano.

'I'm not sure you really want to know,' he said.

26

Irene awoke in the dark in a strange room, and for a moment she had no idea where she was. Then it came back to her. Having returned shattered from a fascinating but fraught exploration of the pre-Roman settlement on the Irish Sea coast, she had let herself be persuaded to stay the night rather than drive straight back to London.

She seemed to have had another of her funny turns out on the beach and, by all accounts, she and Stefano were lucky to have escaped the advancing tide, so setting out for a further five hours behind the wheel would undoubtedly have been rash. She had been given Katie's old room, a plain box with magnolia walls and a swirly carpet, which was where she was now. She was not in bed, though. She was lying on top of a mauve candlewick bedspread, fully dressed, and it was not yet morning, she realised, or even night-time. She looked at her watch and saw that it was just gone six o'clock in the evening, and now she remembered properly: she had been so exhausted that Marion Carter had hustled her upstairs for a nap.

From down below, she could hear the comforting metallic clinking sounds of a meal being prepared. Those were not noises she ever heard in her own house, and she lay still for a moment, enjoying the novelty of being looked after, with someone else taking charge of the domestic chores. Then she sat up, rubbed the sleep out of her eyes and rummaged in her bag for a comb. Something had changed, she thought to herself as she frowned at her reflection in the mirror beside the wardrobe. She felt somehow lighter, as if some inner freight had departed. Had her conversation on the beach really been so successful that she had shed some kind of burden in the process? It was surprising, but gratifying, to think so.

'Are you feeling better, Irene?' called Marion from the kitchen, as she came down the stairs. 'You looked worn out before, and we couldn't possibly allow you to drive back down south like that.'

'Thank you for your kindness,' said Irene. 'I'm sorry to impose like this, but I fear you're right – I was being a little over-ambitious, and I might have been a danger to myself and others on the motorway.'

'Think nothing of it. It's the least I could do, with you coming all this way just to bring a bag of clothing – especially when you'd never hardly met the lad.'

'Well, it wasn't really about the clothes. I'd heard a lot about him and, as I said, I wanted a quiet word. I only hope it's done some good.'

'You certainly had some effect,' said Marion. 'He's gone out on his own. He never normally sticks his nose outside the front door.'

'Although we don't know where,' chipped in Katie, who was stirring milk into a sachet of cheese sauce on the stove. 'Is lasagne all right for you? You're not veggie, are you?'

'No, indeed. Delicious, thank you.'

Later, as they sat around the dining table, with Stefano still not back, she told them about Ollie.

'I knew he was different from an early age, the way a mother can always tell, and it was hard to know what to do,' she said. 'I was on my own, because he never knew his father, and I wanted to let him be himself. For a long time, I blamed myself for what happened. If I had laid down some more rules, stopped him going out so much, not lived in a wicked, tempting city, he wouldn't have got infected when he did. After a while, though, I came to realise that we had both just been very unlucky, Ollie and me. We were in the wrong place at the wrong time, and he was a sitting duck for this terrible new disease at a time when nobody knew anything about it. Maybe things could have turned out differently if one or other of us had done different things, but there's no way of knowing that for certain, because you can't turn back the clock. And if I'd stopped him going out and being himself, I might have lost him in some other way.'

'Like I did with our Stee, you mean?'

'Bluntly, yes. I'm sorry to say it, but it's true. And from what I gather, the reason your Stee is still with us is that he was lucky enough to meet a very responsible older friend almost as soon as he arrived in London, otherwise he might easily have ended up the same way as my Ollie. Don't get me wrong, I'm not saying it's all your fault – I wouldn't be so crass. But, if you'll forgive me for saying so, you have to find a way of getting to know who he really is.'

'If he'll let us,' said Katie.

Marion took a deep breath.

'Who's this Adam, then?' she said. 'Is he going to go back to him?'

Irene chewed a forkful of pasta, thinking carefully before replying.

'Adam is a very nice young man who has been having a difficult time. I'm afraid Stefano has caused him a lot of pain too – so you're not alone in that. As a result, he's very angry with the world and has ended up counting litter, bless him, which really isn't healthy.'

'How do you count litter?' said Katie.

'Good question, but he's been trying. Anyway, I rather suspect his life is going to move in a different direction quite soon, and his focus will change.'

She was thinking of how comfortable Adam and James had seemed in each other's company, which was precisely what she had hoped for. However, she reminded herself of Peg's stern warning that this was entirely their own business, and she must not meddle.

'So, for the moment,' she continued, 'I think Stefano's place is here, with you, as long as he behaves himself and stops moping. That's what I've told him, anyway.'

'Do you think he'll listen to you?' said Katie. 'He doesn't take any notice of anything we say.'

Irene was about to say she could not guarantee it, but she hoped so, when they heard the sound of a key turning in the front door. She noticed Marion and Katie glance at each other nervously.

'Sorry I'm late,' said Stefano, unbuttoning the grey coat that Irene had brought up from London. 'Is there any food left?'

He actually smiled, although cautiously, as if he were trying it for size.

'Sit yourself down here, son,' said Marion. 'Katie, can you get him a plate?'

'Where have you been, Stef?' said Katie, as she cut a wide slice of lasagne for him.

He took a deep breath

'First I went to the cemetery,' he said. He was blushing, and it was clearly an effort for him to get it out. 'Katie, you made me realise that I owed my dad an apology. So I went and had a long talk to him.' He swallowed. 'It's something I should have done before, and it would have been better if I'd done it when he was still... But you know, better late than never, hey?'

For a moment, Irene thought the three of them – mother, daughter and son – were going to sob in unison. She was certainly in danger of joining them. But Stefano had more to say, and he made a visible effort to compose himself as he went on.

'And then I went over to Liverpool,' he said. 'The good news is, I've got a job. In a bar.'

Both his mother and sister's mouths fell open, and the revelation seemed to banish all thoughts of the cemetery.

'That's good news, son,' said Marion. 'But why go all the way to Liverpool? There are bars on this side of the water.'

'Not the kind where I'd fit in. I'm sorry, mum, but I'd

be rubbish in an ordinary pub. I don't know how to act or what to say to anyone. But I do know about the gay scene, and I found a place where they're keen to have me. I can get there and back on the train, or I could maybe get a scooter if I have to stay late. But it's a job, and I'll be able to pay rent, so I hope you'll be pleased. If it's still OK to stay here, that is.'

'Yes, son. I'll be happy to have you.'

Marion grasped his hand across the table, and they smiled shyly at one another.

Irene cleared her throat cautiously.

'And…working in whatever fleshpots they have over there is going to be all right with you? Regarding your immortal soul, I mean?'

'Yes, I think I'm OK with that now.'

'So I must have said something right?'

She glowed with delight at her own unexpected success. She was surely allowed to commit the sin of pride every once in a while, so long as she did not let it go to her head.

'If it was something I said, I'm delighted to have persuaded you,' she added.

'It was certainly something that came out of your mouth,' he said.

She thought she detected a slight smirk, but she let it go.

'I'm pleased to hear it,' she said. 'And I don't mean to keep laying down the law. As I've already said to you, it's not my place to play God…'

He was smirking again, but this time she frowned, and

his expression became immediately more sober.

'But you really do need to talk properly to Adam,' she continued. 'You should let him know where he stands, if nothing else.'

'How is Adam?' he asked.

'I think he may have turned a corner, but trust me, Stefano, it's no thanks to you.'

'Actually my name is Steven,' he said. 'Steven Carter. You can call me Stee if you want.'

Irene noticed Marion's eyes widen. They were brimming with tears.

'But yes, point taken. I'm sorry I'm not coming back with you. This is where I belong for the time being. But I know I owe Adam a big apology. Can you tell him I'll call him very soon, just as soon as my head is a bit more sorted?'

The next morning, when she was folding the overnight things she had borrowed from his mother, Stefano appeared in the doorway of her bedroom.

'I just want to know if...' he began. 'I mean, I wasn't sure if...'

She looked at him askance.

'Go on.'

He seemed awkward, and he was looking at her strangely, as if he were trying to signal something with his eyes. Suddenly he dropped his voice.

'Are you still there?' he hissed.

'Yes, I'm still here, my pet,' said Irene. 'Is everything all right?'

He smiled sadly.

'Yes, I reckon so. Never mind, forget I said anything. I'll leave you to get ready.'

He turned away, but when he was halfway down the stairs he looked back.

'Thank you, by the way. For everything. You did kind of play God, but in a good way. I'll never forget it.'

'You're welcome,' she said.

She had not been looking for gratitude, but it was nice to be appreciated.

27

BACK ON THE BRIDGE of the universe, the creator scanned
his cosmos and was momentarily dazed by seeing all of
it at once. He had grown so used to the tiny perspective
of a hominid that he had forgotten how limited that view
had been.

Getting back had been reassuringly easy. After all that
worry about whether it would be possible, the process
had been entirely straightforward. He arrived back to
find his own end of the tube hanging loyally where he
had left it. When he coaxed it gently, it came speeding
back in a perfect retracting arc from Earth. All was well,
and he could afford to feel more than a little pleased with
himself.

As he adjusted back to his old routine, he realised what
a pleasure it was to leave behind the physical demands
of human existence. No more worrying about refuelling,
garbing or ablution. No more having to coordinate activity
with the rotation of the planet. No more competing for
space with billions of similar beings, all of them desperate
to make the most of their minute span of consciousness
and to leave their mark on the rock.

Part of him felt bad for leaving so abruptly, but it had
felt necessary. He had realised, out there on the sediment,

that the experience was changing him. Not long before, he would have considered it absurd even to think about intervening to prolong a hominid existence. Yet, with the sea encroaching, he probably would have pulled the Special Hominid to safety. It would have cost him nothing and it would have been a generous act. But it would also have set a precedent, which might have had far-reaching implications. Where would all this sentimentality end?

He had enjoyed his first-ever conversation with another being. For a short time he had felt a real connection with the Special Hominid, who had turned out to be remarkably level-headed when the creator had finally revealed himself. For the duration of their encounter, God had entertained the genuine possibility that they might forge some kind of ongoing, lasting friendship. Stefano's obvious shock, however, when the creator revealed his own ignorance of notable hominid individuals, and of the various events in terrestrial history in which he was meant to have had a hand, had made it clear how incompatible their perspectives on the universe really were. Hominids could never have a realistic grasp of how insignificant they were, of the different scales on which they and the creator existed, however level-headed they might be.

Shortly after he got back, he heard the faintest whisper from far below, as the Special Hominid called: 'Are you still there? If you haven't gone yet, just give me another sign. There are so many things I forgot to ask. I wanted you to tell me about the rest of the universe. Are there other forms of life out there? Please tell me. I really want to know…'

Not responding made God feel mildly guilty, but the fact was that he had no means to do so, and this dialogue could not continue now that he was back in his proper place. The Special Hominid would get the message soon enough that the creator was no longer with him. He would doubtless feel aggrieved for a while, and perhaps feel the pain of abrupt abandonment. Then he would have to decide whether to tell his fellow hominids the truth about their precious heaven and hell, and be despised or disbelieved, or to keep the whole thing to himself. It would be a difficult and lonely choice, but God himself had spent his entire existence making solitary decisions, so he was not going to waste too much sympathy. For his part, it was clear that his own time on Earth had run its course. The clinching factor was the prospect of another journey back down the grey thundering trail with Irene at the steering-rotor. That would have been too much to bear.

Glad as he was to be back home, he could not help feeling that something was missing. It took him a while to work out what it was, but then he realised: his solitary place at the bridge of the universe was a good deal emptier than the heaven of the Special Hominid's imagination. He could not quite picture a celestial realm populated by every hominid that had ever walked the Earth, and in fact the idea made him shudder: the logistical problems alone were utterly prohibitive. However, the yawning gap between the hominid vision of heaven and the creator's everyday reality served to underline his lonely situation. One of the Special Hominid's remarks in particular stuck in his mind: Stefano had talked about other gods having their own heavens for different sets of hominid followers. These places were no doubt as fanciful as the one the creator himself was supposed to run. Nevertheless, the idea of additional gods, even imaginary ones, with whom he might share the universe made him wistful. If only they really existed.

But they did not exist, he told himself, and there was nothing he could do about it. He had far better put the thought out of his mind.

As time went on, he wondered how his hostess was faring. He pictured her leading her groups around the city and talking to Emmie the quadruped. She would not miss him, of course, because she had never known he was there, but he felt a great affection for Irene, having shared her every thought, sensation and bodily function in the course of his adventure. Once or twice he found himself reaching for his tube to see what she was doing. It occurred to him that he might perhaps co-ordinate his investigation with the screening of football, which was definitely something he missed. On further reflection, he realised that would be pointless, because she would never have the tee-vee adjusted to the right setting, and he would not be able to control the buttons on the wand from this distance. Nevertheless, it would be nice to look in on her, football or not. After one particularly uneventful day on the bridge of the universe, he checked the time of day on her part of Earth, by looking at the layout of the planet in relation to their sun-star, to see if she was likely to be there. Discovering that it was roughly supper-time, in hominid terms, he was on the point of sending his tube shooting back down in the direction of Earth when his action was stayed by a sound he had not thought about since before the start of his terrestrial escapade. It was a deep, distant murmur – the same oscillating vibration that had caught his attention before his visit to Earth.

It started from his left, then continued on his right, before bouncing maddeningly back to where it had started as soon as he had turned to follow it. It was exactly as it had been before, just as mysterious, just as illogical, just as unnerving.

This was ridiculous. He had always accepted that his cosmos was a noisy place. But noises needed sources, and distant zig-zagging ones were confusing, because it was hard to see how they could have a proper origin. It was time to get to the bottom of this mystery once and for all.

Tube in hand, he cast it as far as it would go towards the source on his left, or what had been his left until he started spinning around chasing it. There was an immediate problem, though. Normally, if he wanted to investigate some kind of noise, he would know where it was coming from and could send his tube to just the right place. That was how he had encountered Stefano. Now, however, it would not work like that. His instinct, or sense of direction, or whatever it was that told him which way to pitch the tube, had deserted him and he found himself surveying his cosmos blankly, without a clue how to proceed.

The noise reverted to the opposite side, and he

attempted to dispatch his tube after it, but once more it was no good. This was getting annoying, and he would have flailed his tube in frustration, had he not remembered just in time how little he wanted to disable it all over again. Instead he let it droop aimlessly, showing a gallery of ever-changing images as it dangled through the heavens.

It came to rest on a damp rock towards the centre of a galaxy about half as far again away as Earth. He glowered out of habit through the seeing-end and found himself looking at a circular expanse of water. It was hard to know the scale without any points of reference, but he could see all the edges of it, fringed with pink and purple rocks, putting the drab geology of Earth to shame. And now there was a point of reference after all: in the middle of the lake was a creature of some kind, with five limbs crossed under itself and four eyes around the top of its shiny yellow head. It was floating on a makeshift pink vessel that looked like it could be a giant leaf. What was clear was that the creature was in distress. It was rubbing three of its limbs together in an agitated fashion and mewing in a manner that communicated alarm.

The distressed pentaped was clearly very young. On one side of the pond, a larger version of the creature was gesticulating and calling instructions, as if to try and effect a rescue. To add to the drama, on the other side, another adult pentaped was waving and mewing too, and it was clear that the adrift youngster did not know which of them to listen to. It turned its four eyes from one to the other in an attempt to keep up, making its pink vessel bob in little twists to left and right as it now pointed at this shore, now at that. God knew how it felt: all that turning back and forth was just what he had been doing with his own oscillating nuisance. Suddenly it hit him. This pond was like his own cosmos – a big circular expanse with himself at the centre. He was the equivalent of the little floating creature on its leaf, trying to follow exchanges from *outside* the expanse. Why had he not thought of that before?

Leaving the yellow pentaped to its fate, he pulled the tube back towards him. As he watched it rattle and retract up into his grasp, he listened hard for the oscillations, and for the first time he noticed there was a definite difference between the noises on the two sides. The one on the left was deeper and more sonorous than the one on the right, which was altogether lighter in tone. The contrast was so obvious, he wondered why he had not noticed it before. Now it made complete sense. He had been listening not to one thing, but two, and they were both outside his own universe, talking across it like the two adult pentapeds calling to their youngster on the pond. The only difference was that those pentapeds were talking to the creature in the middle, whereas these two seemed to be talking over God and his cosmos, without the slightest regard for him or it. That was not the point, though. If they were talking over his universe, they must be somewhere in the Greater Multiverse, and the only entities capable of communicating from one to the other out there were not creatures at all. They must be deities.

God was not alone after all.

The question was what to do about it. Actually, he knew already. Not so long ago he would have lingered and agonised, mulling over the potential consequences as part of a grand cosmic delaying tactic and hoping the whole thing would go away, so he could then rue his missed opportunity at leisure. That was before his terrestrial adventure. The cautious, prevaricating, never-doing-anything deity that he had once been now belonged to a bygone age, which seemed a lot longer ago than the cluster of Earth-days it had actually been. The new God would not hang back. If there were other deities out there, he wanted to meet them, and he was not about to blow the chance by fretting over everything that could go wrong. Now was the time to shrug off solitude and do something he should have done aeons ago. He would go out and explore.

After a brief debate with himself as to which of the two directions to take, he opted for the higher-pitched noise on his right. It sounded the less forbidding of the pair; for all his new-found boldness there was no point in throwing caution entirely to the space-wind. Then he let his tube swing adrift and set out on the journey to the periphery of his realm.

This time he barely noticed the changing configurations of the galaxies he was passing through. As the rocks and burning stars thinned out, it did not occur to him to ponder how much bigger the cosmos had got since he had last been that way. He did not worry whether or not he would be able to get back, as he reached the fuzzy periphery of his own world. He pressed on, the cloud lifted, and he found himself on the outside of his own world, hovering in the enhanced lightness of the wider multiverse. And with it came an equally enhanced hum from somewhere way out in front of him, murmuring confirmation that he had been right to look beyond the confines of his own universe.

The old creator would, once again, have hesitated here, at least to look back on his own world and worry for one last time about whether he was doing the right thing. But the prospect of divine company overcame all his previous anxieties. Without so much as a backward glance, God set out into the void.

It was time to introduce himself to the neighbours.

THE END

Afterword

I got the idea for *The Hurtle of Hell* – a novel which exposes religion to the rigours of rationalism in a light-hearted way – from a magazine about the paranormal.

In 2004, as an unwelcome part of my day job as a newspaper feature writer, I was looking through a publication not unlike the fictional *Paranormal Today*. Headlines such as 'Alien Abduction in Brazil' and 'the CIA and Noah's Ark' made me cringe, but my eye had been caught by the cover story, about near-death experiences.

One of the people the article quoted was Professor Susan Blackmore, then of the University of the West of England, who has made a career of subjecting paranormal claims to scientific scrutiny. Her starting point was that near-death experiences involving tunnels of light are a real neurological phenomenon. She knew that, because she had had one herself. She had then developed a theory to explain the experiences.

It was news to me that anyone could have one, even if they had no religious belief. It got me wondering what would happen if I, as an atheist, had an 'NDE', as they are known. If I was unaware of the neurological explanation, would it suddenly make me believe in God?

This was a time when the churches were among

the fiercest opponents of efforts to dismantle Britain's discriminatory anti-gay laws. In those days, it was barely possible to turn on the radio or television without being told by some senior cleric that homosexual behaviour was a sin. (It is a mark of how much the world has changed in a decade and a half that a party leader who appeared to believe such things at the 2017 general election was pilloried in the media and his career brought to a premature end; in the early Noughties, such views were part of the mainstream.)

What, I wondered, if a credulous gay person suddenly got religion? What would it do to their life? At the time, I was part of the inaugural intake of the City University Novel Writing MA – the first such course where you had to complete a novel to graduate – and I started to base my novel on this idea. As the idea took shape, I had another idea. Would it be over the top, I asked course director Harriett Gilbert, to introduce God as a character, just in the prologue?

Harriett's eyes lit up, and it became clear from other colleagues' feedback that the creator would need to appear in a good deal more than a prologue. By the time I came to work with an agent, Matthew Hamilton at Aitken Alexander, our aim was to tell as much of the story as possible from God's point of view.

The character of God in *The Hurtle of Hell* is obviously not one that any of the established religions would recognise. My aim was to make him consistent with what we now know about the vastness of the universe, just as the authors of the original sacred texts made their

God consistent with the cosmos they understood at the time. Key to this, both as a running gag and as a serious conceptual point, is that the humans of Planet Earth ought not to be as central to the concerns of the creator of the universe, in all its vastness, as previous generations assumed.

Telling an Earth-bound story at least partly from God's uncomprehending point of view presented a logistical challenge. Try as I might, with Matthew's very patient support, I could not make it work and we eventually parted company. By then I had shifted my focus to another improbable-sounding project, dramatising the life of Gerard Manley Hopkins and the plight of the nuns he wrote about in *The Wreck of the Deutschland*, and framing it in a modern satirical comedy.

It took a while to make that one work, too, but when *The Hopkins Conundrum* was published in 2017, its favourable reception encouraged me to believe that these ambitious projects, mashing up tones and themes in a light but hopefully arresting way, were worth the effort.

So I went back to *The Hurtle of Hell*. Originally written when Millennium Eve was still a recent memory, it now describes a time that many potential readers will not remember as adults. In other words, I found that, completely by accident, I was writing a historical novel set in an innocent age before 9/11, the global financial crash, ISIS, Brexit or Donald Trump, where the biggest problems the country faced were the overspend on the Millennium Dome and the illusory threat of the Millennium Bug.

In as much as I have made it work, I have done so with the invaluable guidance of my editor Scott Pack, the support of my publisher Dan Hiscocks and the rigorous input of Clio Mitchell, all at Lightning Books. Thanks are also due to my enduring friends from that City MA, Glenda Cooper, Maha Khan Phillips, David Evans and Sarah Jane Checkland, who read many different versions of the early chapters; to Henry Fitzherbert, who pointed out a plot direction so obvious I had not seen it; and to Tony Bird, who had to read more drafts than any (then) partner should. Also a very big thank you is due to David Shenton, my old colleague from *Capital Gay*, and a long-time friend: for years, unbeknown to David, I have wanted to illustrate the cover with a particular cartoon of his, and when I finally put the idea to him, he jumped at it with characteristic enthusiasm and generosity.

This novel began life as a rebuke to religion. I hope it no longer reads like that, because that is no longer what it is meant to be. Its evolution is testament to the people in my life who are a very good advert for religion – most notably, but by no means only, my late, beloved husband, Ezio Alessandroni, who was a priest before I met him.

A sub-theme of *The Hurtle of Hell* is the relationship of gay people to their parents. This novel is dedicated to mine, who have both been dead for more than a decade now. I am not sure what they would have made of it, but I wish they could have had the option.

Also by Simon Edge:
The Hopkins Conundrum

Tim Cleverley inherits a failing pub not far from the remote Jesuit seminary where the Victorian poet Gerard Manley Hopkins wrote his masterpiece, *The Wreck of the Deutschland*, about a real-life tragedy involving a group of nuns fleeing persecution.

To Tim, the opaque religious poetry is incomprehensible – as if it's written in code. This gives him an idea. Desperate to boost trade, he contacts an American purveyor of Holy Grail hokum – suggesting he write a book about the poet, the area and a recently discovered (and entirely fabricated) 'mystery'. The famous author is suffering from writer's block so he latches on to the project at once. But will Tim's new relationship with a genuine Hopkins fan scupper the plan?

The Hopkins Conundrum blends the real stories of Hopkins and the shipwrecked nuns with a wry eye on the Da Vinci Code industry in an original mix of fiction, literary biography and satirical commentary.

A splendid mix of literary detection, historical description and contemporary romance. Edge's witty debunking of the Vatican conspiracy genre will appeal equally to fans and detractors of Dan Brown – **Michael Arditti**

The novel seesaws between comedy and calamity, present and past. It pokes fun at pretension but also gives an insight into why a Catholic poet such as Hopkins – so weird, so spiritual and so intense – deserves his claim to greatness. The result is a novel enjoyable on every level – **Jennifer Selway**, *Daily Express*

A riotous read – **Nicola Heywood Thomas, BBC Radio Wales**

Also published by Lightning Books, price £8.99